BORN WITH WINGS

THE IMMORTAL LIFE OF PIU PIU

Bianca Gubalke

ARTEBY - Cape Town, South Africa

Arteby Publishing
P.O.Box 653, Sun Valley, 7979 Western Cape, South Africa
www.arteby.com

Publisher's Cataloging-in-Publication data

Names: Gubalke, Bianca, author.

Title: Born with wings : the immortal life of Piu Piu / Bianca Gubalke.

Series: Dance Between Worlds.

Description: Cape Town, South Africa: ARTEBY Publishing, 2017.

Identifiers: ISBN 978-0-620-71491-4 (pbk.) | ISBN 978-0-620-71492-1 (ebook)

Subjects: LCSH: Human-animal relationships--Fiction. | Reincarnation--Fiction. | Future life--Fiction. | Mysticism--Fiction. | Spirituality--Fiction. | Liminality--Fiction. | Girls--South Africa--Western Cape--Fiction. | Western Cape (South Africa)--Fiction. | Magic realism (Literature) | BISAC FICTION / Magical Realism | YOUNG ADULT FICTION / Magical Realism | FICTION / Coming of Age | FICTION / Visionary & Metaphysical

Classification: LCC PR9369.4 .G82 I46 2017 | DDC 823.92--dc23

CONTENTS

DO THIS FIRST:

ACKNOWLEDGMENTS

I am very grateful to the extraordinary people in my life ~ my precious real and extended family ~ for their assistance, advice and unwavering support and faith in my work.

My sincere thanks go first to Dr. Inga Karetnikova, my beloved friend, teacher and critic, who followed the path of Piu Piu into the spiritual realm in 2015. I hope this book makes her proud beyond space and time!

Thanks also to my precious friend and wise consultant, Dr. Thérèse Rodden, as well as to my sensitive copy editor and friend, Alexia Lawson.

Lastly, I thank my husband, Janusz Hajduk, for creating a cover illustration that perfectly depicts the spiritual nakedness that breathes through the pages of this book.

Each of you helps remind me what our journey between worlds is all about through your unbridled spirit, your knowledge, patience, and your open mind.

Bianca Gubalke

To the immortal Piu Piu in you.

CHAPTER ONE

Anata's Choice

Time!

Through the hazy whiteness a soft bell rang. The unmistakable sign.

"I'm ready!"

"Ready for the final review?"

"Yes. I've made up my mind. My time to return to earth has come." As she spoke, her graceful shape emerged from the iridescence of space.

"This is a significant decision!" The silhouette of a dignified man appeared within the pure and formless light. His melodious voice naturally commanded attention. "How well did you prepare?"

"I reviewed a number of life scenarios and selected the one I found most suitable for my advancement."

"How do you feel about the hidden parts within the blueprint? The sections deliberately left out for your own interpretation and improvisation?"

"Oh, those I like most!" She laughed, like a fresh breeze. Her dark eyes sparkled with unrestrained zest. "Any open endings and unknown challenges arising will be dealt with on the fly. In fact, I'm looking forward to them! As long as I can operate freely I'll never . . ." She stopped herself abruptly.

"Yes?" he asked, gently.

She remained silent. But this was a realm without secrets and they both knew she was touching the deeper purpose of her role. Her major challenge.

He smiled. An aura of peace and wisdom emanated from him, indicating his status as the Elder. She was smart, passionate and courageous; but also very young. So far she had always chosen to be the natural heroine: had picked strong independent characters with love and luck on their side. Winners! Now, however, she had decided to play the opposite role.

Was she really aware what that meant?

"There has to be balance." She met his caring eyes in which she saw her own reflection. "For the sake of wholeness," she added, "I want to experience the other side. The irony of being born with wings yet unable to fly. "

He did not move, observing the irregular bursts of energy pulsing through her. She was glowing.

"To transcend it," she whispered. "It seems that in a world of light and darkness we fear what we don't know."

"I understand," he responded, "but most importantly, you need to know who you are." He looked at her intently. "Do you, Anata?"

"I should think so!" She wanted to reply in her vivacious way, but then hesitated under his mesmerizing gaze. Had she really understood what he meant?

She could no longer concentrate. Her eyelids fluttered uncontrollably and her heart started to race. Suddenly, a bolt of energy shot into her crown chakra and flooded her entire being, illuminating it from within. It lasted only a few moments; then it left, whirling her long dark hair and translucent garments around her like filaments in space.

Shaken, she drew a deep breath and released it slowly, centering herself. "My choice to be a bird may seem ridiculous, if not tragic to those who judge by appearance and are inclined to take advantage of it. However, it allows me to enter my new playing field in the physical realm unencumbered and with a different perspective. It is perfect for the challenge I seek; perfect for what I want to embody, experience, express and, ultimately, overcome. I'm ready. I am." She bowed her head with respect. She wanted to say so much more. How she'd always loved creatures and yearned for a deeper insight into their soul. To better understand her own nature by being one of them.

A few moments passed in silence.

He saw she was still trembling but, when she lifted her eyes, he observed an expanded awareness, strength and resolve. She would certainly need all that for what was in store for her. But he also saw that her potential for growth was amazing. Oh yes, he could rely on her; she would not disappoint – least of all herself.

"Very well," he said, his noble face breaking into a smile, "you have our blessings! Let's set the stage then for your new role!"

New role! New life! The message bounced through the luminous realm, which was bright but not blinding, soon to be picked up and repeated by numerous cheering voices.

"New role! New life!" There was a round of applause from the emerging group of entities with whom she was to share her new existence. All of them, expressions of light, were drifting towards each other and into the center. Their energies were high, and were coupled with a spirit of keen anticipation. They formed a half circle around Anata and the Elder, bowing their heads briefly towards them.

The final preview continued.

"Tell us about the location," he asked. "Where does your new life take place?"

"Given my personal affinity for nature, I selected a small village at the tip of Africa that meets all the requirements of the scenario. The surroundings are ideal and my chosen tribe is firmly rooted within them. The name of the place is Noordhoek. These are the coordinates: 34.104°S 18.360°E."

She paused, giving him time to tune his mind into that particular spot on planet Earth. The process was simultaneously mirrored on a large holographic simulation that appeared before them. It zoomed into planet Earth from outer space, focusing on Africa, moving downwards all the way until reaching its southernmost tip, where it closed in on the spectacular Noordhoek Valley, enclosed by high mountain ranges and the endless sea.

"What is the timeframe?"

"Early 21st century," she answered. As she spoke, the entire mountain range briefly turned into a burning inferno. "The story reaches back to the historic fires of January 2000. But only briefly. We will focus on 2009 to 2011."

"Excellent! You may now familiarize yourself with your future surroundings."

During the excitement that ensued while she projected herself into the simulation – sweeping past Chapman's Peak and across the white sands of Noordhoek beach one moment; diving into the turquoise waters of the Atlantic Ocean the next; mingling with a noisy flock of Egyptian geese on the tranquil meadows where horses lazed in the sun; or hovering above a young girl dancing in the rain while a cat with cryptic eyes glanced at her – his gaze wandered thoughtfully from one figure to the next, observing how they interacted with one another. Although they differed in gender and character, there was no mistaking the close bond between them.

This was not their first venture together.

Occasionally, he switched rapidly back and forth between them as if assessing, for a last time, Anata's motive for choosing them as her tribe. He also had to evaluate their individual levels of energy, enthusiasm and resolve carefully, to make the collective project work. This demanded a massive ordered progression of planning and coordination in the background, all of which were his responsibility. Despite the analogy, this was not a stage play where roles were distributed between the most suitable actors and actresses. Here, the blueprints were freely chosen by the individuals themselves. They did so with full awareness that they would be co-creating their own lives within the cosmic plan – from the beginning, to the middle and the end.

As the hologram dissolved and disappeared, everyone turned back to him, their eyes glittering, with a thrill of anticipation.

"I see you like Noordhoek," he said with a smile in his voice. "A unique setting for a unique life." He waited until they had settled down; then addressed the group in a solemn tone: "These are our final moments together before one curtain lifts and another descends. So if you have any concerns, please voice them now. On the other hand, if you commit yourself to this project, do so wholeheartedly! Give your new role your full attention. Do so without attachment to outcome and regardless of the part you play within the whole. Whatever decision you take, the choice is your own."

He paused for a moment then continued swiftly, noting a mutual consensus of commitment.

His glance softened; he had not expected anything else.

"As you step into your new life, you are the director of your destiny. In each moment, you decide how to interpret the blueprint of your role. That is, in as much as you remember it. Sooner or later your conscious memories will disappear. While this may seem disturbing, it ensures that you create a new life based on your unique purpose and imagination; like a poem on a blank sheet of paper. The poem of your life.

It means your divine state of all-knowing will be obscured. You won't remember your true home, but you will always long for it. You won't feel our blissful state of oneness, but you will continue to search for it. As you develop a separate sense of 'I', you eventually forget who you are."

With his main focus remaining on Anata, he not only looked into their eyes, he also read their minds. What he found was a strong desire to create and express, and an unconditional willingness to serve. They knew what he meant; they had lived through it many times before. Regardless of their past experiences, or because of them, they were eager to follow their calling for the spiritual advancement of all.

"You create it all over again; such is the rule of the game," he continued, observing that her calm composure barely concealed her excitement in anticipation of the adventure ahead.

"This time, you chose your biggest challenge, Anata!"

"I'm not afraid," she laughed, "I'm excited! A life where the odds are stacked against me – what a great chance to grow!"

"Courage is not the absence of fear!"

"Let fear then be my teacher!" She raised her arms to brush his concern away: "I can't wait to spread my wings and fly!"

Although her enthusiasm was infectious and her attitude strong, he had to ensure that she was not underestimating the magnitude of what lay ahead.

"Consider, you could fall from the sky and die . . ."

".. . and end up back here?" Her arms sank. She paused, surprised. Was he teasing her or still testing her resolve?

Then her shining eyes locked onto his: "Would you be afraid if there were nothing to fear?"

Her bold words dropped into the silence and confronted his apprehensions. Like ripples in stardust.

"Facing your shadow is not to be taken lightly," he said.

"The more so that before I can face it . . . I have to create it," she replied but, after some thought, added in a subdued tone, "Of course, all this remains to be seen, *after* . . ."

Then she fell silent, still holding his penetrating look until he released her – a bit reluctantly it seemed.

"Yes, your perceptions will differ . . . *after* the cloud of unknowing has permeated you." His smile embraced her: she was well grounded in her new life-centered awareness. Satisfied, he turned back to the group.

"As you well know, without amnesia there would be no change, no growth, no evolution – just predictability and repetition."

He paused, allowing his words to sink in. Most of them nodded in silent agreement.

"For those amongst you who feel trapped within the web of time and space and their faithful ally, duality, remember . . . *be in the world but not of it.* We encourage you to keep connecting with us through your dreams as well as in meditation, prayer and altered states of consciousness. The divine flow of energy is your natural state. There are no coincidences. No accidents. Don't focus on the dancer; become the dance . . . the vibration!"

He bowed his head; then he was gone.

"Here we go again!"

The members of the group were high-spirited as always before a new incarnation. They laughed, joked and cheered, showering each other with cascades of light.

In the midst of the excitement, Anata sensed an irresistible pull. She became quiet. Introspective. Fighting off mixed emotions as she prepared herself to proceed into the unknown –

alone this time as she would be leaving her love behind, but elated by the thought that her twin soul would be playing a dominant role at her side – she gathered herself for her imminent arrival on the grand stage of a brand new life.

As she detached herself from the group, their laughter and encouragements faded and their shapes dissolved in space . . .

"Good luck, my girl!"

"This time, she'll be mean, our angel!"

"Yay! Outrageously mean!"

"*O sole mio* . . . Let's tickle her wicked spot!"

"Don't worry; I'll always take care of you!"

"*Life is a desire, not a meaning*, Princess, this time I'll win the game. You won't escape!"

"Woohoo, I'll be watching you!"

"Good bye, my love! I'll be there when you awake . . ."

Slowly, she drifted away through intelligent emptiness, further and further, alone. She felt some of her essence flowing out of her to remain in the spiritual realm. Although it was too abstract even to imagine, she remembered that this would be the hardest to endure: the loss of home, the perception of separation.

The pace increased. Floating through veils of shimmering whiteness, she was carried on the billowing wings of a magic symphony. It swept her along, faster and faster, until everything blurred and the music rose to an explosive crescendo. Moments later, all came to an abrupt halt. Then, there was absolute silence.

Through the sensitivity of her unborn eyes she saw herself immersed in fluid darkness. It felt warm. Pleasant. There was a dull rhythmic beating that intrigued her. Its presence became louder.

Was it outside her or within?

It took a while for her to realize that it was her heart. Her new life was about to begin!

CHAPTER TWO

Leap of Faith

Ploff!

Pippa heard a muted peep as she stood under the tall, old, stone pine that was stretching its many branches into the fading evening light. She looked down. MadMax had heard it too. His ears had pricked up and his whiskers were shimmering as, on soft white paws, he inspected the grass, his body melting into the shadows. Suddenly, his tail tip twitched, indicating an exciting discovery.

The delicate child brushed some unruly curls out of her face and knelt down next to the tomcat. There it was, a tiny chick! It was lying in the grass, its head slightly to one side.

"Phew!" Pippa's eyes scanned the huge pine, all the way up as far as she could see, trying to spot the nest from which it must have fallen.

"Phew," MadMax echoed, looking down at the little bundle of misery.

Gently, Pippa took it in her hands. Holding it with her eyes closed, she felt a stream of life energy pulsing through the tiny feather ball. She got up and hurried to the house with MadMax following her. She did not even notice when he stopped and turned, piercing the darkening shadows with utmost attention.

The blood-thirsty beast was definitely out there, following them with evil intentions and watching their every move.

He gave off a warning growl. It was not the first time they'd clashed and his hunting juices started to flow. Hearing Pippa reach the terrace in the background, he hesitated, torn between a basic instinct and an ageless bond. It only took a few moments. He was back at her side just as she opened the door.

Once in her room, Pippa switched the light on and they saw it was a gosling. Each winter, a couple of Egyptian geese came out of nowhere to take up residence in the garden. This was often preceded by violent territorial fights on the roof and on the lawn until, eventually, the winning couple would parade on top of the chimney, honking away loudly and triumphantly to make their presence known to the entire neighborhood. From that moment on, they owned the place and protected it fiercely. Nothing escaped their sharp and enquiring eyes. Better than a watchdog, they would announce and scare away intruders with their clamoring voices, while welcoming friends with wide-open wings. They even announced Dad's car before it actually arrived on the property.

Paired for life, they'd soon build a nest, concealed in a tree, and the female would disappear during breeding to incubate the eggs. While they shared nesting duties, the gander kept a close eye on Pippa who secretly saved the soft parts of her breakfast roll for him – a treat he took very gently from her hand.

When spring arrived, the feathered couple would suddenly appear on the terrace and proudly present eight to twelve goslings. Pippa loved the new family members, but was always a bit nervous as to how her parents would react.

In common with most South Africans, they were great animal lovers, but Dad would always pull his eyebrows up and shake his head rather disapprovingly. "We don't know how to get rid of them on the golf course and you invite them into the house. They're a bloody nuisance," he would say with a deep sigh, looking at Mom.

Mom always smiled at him lovingly, with her almond-shaped eyes sparkling in shades varying from a bright blue to midnight blue to black, like a barometer of her soul. Despite the fact that they had been together for over a decade, he had not been able to fathom exactly what triggered those subtle changes. Perhaps they were simply part of her African heritage or her feminine mystery. Or both.

"Aren't they just too gorgeous, Pete?" he'd hear her rejoice, after which she usually turned to her daughter. "Patricia Phoenix," she would say strictly, with a hardly noticeable wink, "you know what that means, don't you?"

"Yes, Mom." Pippa always nodded dutifully on the rare occasions when Mom called her by her full name. "I will keep the terrace spick and span."

"Well, just one more time then," Dad would concede.

"As last year!" Mother and daughter completed in thought, winking at each other and laughing as father goose ejected a messy comment from his pompous backside.

"They will keep you busy, my girl!" Dad added. "The question is, for how long?"

That was indeed the big question as many animals were keen on tasty gosling snacks – be it owls, lynxes, dogs, mongooses, snakes, various birds of prey, and cats. These were just a few of the dangers lurking every single day and night, giving mother and father goose challenges in raising their brood.

Pippa looked at the limp bundle in her hands. The next hours were decisive for death or life. She brought it close to her face and blew gently over the greyish fluff: "Poor little orphan, wake up!" It weighed almost nothing; yet its heart was beating.

"It needs water, food and a warm place to sleep," MadMax said drily, keeping his sight on everything Pippa did as she prepared a nest in her duvet and a cushion to keep the gosling warm. "I didn't mean your bed," he remarked with a sulky undertone.

Pippa smiled. Sharing her bed had been her tomcat's exclusive privilege during the past seven years, from the day she'd found the abandoned kitten nobody wanted. Now, however, she had to do everything possible to help the newborn gosling survive. "It's too late to call the bird park," she thought, "but let's check 'Egyptian Goose' on the Internet. I've always wondered why they call them 'Egyptian' anyway. They've been with us down here for as long as I can remember. That's a pretty long time. And pretty far away from Egypt."

"Ask me," MadMax purred, his gooseberry green eyes glistening with a regal pride. He waited until he had her attention, then continued, "They go back to a long, long time ago when they still lived along the Nile in Egypt. Like my ancestors, the Great Cats, they were considered to be gods. GODS! Oh yes, we were eternalized in many ways. Even in hieroglyphics . . ."

"You are so clever," Pippa responded admiringly as he jumped onto the desk and sat next to the screen. He beamed.

"I'm sorry to say that some barbarians enjoyed goose on their dinner plates. Sadly, they do so even today," he added, absorbing the incredulous look in Pippa's eyes.

"Of course," he continued, lowering his voice, "they would never dare do that to us. Whoever killed a cat had to die – that was the law!"

"Oh," Pippa sighed, spellbound.

"In those days," he hissed, his whiskers vibrating, "we enjoyed a status that was equal, if not superior, to that of humans. We were treated like royalty. Admired, mummified and buried in tombs to accompany our beloved owners through space and time, forever!"

"Forever . . ." Pippa whispered, meeting the tomcat's mesmerizing gaze. She shivered.

Satisfied with the impact his words had on her, MadMax rubbed his head against hers, fondly. Time melted into the magic of this symbiotic moment.

"Look," he remarked lightly, "there are just a few thousand years in between, but I still feel like . . ."

". . . my Pasharotti!"

She laughed in her vibrant way.

"When will you sing for me again?" She loved to tease him. "Let's hear your magnificent voice."

"Hey, you'd better check out the chick before it's too late," he reminded her.

"Right!" Pippa sat up straight, got hold of the mouse, typed a few keywords into Google and shifted her focus onto the screen. Soon she found the information she was interested in.

"According to what I read here, the Egyptian goose is a member of the duck, goose and swan family, *Anatidae*. Oh, and you are right, they say that it is native both to Africa south of the Sahara and the Nile valley. But they also live in Europe, mainly in countries like Germany, the Netherlands and – "

Suddenly, there was a timid chirp; the gosling tried to get onto its feet, calling desperately for its mother.

Pippa was immediately at its side. "The poor thing must be so hungry. I found nothing on gosling food. Shall I give it breadcrumbs or some of my seeds?"

"Try squashed snails," MadMax suggested, "or worms."

"Very funny! How could I find those in the darkness outside? But let me try something else."

She put some water into a saucer and placed it close to the gosling. It didn't react. Then she dipped her finger into the water and offered some drops in the palm of her hand, holding it right under the little beak and making encouraging quacking sounds.

MadMax squinted: "She thinks she's mother goose now!"

The gosling, however, opened its beak and slowly slurped up a few drops, after which it continued to chirp and chirp and chirp.

"OK, OK, let's try the seeds!" She opened her cupboard. There were dozens of glasses filled with seeds, all labeled and arranged in perfect order. It took her hardly a second to make a choice, then she offered some minuscule poppy seeds on the tip of her finger.

But the gosling did not even look at them.

"Hmm," Pippa said, "it doesn't like them. Sunflower seeds are too big. Perhaps I should try dill?"

"Soak them first," MadMax advised, which Pippa immediately did. After a while, she put a few soggy bits on her finger and tried to stimulate the chirping chick. There was no reaction. The chirping got louder and more demanding.

"I have an idea," Pippa said. "You watch the chick, I'll be right back!"

"Just what I always dreamt of: a delicious chick right under my nose." MadMax licked a paw, displaying an impressive array of claws.

"Don't you dare touch it!" The door closed behind Pippa. MadMax grinned. He knew how much Pippa had always wanted a cute little gosling like that. Meanwhile, on shaky legs, it looked at him with dark button eyes, chirping incessantly.

"Now don't you take *me* for a goose," he grumbled. The fluffy creature probably weighed less than 60 grams. How could a grey, helpless ball of fluff like this grow into a strong, magnificent being with a wingspan of over 140 cm? Grow into a wild goose that could fly over vast distances, swim with ease and even intimidate him – an adult tomcat – in his own garden?

He decided it was definitely smarter to become friends right away. Boy! These geese could be very aggressive! MadMax still remembered the pain when he was pecked in his hiney by a young gander. At the time, he did not take the stupid hissing of the male goose too seriously, instead kept his distance from the smaller, yet much noisier, female, which honked raucously whenever she saw him. The recollection still made his ear twitch quickly. Even then he had found the mere sound and frequency to be an assault on his fine hearing.

No doubt, this gosling was a female!

"Let's try some greens!" Pippa arrived with a small bowl. "Chicken soup with finely chopped broccoli, how about that? Mom said tomorrow we will get some chick starter crumbles; this must do for now."

The moment the gosling saw the wet, green bits on Pippa's finger it devoured them and chirped enthusiastically for more. Eventually, Pippa could guide her new fosterling towards the bowl. She was overjoyed to see the rescued gosling gobble up all the green bits. It also sipped some water; bending its head so far backwards it almost lost its balance. It stretched, flapping its ridiculous wings a few times and, finally, settled into its new nest, giving off a last satisfied chirp.

"Phew! That was close," MadMax whispered, rubbing his head fondly against her.

"Piu!" Pippa exclaimed, stroking his fur and yawning. "That's what we will call him."

"Her," the tomcat corrected and yawned as well.

"Piu Piu!" Pippa whispered. "Welcome home."

Later, when the moonlight fell through the windows, they were all happily asleep.

"This is funny," Piu Piu thought while she was dreaming. "I fell from the sky, but I didn't end up back here! Perhaps earth isn't that bad after all? As long as they leave me alone with chicken soup! I mean! Get me some *escargots sans* shells. How difficult is that?"

Somewhere out there, the mongoose was beside herself with rage, and thirsting for revenge. Her babies were hungry and she could not return to the den without food. She had missed the gosling by seconds. Her only consolation was the enticing thought that – one day – it would be so much juicier with some real meat on the bones. And the blood! What a feast that would be. The thought alone caused saliva to flow in her snout and, suddenly, an audacious idea hit her. Nothing inspired her more than the dull sound of a neck cracking between her jaws and the taste of fresh warm blood spurting over her tongue.

Ah! She had to have it. And soon!

A string of hysterical giggles bubbled up towards the moon just as it hid its face behind dark clouds. Then a blanket of velvet blackness enveloped the garden.

CHAPTER THREE

Spirit of Survival

The fine silhouette of the full moon was still shimmering in the fleeting mist above the Atlantic ocean when the first glittering rays of the morning sun crept over the mountain ranges in the east. Rising high above the dark and dreaming valley, Chapman's Peak glowed as if dipped into a pot of gold. The ridiculous little cloud floating around it like a puff of smoke, slowly turned pink. Almost magically, the light drifted downwards over steep rocks and cliffs, hidden gorges, undulating hills of fynbos, leucadendron and proteas, pine forests, vineyards and gardens, into the enchanted valley with its whispering oaks, luscious pastures and streams.

"Ek sê! My word!" gulped a dainty frog as a drop of dew splashed down the chalice of an arum lily, right onto its head. "I'm still sleeping!" Not amused, it hopped out of its obscure retreat and opened its eyes to a world of wonder reflecting in millions of crystal beads.

"Ek sê . . ." it whispered in awe, "is this another dream?"

They were sparkling on graceful restios, reeds and grasses, interwoven with blue morning glory. Some shimmered like broken ice in rockroses; others were hanging onto the perky snowbells that had survived the recent winter storm that had swept through Pippa's garden.

"It must be spring!" the tiny being exclaimed, holding on to a leaf swaying in the breeze.

Suddenly, it turned its head: "Oh, there she is! Ready to feed the chickens."

Pippa stood on the terrace with a bowl of peels and leftovers in her hands. With her eyes closed, she drew the fresh, cold, morning air deep into her lungs. Then she looked up towards the mountains and called: "Where are you?" Filled with the thrill of anticipation, she waited for the answer – her cue.

Promptly it came, as a group of hadedas announced their imminent arrival. Their loud distinctive calls echoed through the vast amphitheater formed by the Silvermine mountain range. Just as Pippa set off towards the compost heap, five large shadows landed on the lawn.

After greeting her with a soulful "Haa! Dee! Daa!", the grey ibises pursued their breakfast snails by following their slimy trails on the frosted lawn. As they stalked along, their curved bills pierced the grass to extract delicacies sheltering between the roots.

Pippa studied their hunting strategies and admired the metallic glow of their wings as they caught the light. "If only you could show Piu Piu how to catch snails," she sighed.

"Teach her!" One of the hadedas croaked, choking down a wildly wiggling worm.

"Me? I can't do that!" Pippa shuddered at the mere thought. To her, nature was a magical place filled with light and energies well beyond the perception of a human eye. She had not yet completely lost her memories of that blissful state of oneness from the time before she was born, although she saw herself increasingly challenged and – sometimes – felt her ability to recall dwindling away, a little bit at a time.

"Wake up, my girl. Get real!" Dad tried to hammer into her brain over and again. "If we want to survive we've got to stay on top of the food chain."

The more he insisted, the less she understood.

"Lions, vultures, sharks, crocs, why are there so many predators around?" she asked at the dinner table one night. "I don't remember it that way?"

Mom and Dad exchanged a quick look. They had agreed not to discuss their daughter's sometimes strange questions any longer; talking about it usually led to disputes between them. Dad shrugged while spooning mashed potatoes onto his plate. "Because . . . because . . . perhaps because of us? Like attracts like. We're the worst of them all, are we not?"

With her eyes glued to his plate, on which blood streamed around islands of green peas and swamped a continent of mashed potatoes, she opened her mouth to object. Then she felt MadMax leaning against her shin to quieten her rebellious temper.

"Hmmm, this is so tender." Dad closed his eyes, chewing with zest. "I eat lion before lion eats me! One's gotta stay in control. Without that . . ." The mashed potatoes disappeared; there was only a lake of blood from which his fork lifted the last peas, no matter how hard they tried to escape.

"There's no pity out there, my girl!" Pippa heard him say. "But don't worry, you'll find that out soon enough. There's a war; there's always war. Believe me!" He licked his lips and gulped down his beer. "But, what doesn't break us makes us strong . . . Right?"

Pleased with himself, and not really expecting an answer, he poured himself another beer. "Right! War is good."

He gave them a lunatic grin, adding in a subdued tone: "Cheers . . . to the dark side of the moon!"

Pippa felt sick. Her hand formed a fist around her fork. Forcing her teeth apart she bit into a piece of spinach quiche, feeling the tip of the fork on her tongue. As she glanced across the table she met Mom's eyes just above the rim of a glass filled with ice that she pressed to her burning cheek.

"And now for a juicy mouse." MadMax purred, his whiskers gleaming, catching Pippa in her reverie as she rinsed the bowl. He loved to tease her.

"As long as you leave my birds alone," Pippa shot back. "Or else!"

"Or else?" he inquired with an indignant undertone, "or else? Could you possibly turn into a predator? You?"

She looked up. "Hmm," she said pensively, "do you think I could?"

"Could what, exactly?"

"Oh, never mind!" The idea confused her. Besides, she preferred not to even think of all the mice, rats and even the odd mole he had killed during the course of his life. Many times he brought his trophies to her to show off his heroic accomplishments, triumph and pride beaming all over him. He would devour them from head to tail, leaving nothing but what looked like an internal organ.

"Why don't you eat this . . . this thing?" she once asked, staring a little disgustedly at the greyish piece of flesh.

"The stomach? No, never," he had replied, "one never knows what's hiding in there." The tomcat yawned and stretched his body luxuriously, his fluffy tail high in the air. He watched as one of the hadedas speared a snail, got to the soft part and gulped it down, leaving nothing but an empty shell on the grass.

"One day, you will have to squash a snail to teach Miss Pancakes what geese do."

"Geese don't squash snails." Pippa objected.

"You're right. They eat them alive. Snails, slugs, mice, worms, froglets, hamsters –"

"– cats!" she cut in boldly, "preferably kittens. Sweet, mummified, little kitty cats!"

"That's totally tactless." He turned his back on her as if she did not exist. How could she be so mean?

Unmoved, Pippa poured fresh water into Piu Piu's red plastic bath. "She can swim in here while we keep an eye on her," she said, amused that the tomcat was ignoring her, but knowing all too well not a single word she spoke, or even thought, would escape him. "Once she's bigger the whole dam will be hers."

"That dam." MadMax twitched his tail. The mere thought of it gave him catbumps, even after all these years. His mind drifted back to when he was a little kitten playing in the evening light at the dam. He saw it all vividly before his eyes: suddenly, out of nowhere, a large shadow sailed down, grabbed him with deadly claws and hacked into him, fracturing his skull. He felt himself erupting from within and screamed so loudly that everybody shot up from the dinner table and rushed to his rescue.

Meanwhile, a magnetic force lifted him out of his head and he felt a great sense of liberation and space. It was neither new nor surprising to him; rather something he instinctively knew. The pain was gone! He was free!

Far below him, the giant eagle owl realized she had become the target herself. She dropped her prey and flew off just as Dad arrived at the scene of crime. He glanced at the little tomcat and briefly inspected his limp body while Pippa, trembling like a leaf, watched from a distance.

"Bloody bastard," he cursed under his breath, "must've taken him for a stupid rabbit."

He got up and shook his head. "This is Africa. Pets belong inside the house after dark. Think I made that clear often enough. Will bury him tomorrow – that's if he's still around by then."

Filled with horror and guilt, she hid in the shadows. Once everyone had gone to bed and the light in the kitchen was out, she slipped over to her injured kitten and took it into her arms, hugging it as if she would never let it go. "Come back, my Pasharotti," she sobbed, "don't leave me behind alone."

She lifted her glazed eyes and looked beseechingly at the sky. The stars were coming out, one after the other, connecting with her in some mysterious way. She kept counting them, counting them until she felt his little heart beat again.

"I am now here," he told her, mentally.

Her soul soared in jubilation. Wrapping him in her energy, she took him along in her dreams. He hovered between life and death for a while, but finally she convinced him to stay.

"Oh, happy day!" The sunbird tweeted from a red watsonia, losing itself in a psalm of joy.

"Oh, happy day!" MadMax tuned in, following each note with an inaudible 'meow'. It had to be cosmic humor that he of all beings was equipped with the finest hearing, but such a ridiculous voice. His only consolation was that he always felt his music within – oh yeah, he remembered that well! He stretched and arched his back while keeping an eye on the sunbird. It was collecting cobwebs glistening between twigs, which it carried into the strelitzias on the terrace where it was building a nest.

"Sweetheart! It's getting late." Mom's voice resounded from the atrium.

"Oh! Poor chickens, they must be hungry." Pippa grabbed the grain-filled bowl and walked past pink clouds of scented flowers that were still in the shade. She smiled. A few more storms and spring would be in full swing. But then she hesitated.

"Something's missing," she thought.

"No wheelbarrows," MadMax observed drily from behind her. Pippa stopped and listened. "You're right," she said. "No wheelbarrows. That's weird!" The noisy voices of guineafowl were missing. Dad called them 'stupid old wheelbarrows' as they sounded like rusty wheelbarrows needing to be greased. Usually, a few of them hung around to snatch some of the grain Pippa brought each morning, before the greedy Bantam chickens stormed through the door to chase them away.

"And no chickens!" she suddenly realized. By now, the roosters normally would have flapped their wings and crowed a few times. There would be an excited cackling commotion in front of the door. But today there was total silence.

"Something's wrong."

She clutched the bowl to her heart and continued on her way with a sense of foreboding. As she came closer to the hen house she started to panic: "Oh no! They're gone."

"No no . . ." MadMax said, "they're here!"

"Oh . . ." she sighed with relief. "There they are!"

The chickens had clustered on the top bars in the corner that caught the first light on cold winter mornings. It was nothing unusual. What was alarming, however, was their total lack of reaction.

"They don't even turn their heads. They look, like . . . numb!"

Pippa peeped through the wire netting, her eyes scanning the spacious and solidly built chicken pen under the huge acacia tree. What could have panicked them? She unlocked the door and opened it. The chickens remained completely still; the silence was eerie. Then it hit her: her favorite hen was missing!

"Popcorn!" she called. "Popcorn, where are you?" The white hen would normally fly onto her shoulder and nibble her ear to greet her while the rest of the noisy lot dashed out of the door.

"Popcorn! Popcorn!"

As there was no response, Pippa stooped to peer into the lower boxes of the hen house where they usually laid their eggs.

It was deserted, but there were a few suspicious feathers on the ground. Her eyes followed them to the other end of the enclosure, and then a strange noise made her look up.

What she saw was so horrendous she dropped the bowl. The grain scattered all over the ground, but none of the chickens reacted. They just stared into nothingness, as if into a void, while, higher up above them, a mongoose was desperately trying to pull a white hen through a narrow gap between the wire fencing and the shade-cloth roof. The hen's head was outside the fence, the mongoose had her neck locked in a deadly grip, while her body was stuck inside. It was bathed in blood, with two lifeless feet dangling in the air. Blood dripped along the wire fence and collected on the ground.

As Pippa stared upwards, her disbelieving eyes locked with those of the beast. Cold ripples ran up and down her spine. Her muscles tightened. Her heart started to race.

The mongoose realized her crime had been discovered; now she was pulling and struggling even more fiercely to secure her prey, determined not to lose it – again.

Popcorn's feathers were flying in all directions.

"Youuuu!" Pippa snarled, a wave of grief and rage welling up within her such as she had never experienced before. She looked around frantically; she needed something to . . . to . . . Ah! That's when she saw the big fork. She hurled herself forward, grabbed the tool and turned it around, aiming the sharp metal spikes at the murderous mongoose that kept on dragging and ripping poor Popcorn apart.

"You're not going to have her . . . you . . . youuuuu . . . !"

To Pippa's dismay, the beast was evading the blows from below it with great agility, occasionally giggling hysterically at her clumsy efforts.

By now the young girl was almost blinded by tears. She hated that dark force – that raw brutality – exploding within her, while feeling so terribly powerless at the same time.

There was an unexpected twist of events and the course of the drama changed when a ferocious growl resounded from high up in the tree. Startled, Pippa spun around and stared upwards: the tomcat was crouching on a branch leaving no doubt that he had the mongoose in his sights. In the heat of battle no one had noticed the old warrior maneuver himself strategically into the best position to put an end to the butchering below.

"MadMax . . . " Pippa whispered in awe, "I never noticed you were that –" Her words got stuck in her throat and her mouth went dry when she saw his muscles contracting, preparing for the lethal strike. With his eyes firmly fixed on the target, he flung himself down.

But the fully exposed mongoose had instinctively understood her potentially fatal predicament. It was with extreme reluctance that she let go of her prey and disappeared – just a fraction of a second before MadMax catapulted with full momentum onto the wire fence; a feat he hardly noticed as he was already at her heels.

Slowly, Popcorn's head slipped back through the gap and the dead hen dropped to the ground.

"Keck-keck-keck!" a squirrel applauded from amongst the tree's soft yellow puffs of mimosa flowers, its tail jerking nervously.

Shattered, with tears all over her face, Pippa looked up through the netting. She squinted into the sun as it danced in translucent halos of light through the blossoming tree.

"Popcorn?" She seemed to see the white hen calmly perched on a branch. She appeared to be completely detached from the murderous scene below.

Was she real or a fantasy?

When Pippa felt the familiar little bites on her right ear, she put her hand against it, drawing comfort from the tender caress. "You are still here?" She closed her eyes, listening to fragments of a distant melody that reminded her vaguely of something she no longer remembered, but she desperately held on to it as the sound soothed her heart.

"I'm fine, sweet Pippa, don't worry about me. I was on my way home anyway."

"Home?" Pippa was confused. "This is home?"

"Yes, it is," Popcorn said, softly.

When Pippa opened her eyes, the hen had gone.

As if a button switched them on, the Bantam chickens stormed out of the door, leaving the grain untouched. The roosters stood tall, flapped their wings and crowed with exuberant joy, their bright red combs and colorful feathers sparkling in the sun. They started to scratch on the ground, ignoring the guineafowl who sneaked in through the door and gobbled up all the grain that Pippa had spilled. The old yellow hen blew up her feathers and snuggled into her favorite spot under the blueberry bush, where the sun had already warmed the sand. She closed her eyes and dozed off. *Life was a blessing!*

But Pippa had lost a friend; she cried bitterly all day.

"One day, I'll get that bitch," MadMax swore under his breath, slowly flexing his claws. He could not bear seeing Pippa in tears.

"You keep out of the way," Mom told him firmly as she poured fresh milk into his bowl. "Don't you even dream of it!" A mongoose was determined, patient and tricky, and always found a way – especially if there were babies to be fed. She was a strong little predator, able to kill a Cape cobra many times her size and weight, and could well harm – if not kill – even a cat. "Dad will deal with this. You stay inside!"

Grinding his teeth, MadMax looked right through her, a savage blaze in his eyes.

At that very moment, the mongoose lifted herself slightly onto her hindlegs and peered inquisitively into Pippa's window. The young girl looked up from her desk and their eyes locked. Pippa had never seen the notorious chicken killer, with her round little ears and horizontal slit-like pupils, so close up before. The animal showed no fear, but rather a form of boundless curiosity . . . even trustfulness. Pippa could hardly believe her impudence. After all she had gone through, why was she here? Why now? What was she looking for?

Piu Piu!

Pippa felt her blood drain from her face. Her mind went into overdrive. Was she coming back to get her revenge? Was this war? Her thoughts raced feverishly. She glanced at her door. It was usually wide open during sunny days. Anyone could walk in from the garden. It was unlikely that the cheerful chirping of her tiny feathered fosterling had escaped the ravening mongoose. While Piu Piu was, as yet, nothing compared to a fat chickenburger, she was nevertheless a much more substantial delicacy than insects, mice, lizards and the odd snake – bearing in mind her diet of Mom's sumptuous meals!

In the blink of an eye, Pippa reassured herself that the little gosling was resting safely on its favorite spot: Pippa's right foot. Dad had built an enclosure around her desk where Piu Piu had her box with fresh water, food and a soft nest. Here she could move around freely. She loved to stand up tall and flap her tiny wings, chirping out loud: "I am here! I am here!"

As Pippa was her adopted mother, she followed her everywhere, leaving 'pancakes' along the way that grew bigger from day to day. Whenever Pippa sat at her desk, Piu Piu nibbled her toes, chirping away happily, and then settling on her right foot.

Being unexpectedly eye to eye with the enemy got Pippa praying that the little gosling would not wake up and start its exuberant chirping, thereby attracting the predator's attention.

"I am here. I am there. Piu Piu pancakes everywhere!" Piu Piu chirped promptly.

"Oh! Shut up!" Pippa's heart almost stopped and the face at the window pane broke into a gloating grin. But then it softened. It wrinkled up to that of an old woman holding the night sky in her eyes and a tiny baby shoe in her hand, gleaming softly.

There was a sudden blur when MadMax jumped onto the keyboard and brushed his bushy tail over her face, tickling her nose. Pippa sneezed and when she opened her eyes again the mongoose was gone.

"Phew!" MadMax said quietly.

"Phew!" Pippa stared at the white feather in her hand.

They both knew what this meant.

Much later when everything was dark and quiet, Piu Piu heard Pippa toss and turn in her bed. Whenever Pippa's eyes closed from exhaustion, the traumatic images returned. She leapt out of bed several times; in her dreams hearing the chickens fluttering madly and cackling with panic as the murderous mongoose went for her next victim: Piu Piu! There were feathers flying all over. Among them, the beast's grizzly face appeared, its black abysmal eyes burning with greed: "She's mine!" Nothing was going to stop her!

It was during this feverish state that the door opened. Wrapped in a traditional African garment that hugged her feminine shape, Mom stepped into the somber room. She hesitated for a moment – MadMax was not in his usual place on the bed – then spotted him on the chair, snoring away. It had been an exhausting day for him and, in her restlessness, Pippa had kicked him off

A brief glance at the little gosling: Piu Piu looked up at her with her head tilted, absorbing the fragrance of fresh floral notes Mom left behind as she turned away and sat on the bed, taking her child into her arms.

How hot and miserable her little girl was.

"Oh Mom . . ." Pippa cuddled up to her tightly, releasing some deep sobs while her mother rocked her gently and hummed a soothing melody, her lips in Pippa's hair.

Trembling with empathy, the little gosling gave off a few little chirps.

"Relax, my angel, all is well," Mom whispered, brushing away the tears and looking at her as only a mother does.

"She just went home. She's OK."

Pippa stared at her with unfocused eyes. Mom wished she could read her mind. Something was bothering her child.

"What is it?"

Distracted, Pippa glanced at the feather in her hand.

"She's in the shed," Mom said. "We'll bury her tomorrow."

Pippa wanted to say something, but then bit her lip.

"Yes?" Mom encouraged her gently.

"So . . . she grows into a tree with many branches?" Pippa whispered. "Like my tree."

"Which one, sweetheart? You have so many?"

"No, Mom, the one in the song."

"Ah, your birth song?"

Pippa nodded.

"You remember it?"

Pippa shook her head.

"No?" Mom smiled. She had told her the story many times before, but she knew that, right now, her child needed to hear it again. And so she began: "According to Grandma's tradition, in Namibia each newborn baby is gifted with a birth song by its mother; a song that has a special meaning for that child." And so Mom began to sing Pippa's birth song in her mellow voice:

When I felt that my time had come
I went out into the night
Long long before you were born
Long before you were in my womb
You were just a wish in my heart
An idea in my mind
It was when I met your Dad.

Down in her nest, Piu Piu absorbed each note, each word, as if it were meant for her. It seemed to her that even the stars descended to caress Mom's mahogany face while she recalled those magic moments that had transformed her life:

I went up into the mountains
Waiting under the stars
Long long before you were born
Long before you were in my womb
You were just a wish in my heart
An idea in my mind
A memory of what should be, I had.

After listening for a while, Piu Piu added some warbling notes in the background. Moonlight flooded through the windows and flirted with the shadows dancing across the ceiling and the walls.

On a night like this
In a state of bliss
I drank from the sacred source
Through time shifting
A dream was drifting
To meet with destiny's course.

MadMax opened his eyes, absorbing Mom's silhouette as she cradled her child while she sang: the curve of her neck, her smoothly chiseled head, the fullness of her lips.

Suddenly
It imbued me
A light of magic blue
Recalling a distant melody
Water running through my fingers
Knowing you.

As Pippa listened, a great calm came over her. Gradually, the walls around her, the ceiling above and even the floor lost their solidity and morphed into the mystical scenery depicted in her mother's words.

Finally
It was revealed to me
Within the mirror blue
A tall and ancient tree
With many branches reaching out
Healing through you!

Pippa still heard the brook gurgling when the landscape changed into the wide expanse of the garden. Shimmering above the distant sea, the moon laid a blue trail that stretched all the way from the horizon into the room. As Pippa followed it dreamily into the distance, she saw the white hen appear. A soft vibrating light emanated from her as she came strolling towards her bed.

That night
My love flew to me
Past fields of flowers blue
Where our passion's heat
Gave rise to a seed –
The sacred koan
That is you!

"Popcorn . . ." Pippa smiled, with her words still inside her. "Where are you now?" The hen looked up at them for a while as though listening to the song, but then she turned around, distracted by a slight noise. It was MadMax, who was stretching and yawning in his sleep, apparently totally oblivious of her presence. Eventually, she flew onto the moonlit desk, ruffled her silky feathers and looked around with an air of curiosity so typical of her. Tilting her head, she discovered the little gosling in the nest below her.

Piu Piu was looking up at her, wide-eyed. She recognized her clearly but kept still while listening to Mom.

"This was the song I sang when you came into this life. This is your song. This song will be sung when you go home."

After a while, Popcorn's etherial form became even more transparent and, when Mom hummed the final notes, she faded away. Silently, the room returned to its normal dimension.

Blowing the soft white feather from her hand, Pippa asked the question that had been tormenting her: "Did she suffer?"

Mom's eyes followed the feather as it wafted away along a silver stream of memories.

"No, my sweetheart," she said. "Her soul popped out in time and flew away, leaving her body and feathers behind, like old pajamas. That's what animals do. They don't hold on to life the way we do."

"Like Great-grandfather?" Pippa whispered.

Mom's lips curved in a smile but she remained silent.

"Is he still up there?"

"Maybe," Mom said, lifting her face towards the moon just as it was balancing on Chapman's Peak like on a wizard's hat.

"He loved this magic mountain. He told me about the crystal source when I was a little girl like you . . . I remember it well. He caught me by surprise by asking me to tell you, too. Great-grandfather already knew your name!"

All this was too much for Pippa to grasp.

"Where did he go when he died?" she asked, drowsily, her eyes closing.

"I don't know. It's one of life's mysteries . . ."

A moment of quietude enveloped them, broken by the hooting of owls.

"What I do know is this," Mom continued, steeped in thought, "to be really sure about something – anything – you must feel it inside. You don't need eyes to see, you can see with your heart." She was puzzled by the serene smile that spread across Pippa's face as she was slipping away into sleep.

Relieved, Mom nestled her back into the cushions and kissed her: "Good night, my angel. Fly . . . fly . . . fly . . ."

Heaving a happy sigh, Piu Piu put her head under her wing and fell asleep, following Pippa in her dreams.

"Woohoo!" said the owl and turned her head. It was well after midnight and very dark and quiet, but something had stirred her up. She was too familiar with all nocturnal activity in the garden to ignore this most unusual sound. All her senses were alert.

"Hoowoo!" her partner signaled from the big pine; he was aware of it, too.

There it was again! She saw something move. She caught brief glimpses of a dim light flickering across the narrow path, snaking between the plants and bushes. Intrigued, she swept noiselessly down into the quince tree, closer to the path.

"Ouuuuu!" she expressed her surprise when she recognized a human form brushing past; a ghost amongst the shadows.

At this time? All was silent except for the melodious call of the fiery-necked nightjar. Her eyes followed the light that rushed forward with a definite sense of direction. Then she lost it in the darkness.

"Hoowoo!" Now the other owl picked up the light beam of a torch zigzagging through the plants. *How exciting!* Something was happening in the garden.

The light faltered for a moment, but then came to a halt and the silhouette of the weathered shed beneath the syringa tree peeled from the darkness. There was the squeak of a rusty door handle being turned very slowly, after which the creaking door was carefully pushed open.

Driven by an irresistible curiosity, the owl landed on the wooden roof of the shed and found a gap through which she could peer. A wind chime was tuning with forlorn sweetness in the sudden draft of the open door. Her intense gaze followed the light beam as it moved across a range of rubber boots on the wooden floor and past some empty wicker baskets of different shapes and sizes. A large orange lawnmower, a wheelbarrow, garden utensils – rakes, forks, spades – all leaning against a shelf with many little drawers.

The light danced across a collection of mushrooms strung out to dry in the air, their shadows swinging like mischievous tokoloshes suspended above a fragrant field of freshly cut lavender on a table. The owl gave off an intrigued click when she discovered a white object, a box, shimmering in between the flower bunches. The torch was closing in on it, trembling . . . but just as the lid was being lifted, there was a sudden commotion. A large bat swept past and out through the door. The wind chime resounded wildly and the torch dropped to the floor with a bang. Slowly, it rolled underneath the table. It flickered a few times and went out. Undeterred, the nightjar sang.

Gradually, the darkness in the shed took on a different quality; the white box seemed to be floating, exuding a soft haze.

Then a shadow obscured the view.

"Wooooo!" The owl ruffled her feathers in frustration.

Moments later, the door closed. Footsteps retreated. The owl peeped through the gap once more; the box had gone!

Each morning at three o'clock, the old rooster crowed and MadMax woke up. It was no different this night. He yawned, and looked towards the window. The clouds had disappeared and the moon shimmered above the sea. Everything was quiet and seemed infused with a divine breath.

Obeying an instinctive reflex, he turned towards the door with his ears pricked up and the tip of his tail twitching. Something was going on out there! His large gooseberry eyes stared into the distance, past the big old pine, the chicken house and the vegetable garden, and then all the way up the slope where massive rock formations cropped out of the earth.

"I know she's out there!" He could sense her, somewhere amongst the shadows. His teeth chattered from excitement. He gave a low growl when he saw her scurrying on her short legs; her long, tapering tail visible amongst the stones. She paused from time to time, lifting herself up on her hindlegs to have a better view around and to sniff the air.

"The bitch!" he hissed, watching her closely. "She's picked up something . . ."

Dipping in and out of sight, she climbed quickly towards the top of the property where the driveway reached the road. Again, she stopped to reassure herself that there were no tricky traps or any possible dangers lurking.

What was she after?

Once she had reached the big flat stone at the top, he saw her stop abruptly in her tracks. She stared . . . She seemed completely transfixed . . . And then he saw it, too: right there, stretched out on the rock and bathed in silver moonlight . . . was *her* hen!

The spell lasted only a few seconds, then her hunger and greed got the better of her. In one swift movement, fixing the object of her desire firmly with her eyes, she hurled herself forward like an arrow and grabbed it by the throat.

The hen was hers!

Triumphantly, she checked in all directions. Then she dashed off with her prey as fast as she could. For now, her young would eat! *And to her, all there was, was Now.*

CHAPTER FOUR

Pippa's Secret

Once the worst winter storms were over and a new season had begun, MadMax noticed how the little gosling grew and followed her surrogate mom. "She really takes note of everything Pippa does," he thought, "not that she understands it, of course. After all, she's just a bird!" But it was obvious: nothing satisfied her more than having Pippa all to herself. "One of two things we have in common," he mused while stretching his hindleg skywards to continue his grooming routine. "*Allora*," he grinned,"I should've tried this *asana* when I was one of Italy's greatest . . ."

He stopped himself. "*Tempi passati*, old fool, forget the past!" he mumbled, then uttered a sigh, "As long as I have her."

But Pippa was not one to be bound by attachments. A true child of nature, she loved to be outside in the garden and in the mountains. Although she was not supposed to venture beyond certain boundaries, her curiosity – her passion to explore the unknown – had taken her much further afield than she would ever admit.

While he often gave himself the appearance of being asleep, MadMax observed her through half-closed eyes. "*Certamente...*" he grinned, "*il nostro angelo* is on a new trip. That magic place in the mountains . . . She won't be able to resist!"

And sure enough, one day he saw Pippa sneaking away on the path that led up into the gorge. All along, Mom's song had kept ringing in her ears; it had awakened a restless longing that gave her wings. She was not sure what exactly it was, but something had touched her soul. She had always known that part of her ancestral roots was here; and now, with each step, she felt them reaching deeper into the ground. The mere possibility of getting closer to her great-grandfather spurred her on – quicker, faster – and soon she reached the granite rock formations and the big old trees. She could hardly wait to be drinking from the source! *Oh, to see the blue light and find her tree!*

Finding the spring was easy; Pippa just followed the stream. But when the big moment came and she sank onto her knees, letting the water run through her fingers before bending over her hand to drink, the unearthly blue light that had become her inner compass was nowhere to be seen! How could this be?

She lifted her head in disbelief and glanced up at the trees, wondering which one was hers: "You? Or you? Are you my tree?" As there was no answer, she looked back at the water – but all she saw was herself. She puckered her lips in disappointment. "This is just me!" Feeling somehow betrayed, she turned to leave. But then she hesitated. *There was more to this place than met the eye . . . but what was it?*

With her senses alert, shivering slightly, she glanced around listening to each sound – the birds and frogs, the water gurgling past, and the whirr of dragonfly wings near her ear. Only when she closed her eyes did she become aware of a subtle range of overtones in the air. Suddenly, the rhythmic chanting increased dramatically, bouncing back and forth in a spinning motion between resonating rocks. Her body started to vibrate and, before she knew it, a multidimensional wave almost swept her off her feet.

What was that?

Although trembling, she was too overwhelmed to be scared and felt compelled to open her eyes and look up. Boulders were towering around her: some cloaked in shadows, others bathed in light, all glimmering in shades from ochre to grey to white. Her eyes followed the cracks and fissures, the holes and lines. Tree creepers and lichen were emerging from them like swollen veins and untamed hair in which birds had built nests.

Was the ground still vibrating – or was it her?

Then it struck her: there were faces! They were staring down at her. Grotesque, so real and intimidating that she stepped backwards, stumbled, and plunged into the stream.

Sinking . . . sinking. Then silence. It seemed to come from her heart. In the fluid darkness that engulfed her, air bubbles rose higher and higher towards a radiant source until she felt herself expanding into light. All moments were melting into one and everything seemed to be flowing from her and through her. Within the radius of her complete vision, she observed a small body floating down below . . . like a twig.

Oh, is that me? Am I drowning?

Her soul stretched towards the magic mountain, the gorge, the trees, and the plants. Everything was so vivid and intrinsically connected and she was part of it, too.

No, no, I love you too much! I'm not ready to leave.

She did not know what happened then, but when she opened her eyes she found herself lying on a patch of moss. Water was babbling nearby and there was a bluish haze in the air. She glanced upwards focusing on a furrowed stem from which moisture and sap were dripping, drawing viscid trails across her skin. Sunlight filtered through the canopy of trees, palms and ferns, just enough for her to see. But what really struck her first was a distinct sense of timelessness. Doves cooed sweet nothings at the water's edge while dragonflies poised on reeds. She got up and stretched, feeling refreshed, and now she remembered the faces.

Were they real – or had it been a dream?

She looked up and around, trying to catch another glimpse of those mysterious boulders and could not believe what she saw: "Giant ferns! I've never seen those before!"

She stopped abruptly: "Or did I? Perhaps I did?"

She waded between the fibrous tangle of roots and marveled at the pattern of fronds fanning out above her head. There was this omnipresence of being . . . the constant flow of becoming.

Was it within her or . . . without?

"Great-grandfather?" she called out tentatively. "Great-grandfather, are you here?" There was no answer.

"It's me, Pippa! Don't you remember me?" She shrieked when two blue flamingos flew up with a harsh croak. "No, no. This isn't real," she thought, "flamingos are pink!"

She squinted against the light and now she saw that they were pink. But when the dome of emerald fans undulated to open a passage for their wings, she no longer knew what to think. "Great-grandfather! Where are you . . . please?"

She spread her arms and turned and turned and laughed and tumbled until it made her dizzy, while her voice continued to spiral upwards with an echo in its wake.

There still was no answer, but when she tried to center herself again, something tickled her neck and she giggled: "I knew you were here!" She turned around but there was no one; it was only a young frond from a fern with the coil at its tip still uncurling. She stared at it for a while, swallowing her disappointment, "Great-grandad, why do you call me and then you don't appear?" No longer expecting an answer, she picked it. "Sorry," she said, "but I need you to remind me that I was here."

When she held it up against the light to contemplate its pinnate structure, she noticed that the sun was sinking; in fact, it was almost gone. "Oh! It will be dark soon! I have to go!"

She looked over the edge of the cliff where the water cascaded on its way into the valley. The sun had already disappeared behind Chapman's Peak, feathering the sky with golden hues. Climbing over rocks and roots, she wove her way through undergrowth until she reached the creek. Hopping light-footedly from stone to stone, she followed it all the way down the mountain. By the time she got home her hair and clothes were dry, raising no suspicion.

Later that evening, MadMax watched as she placed the delicate frond between two sheets of blotting paper at the back of a thick old telephone book.

"Ferns are so . . . primeval," she said matter-of-factly.

"Yah. Especially those from our garden," he replied with a devious glint in his eyes.

"There are no –" she started off and quickly bit her tongue. She closed her 'plant press' and put a book on top for more weight. Then she looked at him.

How on earth did he always know?

MadMax sat quietly, his eyes shrouded in mystery. Once again, he had her wondering. Did he secretly accompany her on her excursions, wrapped in an invisible cloak? Did he follow her footsteps back in time, right to that gorge . . . to those faces that had imprinted themselves onto the memory card of her mind?

Little did she know that she would be seeing them again . . .

Year after year, Pippa observed the seasons. What fascinated her most was how the winter rains in June gradually restored all life that the summer heat had withered. Watsonia and chasmanthe broke through their corms, shooting arrowheads of green into the gloomy sky. These were soon followed by long erect spikes with gorgeous flowers, covering the mountain slopes in reds and pinks.

Pippa discovered something new each day. Nothing could stop life from breaking barriers on its mission to create, to expand and to thrive. She saw ericas and even dainty orchids bursting through solid pathways to get a place in the sun. They swayed on their long and slender stalks resembling tiny butter-flies with flashy wings, and triggered in her an irresistible desire to capture those perfect moments forever by preserving them in time. They were ideal specimens to press and dry. After a few weeks, she transformed them into floral compositions mounted on handmade paper from the valley. Mom framed her creations behind glass; that's the maximum Pippa agreed to as she hated frames.

Too small to hang them up on her own, she obediently accepted Dad's help and, with it, his imposed monotony of order.

"A straight line's a straight line, even in Africa!" he preached from the ladder with a level in his hand. "Where would we be without that? Now look carefully and tell me if any picture is out of line. Hello? Knock, knock, Miss Pippa!" His commanding voice forced her from her thoughts as she gazed across the neat new gallery, intrigued by the way her flowers and plants now dissolved in reflections. They almost disappeared! She so much wanted to stop him but what came over her lips was a meek: "It's perfect, Dad!" trying to sound convincing.

"No, no, my girl, you can't see like that! Go to the opposite wall and tell me!" he barked, annoyed by her sluggish gait. "Quicker! Quicker! That's it. And now?"

Pippa gulped. She felt suffocated. Her breath got stuck in her throat, and that was not all.

"Can't be that perfect," Dad grumbled impatiently and climbed down, joining her. Stooping to look from her perspective, he immediately spotted a picture slightly out of line. "Ha! See that one over there? That one's gotta be adjusted! Don't you see that? One's gotta be blind not to see that!" He looked at her. "Hey, what's wrong?"

Pippa held her breath to escape the vile smell of tobacco from his mouth. "They can't breathe, Daddy," she muttered. "They need light!"

"Nonsense! They're dead! Light won't change that. Get the spiritual pollen out of your mind! Think straight!"

Shaking his head disapprovingly, he walked back and moved the ladder to correct the picture. "Now . . . this is level. That's all it needed!"

"Wow!" Mom exclaimed as she came into the room. "We have a real artist here."

She smiled at Pippa and gave her an encouraging hug. "I'm so proud of you . . . !"

"Thank you!" Dad answered from the ladder, measuring and pushing another picture two ticks higher and one back again. "Nothing's perfect, of course . . . but . . . this should do the trick!" Now it was all aligned. "Art," he said intermittently while scanning the lines for the umpteenth time, "they say . . . is 1% talent and 99% hard work. If you ask me, it's all in the lines!"

"Your flight captain is speaking," Mom smiled.

"As I told you, there's only one shortest line between two points." He stepped down and joined them, looking proudly at his oeuvre. "Voilà, my girl! Now we've got something to show!"

Mom sighed quietly, giving her child a squeeze. Pippa hardly noticed it; she was staring through the window, out . . . out into the garden. It took her some time to get used to the subliminal intrusion into her space, but as the content of her pictures was so much part of her, she soon hardly noticed it anymore. Now and then, when she felt patronized or belittled, she knocked a picture out of line, drawing from it a dose of instant relief.

Sensing her inner revolt and anger, Piu Piu stood up tall and proudly flapped her fast growing flight feathers, chirping ever-lasting support and making her laugh.

"She's a scream!" MadMax grinned, always with an eye on the bird and amazed by its rapid transformation.

"Yes, she is. Always simple and herself. She brings such joy."

"Especially those . . ." and he pulled a funny face, upon which Pippa promptly burst into peals of laughter.

As time went by, Pippa's interest shifted. While she kept adding new pictures to her collection, she now developed a strong desire to know more, to identify what she found, and to classify it according to the scientific sources she researched in books and on the Internet.

There was also nature's real treasure trove, Kirstenbosch Botanical Gardens, situated on the other side of the mountain. Whenever she had a chance to go there, she slipped away into that other world. Despite the wide expanse of the gardens, she never got lost.

"I'll bet she's in 'The Dell'," Mom thought to herself as she stepped into the mist that hovered around the mystical forest, just where the gardens originally started, some hundred years ago. "She loves these living fossils, the cycads. Bit strange for a young girl. . . " She shivered; but then this place had always held a strange fascination for her as well.

Pippa did not even notice her. Her silhouette popped up and down between the prehistoric seed plants. She seemed to be picking up something that she stuffed into her pockets.

"Maybe they triggered Pippa's new passion?" Mom wondered. "She always collected seeds . . . usually just a few to integrate into her pictures – but this? She's almost obsessive about it." When she observed how her daughter stored her seeds in jars, labelling them diligently – presumably as she had seen it in the conservatory of the Botanical Gardens – it hit her right between the eyes: "Just like him!"

"Why are you squirreling away so many of them?" she asked her child one day while cleaning her room. "Do you think the earth will run out of seeds?"

She shook her head, looking into Pippa's eyes. "Don't ever worry, sweetheart, there's always enough for all."

Pippa nodded obediently – and continued undeterred.

"What do you want," she overheard Dad say to Mom one day, "they're carved from the same tree. It's in her genes. Don't worry about it. Just a matter of funneling it into something that makes sense."

Mom always said that Pippa took after her great-grandfather who had created many famous parks in Europe. But, once he had set foot in the Cape of Good Hope and discovered what today was depicted as one of the richest floral kingdoms in the world, he never left again.

"Of course, there was more to it." Mom had confided to her one day. "There was a secret! He had fallen in love with a proud African woman. It was her free untamed spirit, her open heart and, above all, the way she lived the life he had always longed for." Then Mom fell silent. Her gaze wandered up towards the distant mountains.

Pippa did not dare to interrupt although there was so much she wanted to ask.

"She was that one wild flower he couldn't analyze, dissect, and tame." Mom went on. "She fascinated him more than any-thing else. And, as Grandma would never leave Africa, he had no other choice but to stay. So he spent the happiest part of his life studying the unique diversity of the Cape flora . . . absorbing its constant change . . . its fearlessness . . . its power to reinvent itself and . . . thrive."

She turned back to Pippa: "That's why it's in our blood, yours and mine. This is where we belong. Do you understand?"

"But Mom, I don't even know where they are! You never showed me their –"

"There are none. They were never found. They're just . . . up there! Like nowhere . . . and everywhere."

They fell into each other's eyes, and beyond – wordlessly searching, connecting and sealing their bond.

Pippa immediately searched the Internet: there were over 8500 plant species in the specified area, most of which were not found anywhere else in the world. Almost 70% were endemic. What she did not know at the time was that her great-grandfather had compiled all his work and findings in his *Botanical Encyclopedia*, a magnificent oeuvre that Mom had treasured dearly, but that Dad had wanted her to donate to Kirstenbosch Botanical Gardens – at a time before Pippa was born.

"Com'on, Grace! That's where this kinda stuff belongs!" He'd kept nagging her, time and again. "At least, there it'll get the recognition it deserves! It's part of your roots – and you never know what may happen."

"If only I had listened!" Pippa heard her say one day in such a broken tone that she looked up from her desk with concern. Mom was staring at a brochure she had picked up from the floor; Pippa recognized it immediately. She saw her eyes flood with tears as she sat down on Pippa's bed. "Now it's too late."

"What, Mom?" Pippa trembled; she had never seen her mother in such a state.

"I . . ." Mom whispered and stopped, her jaws grinding. Then she took a deep breath and Pippa saw her gaze wandering beyond the barriers of time.

"Long ago, before you were born, there was a fire. It was a big, devastating fire." She was lost in some potent memories that visibly shook her to the core.

Walking up and down in her 'kraal', Piu Piu stood on her toes and gave a compassionate chirp. Pippa bent down and took the gosling into her hands, gently caressing its newly sprouting feathers and putting her cheek against its fluff.

"I should be grateful," she heard Mom say to herself as she continued to sweep the floor. "I could have lost so much more."

Suddenly, there was a rumbling noise. Pippa froze, feeling the mountain trembling. Even Piu Piu was holding her breath.

"Good grief, Pippa, you must have gold in there!" Mom looked down at the wooden chest she had just bumped into while cleaning underneath Pippa's bed. "I didn't even know the old thing still existed. Where did you get this from?"

Exchanging a quick look with MadMax, Pippa turned away and put the gosling down, feeling her mother's iron stare on her back. As she came back up again, their eyes met. Her mother's were black. Bottomless. Without saying a word, Pippa put her finger to her pursed lips, holding Mom's glance, willing the question away. Mom raised her eyebrows, sighed and pushed the chest back. Gathering her cleaning utensils, she left Pippa's room without saying another word.

"Phew!" MadMax commented.

Quietly, Pippa let the gosling out and walked into the garden. Piu Piu followed her and enjoyed herself on the lawn. Meanwhile, Pippa's mind raced. She got away with it today, but her mother would still want an answer – sooner or later.

"You'd better come up with something that makes sense," MadMax echoed her thoughts.

"I'm not worried about the chest."

"I know; it's about what's within."

"It all happened so quickly."

"One of those coincidences."

"Coincidence?"

They looked at each other, thinking of that fateful day. The South-Easter had been blowing so fiercely that the door to the attic sprang open and, as Pippa was passing by at that exact moment, she'd slipped in! It looked as if nobody had been in there for a long, long time. Dust particles danced in the light that filtered through a small roof window. With the storm still howling and her heart thudding in her ears, she waited until her eyes adjusted to the gloom beneath the slanting roof. She had no doubt that ghosts were crouching behind the piles of books and boxes, while horrible spiders with long hairy legs, and who knew what else, were hiding in the dark corners.

Suddenly, her heart skipped a beat: she spotted something golden shimmering on the floor. She loved gold! As she got closer to it, she saw it was on a big book lying at the bottom of a pile. The book was wrapped in a white cloth, visibly falling apart. She shuddered. Everything was coated with thick, sticky dust. Plastic covers looked as if they had melted into the books ages ago. Cobwebs were swaying in the draft, just as a violent gust of wind revealed another glimpse of gold.

Gold!

Pippa was magically drawn to it. She did not know nor even care what the book was about; all she knew was that she had to have it. Her whole focus now was on getting the heavy book down into her room – undetected. And before the attic was locked again! She started by removing the books off the top, one by one. She held her breath when the pile collapsed, whirling up dust and making quite a noise. She waited and listened.

As nothing moved in the house and all she heard was the storm, she continued feverishly until she could finally hold the heavy object of her desire in her arms. She slipped back onto the mezzanine, down the spiral staircase and into her room. She opened her treasure chest, praying it would be big enough for the book – and lo and behold, it was a perfect fit! It seemed that all was as it was supposed to be. But then she heard some commotion in the house and rapidly closed the lid. Breathlessly, she sat and listened. There! Somebody had just locked the attic.

"Phew!" Pippa let out a sigh.

"What's up?" MadMax watched her shove the chest back under her bed.

"Hush, it's a secret!"

"Ah!"

"Shhh! We'll look at it tonight."

They didn't realize that Piu Piu had overheard every word and was frustrated that she could not see through her enclosure; not even by standing on her toes and paddling with her wings. She walked up and down, up and down – but not a glimpse! The irony was that it was all happening right under her beak. But, having a happy nature, she was far too excited to sulk. Today, she would certainly not fall asleep after dusk as was her habit; she would be waiting for the secret to be revealed!

It was close to midnight when all went quiet in the house. The wind whistled outside, rattling at the windows and doors. Dark clouds raced across the sky, inking out the moon and the stars. The owls hooted angrily, tired of storms. Pippa shivered a little when she climbed out of her bed. She lit a candle and put it on the floor. MadMax yawned and glanced down at her from the bed as she pulled the wooden chest with its copper trimmings carefully out into the flickering light.

Wide awake, with her heart throbbing in her ears, Piu Piu waited for the clicking sound when Pippa opened the lid.

Removing the mothy cloth and the layers of dust with her hands, Pippa held her breath as the precious leather-bound book appeared. "Oh . . ." she whispered, "this is –"

"A book!" MadMax observed drily from the top. "Now isn't that something."

"Carved geometric lines along the borders," she said, ignoring his facetious tone. "Gilt decoration! Oh, and the title . . . how elegant it looks! It's slightly embossed in gold: Encyclopedia Botanica!" She looked up at him, her eyes sparkling.

"Not bad," he said, "by whom?"

"Who? Ah, wait . . ."

Pippa raised the candle to decipher the longish name of the author, carved into the leather.

"No!" she exclaimed, mystified. "Holy smoke!"

The candle flickered, sending shadows across the ceiling. Piu Piu was strung to breaking point.

"That's his name." Pippa looked at MadMax, gobsmacked. "Do you know what this means?"

MadMax got up to have a closer look from the top. "Are you saying it's . . ."

"Yes!"

"Hmmm . . ."

"If I see what I see, it must be."

"Not bad."

"Shhh!" Pippa hushed him.

"So it didn't –" MadMax whispered, "– after all?"

"No! It didn't!" She shook her head, tracing the embossed title on the delicately carved leather with her fingertips. "This goes a long way back. It's so . . . cold."

"Cold? Like . . . petrified?"

"No, not that. More like . . ."

"Mummified? Fossilized?"

"Perhaps. I don't know!"

"Whatever," he purred, watching her closely. Her eyes were closed and the palm of her hand hovered just above the leather landscape; vibrating slightly. He narrowed his eyes to slits. "I know someone who'd be ecstatic . . . if she knew!"

"No!" Pippa flared up, "no!"

"Shhh!" MadMax hissed.

"No!" Pippa hissed back. "It's mine! Don't you dare tell anyone!"

"OK, OK!"

Piu Piu got real goose bumps. Rooted to the spot, she absorbed each word.

"Promise!" Pippa insisted.

"Promise!" MadMax lifted his paw.

The ensuing silence was broken by a gust of wind that pulled at the door.

"It's not because of her," Pippa whispered, "it's . . ." She broke off. It always irritated her when MadMax stared off into a space where she could not follow him. She wondered whether she had offended him?

"Look at me, don't you see? I was meant to find it!" she said and, as he still did not move, added: "I'm not giving it away."

"Yah . . . got that." He turned his head and looked at her, his eyes suddenly glistening like One Thousand and One Nights. "So what are you waiting for? Open it!" He jumped down and sat beside her as she heaved the book carefully onto the carpet. Once she had dusted it down completely, they saw it had gilt lines and decorations on the spine, and brass clasps on the side.

"Gold-rimmed pages. I love that!"

"*Noblesse oblige!* He was –"

"– an aristocat, like you!" She teased him while opening the book. She went carefully through some of the slightly yellowed pages, getting more and more excited. "Oh," she repeated over and over again, "look!"

"Shhh!" MadMax kept warning her, while poor Piu Piu ran up and down in her 'kraal', watching the shadows on the ceiling which were now flecked with golden glints. She was on the edge of despair. Her beak was burning hot and her nostrils perspiring. "I want to see, too!" she wailed. "Let me out, please!"

"Not for you!" MadMax barely twitched an ear.

Oh, that conceited faun! How could they be so mean and shut her out? "I don't like this secret," she thought, "it takes her away from me."

"Perfect!" Pippa said, bent over the table of contents in the book. "It's in alphabetical order. Each plant has its description. Look, all these delicate drawings, the details, down to the seeds." She was beside herself with joy.

"I guess they used a quill in those days. Perhaps a quill from a goose?" he purred, shooting a sardonic grin at Piu Piu, who vented her feelings with a burst of ridiculous chirps.

"What did you say?" Pippa asked, ignoring Piu Piu.

"I said – there are a lot of pages. You don't mean to read all this?"

"Poppycock!" Piu Piu snapped, "that's not what he – "

"What do you think?" Pippa laughed and returned to the book. "Oh! Here he writes about the seasons . . . winter plants. Listen to this: . . . *many varieties of geraniums, thyme, rosemary, rockroses, flowering buchu and the numerous fynbos shrubs with aromatic foliage, mixing into bouquets of fragrances . . .*"

Pippa looked at him: "Sounds like our garden, doesn't it? *Winter is the time when the crane flower (Strelitzia reginae) – also called the bird of paradise – starts to bloom again. Orange flames with dark-blue spikes . . .* Hey! He forgot the yellow one that grows under my window, the 'Mandela Gold'."

"Hey!" MadMax gave her a nudge. "He wrote this well over a hundred years ago."

"Hmm," Pippa said and continued to leaf through the pages, "you're probably right."

As her fingers glided through the pages, they opened at her favorite plant: "The poppy. Did you see? It opened all by itself." After considering the drawings for a while, an idea struck her: "Wait, wait . . . I'll get my 'press'."

After rummaging a while in the background, she came back with the thick telephone book. She opened it carefully, locating the protruding edges of white blotting paper. "Here we go . . ." She inspected a few delicate red poppy flowers that she had pressed and dried between the pages of the book. Some had stalks and a few leaves attached to them, as well as tiny bits of pollen.

"*I will dance. . . I will fly. . . like a petal in the sky. . .* " she sang in a low voice. Suddenly, she beamed with excitement: "I think I've got it. Look. Isn't it amazing? The petals are almost transparent, but the colors are still quite well preserved. Now let's compare their shapes with the drawings." She chose one specimen and placed it carefully on top of the drawing. Now it was shining through the real flower on top of it as if it had always been there.

"Now it has some life to it," she whispered.

"It needs more than that," MadMax replied, sniffing the air. "I still smell it . . ."

"Smell what?"

"Shhh!"

They froze and stared at the door, listening. Everything remained quiet, so she turned back to him and signaled: "Don't tell me. I don't want to know –"

"Ashes!" he said ruthlessly. Fired up by a sudden shriek from Piu Piu, he continued, "Ashes and smoke. It's everywhere."

Pippa looked into his mysterious eyes. They went right through her, and beyond. He was here and not here because he was somewhere else at the same time. "Hey!" she said, pushing her head softly against his. "Where are you?"

"*I am lost in that other reality. It's sweet not to look at two worlds, to melt into meaning as sugar melts in water*", he declaimed. "That's . . . Rumi."

"That's . . . nice," she replied laconically. "I remember you used to quote him . . . or wasn't it you? I know someone did . . . Anyways, I have no clue what you mean."

"You do." He nudged his cold nose against her burning cheek. "You just don't remember."

"It seems I'm forgetting a lot," she said sleepily, "so much is slipping away . . . these last years." Suddenly, she felt tired.

"You're growing up," she heard him say and off he went to curl up on her bed.

She closed the book and heaved it back into the chest. She could not resist gliding her fingertips one more time across the leather landscape. The title snaked through it like a river of gold. She closed her treasure chest and pushed it back under her bed. Then she blew out the light.

Miserable and resentful, Piu Piu plunged into her nest and wept. Her happy world was crumbling, leaving her behind - alone once again. No doubt it could only get worse!

Hooked by her great-grandad's book, Pippa could not rest. The tome opened in her mind's eye and the drawings started to oscillate and stir. Like glistening threads, the delicate lines took on a life of their own. Tender sprouts wiggled through the gold-rimmed pages, dreaming of freedom and of space. Rising from the chasm of oblivion, they cracked open the leather landscape like scorched earth. Stimulated by the air they touched, they grew leaves, and then more leaves opened, and tender blossoms unfurled.

Mesmerized, she watched as a forgotten universe unfolded, while pages turned to the rhythm of a magical hand. With her mind engrossed in her reading, past and present, memory and dreaming melted into one. Her eyelids fluttered as she drifted to the next page:

Fynbos wouldn't be fynbos without its most defining compo-nent: the graceful Cape reeds. These are tufted restios including feathery grasses, sedge, rushes and even papyrus in the swamps and marshes.

As she studied the detailed drawings they seemed to come alive, with a languid breeze making them undulate. It seemed as if her great-grandfather guided her through the pages, showing her how, after showers, the restios drooped tragically, heavy with crystal beads. Then, when the days became longer and warmer, delectable golden nuggets emerged. Soon they were abuzz with bees whirling up pollen as they foraged through the culms, whispering: "Winter is over! This now is spring!"

Almost overnight, the slopes of the mountains exploded into lavish yellows, oranges and golds as pincushions and leucadendrons started to bloom, with pockets of silver trees and proteas in between. Then there were more proteas!

"Oh, Great-grandad, I see they fascinate you as much as me!"

She saw herself following him through the veld and the mountains, discovering new species while he shared his wisdom with her: "Plants have a strong sense of place. A plant and its location belong intricately together. A similar plant in a different place naturally has a different vibration; hence it is not the exact same plant. "

She watched him take notes and make sketches of plants within their natural environment – and indeed, he used a quill!

At times he added an insect, a butterfly or a bird, depending on its relationship with the plant, often as its pollinator.

He collected the seeds and he cut flowers and leaves at different stages of growth for further studies and to execute the more detailed drawings later at home. She walked on air within the timeless space they shared, absorbing his knowledge like a sponge.

Look at the name of a plant for identification and classification purposes only. Beyond that, remember that a plant is not a name.

From the many species growing in the garden, Pippa already knew that proteas exhibited a wide variety of shapes. Their name had never meant anything to her.

"Did you ever notice how easily they adapt to any condition?" Pippa nodded.

"Now think of their name: protea. Protea! Where does this come from . . . do you know? You tell me!" As Pippa shook her head, he continued: "Well, then let me tell you: they were named after the shrewd Greek sea-god, Proteus! Proteus stood for change; the constantly changing nature of things. Imagine," he muttered under his breath, removing his hat as he bent down to her, "imagine, the god could take on any form at will!"

Hidden behind unruly brows, his blue eyes were alert and shining as if he were the mighty sea-god himself.

Pippa was gobsmacked. She stared at him incredulously.

"Oho ja! He could well be the stone over there . . . a pie in the sky . . . or this noisy cricket on my hand!"

Great-grandad gazed intently into her eyes and nodded: "He just focused on it and, voilà!" He snapped his finger and laughed. "Knew a lot more than we do, da jolly old Greeks. Besides slipping in and out of their roles all the time, creating nothing but human drama."

Pippa looked up at him wide-eyed, brimming over with new sensations that sent her imagination spinning.

"Beware what you focus on or wish for, young lady," he cautioned her, "it could well come true."

"I want to be like you, Great-grandad!"

He patted her tenderly on the head and smiled. Then he put his hat back on. "Where was I? Ah, the seeds, the seeds . . ." he said more to himself than to her, putting the cricket onto a twig where it continued to chirp. He had been focusing on a more mature protea. The flowers changed their colors and structures once they'd withered and dried, at the same time holding on to their precious seeds.

The page turned and Pippa saw some exquisite drawings of birds, which she knew well from her garden: "Oh, how lovely . . . a sunbird . . . a sugarbird!"

Then she read: *The seeds attract a multitude of little spiders and insects, which in turn attract the double-collared sunbird with its green metallic head and throat and a bright red band across the chest, and the long-tailed greyish Cape sugarbird. They are equipped with long down-curved bills and brush-tipped tubular tongues to reach the nectar hidden in all kinds of different protea heads, although they don't mind catching an occasional insect cookie – sometimes right in the air.*

And, of course, there were ants! Living in large colonies, they sometimes built anthills from sand and clay at the base of the big plants.

"If you watch closely," he said, "you will notice that they are looking for seeds that have little fleshy parts attached to them, the *elaiosomes*. These they carry into their nests to feed their babies. This is how seeds are dispersed underground. At some point in the future, when they know their time has come, they will germinate and grow." There was an appraising look in his eyes when he added: "As with many things of value in life, first they have to go through fire."

"Do plants know that their time is limited?" she asked after a pause. "I mean . . . that they die?"

Bending down to her, he gave her an enigmatic glance: "You have to become the plant if you want to uncover its soul."

"How on earth would I do that," she thought to herself, her eyelids fluttering under his stare.

"What you are the vibration of, appears. What you ar not the vibration of remains invisible to you. That's the secret," he said.

She felt something creepy running down her spine and quickly sat up in her bed. Was it perhaps Proteus disguised as a noisy cricket getting on her nerves for a while? She listened into the darkness and, just then, the obnoxious noise stopped. It really stopped!

"Spanakopita," MadMax said, licking his paw, "tasty stuff. He won't bother you anymore."

Her eyes closed drowsily and soon the magic realm had her back: *Fire is an essential stage in the life cycle of most fynbos plants, ideally in late summer. My research over years showed that many proteas keep their seeds for at least a year. They release them only once they are literally on fire!*

Pippa's vision blurred and she gasped for air, kicking her blanket away.

"You're hectic!" MadMax hissed, "calm down. Sleep!"

"I'm becoming the plant . . ."

"Indeed," he groaned. "I smell the ashes . . ."

She no longer heard him. She felt a stream of energy rising and sinking that was much stronger than her. It invaded her veins, her cells, her entire being – it even filled her ears. It became her. Or was she it?

Too tired to think, she sank into its regular rhythm, hoping it would lull her to sleep. But, suddenly, the unthinkable happened: she saw herself engulfed in flames! A blaze of blistering heat devoured her hair, igniting her like a candle. But, instead of resisting, she reached out through the flames to surrender the last barrier, to give it away, to offer it all like a prayer. One last time, life's ecstasy escaped from her lips, rising, rising higher and returning into the light. Shrouded in acrid smoke, the empty vessel cracked, it broke and crumbled – down, down, down to ashes, to darkness, to dust.

"Awake! Awake! Winter is over now!" The seeds rejoiced as the heat exploded their shells. Patiently, they waited until the first rains with an essence of smoke in it tickled them and their juices started to flow . . . and flow more . . . and they anchored themselves in the soil. Hungry for life, they thrust themselves through the earth's crust, the dust and the ashes. They pushed and sprouted, rising up, up, up towards the light.

"A plant is not a plant," Pippa whispered, "it's the sun, the earth, the rainbow and even the fire. It's the whole universe vibrating."

MadMax opened half an eye and twitched his ears. Her voice was barely audible.

"There's always a space to stretch beyond, there's always something new to become."

He covered his face with the tip of his tail. "That's as it is."

"That's as it is," she murmured and floated away into Morpheus' realm.

Starting up from her own blazing nightmare, Piu Piu was relieved to hear Pippa's voice again. "If a plant is not a plant," she wondered, "who am I?" It was something she had to find out. But when she glanced at Pippa, and saw the pompous tomcat snuggled up against her, a pang of jealousy consumed her, like a fever. It wasn't long before a mad, destructive, idea possessed her: There had to be a way to win Pippa back - no matter how!

"Are you OK, sweetheart?" Mom asked Pippa the next morning as she prepared for school. "You look tired. Did you sleep?"

"Yes, Mom," she said, without looking at her.

"Are you sure there isn't something I should know?" Mom insisted.

"I'm OK, Mom."

Grace knew her child too well; something was going on.

"It's a beautiful day," she said, as she looked out of the window, "and did you see? Your trees are in full bloom! How about taking some pictures when you're back?"

Pippa looked up, her face suddenly beaming: "With your cam?"

"OK," Mom smiled, "hurry up, I'll take you through just now." Her eyes followed the young girl as she skipped away to her room in her new school uniform.

Perhaps it was just her imagination?

"She seems so . . . aloof," she said to Pete before he left for work. "It worries me. I hope it's not a fever or something."

Dad shrugged her concerns off. "Always a lot going around at this time of the year," he said. "Kids pick it up in a snap. You should hear them bark and sneeze on the plane."

"I didn't think of that. She's never been affected by seasonal changes. My feeling is that it's more on the emotional side."

"Well, that's in your department . . ."

"I'm not sure."

"Don't worry, my angel," he kissed her good-bye. "Let me know how she is later this evening. I have to fly."

Mom watched him walk away towards his car. "How different we are," she thought, folding her arms. "Quintessentially, men are a different species. In Africa, we've always known that."

He stopped and looked back, "Don't fuss too much about it. Worry is a misuse of imagination!"

"Really. Did you come up with that one all alone by yourself?"

He cracked up with laughter, now anxious to get to his car. "Of course not! Why should I? Since I have you!"

"Love you, too!" She waved a kiss as he drove off, with the pair of Egyptian geese on top of the chimney honking a noisy goodbye. As she returned to the house, her thoughts drifted back to Pippa. What had become of her bubbly child?

She knew something was wrong.

CHAPTER FIVE

Bitter Taste of Freedom

"Piu Piu, we have to talk!" Pippa blurted out, a few months later, when she came home from school. Flinging her bag onto her chair, she ranted: "Instead of going for my ride I have to clean up all this . . . this mess! This isn't fair!"

"Fair?" Suddenly, everything revolted in Piu Piu. "Do you think *you* are fair?" She did not dare express her indignation yet, but her awareness of being manipulated against her will grew. All this prevented her from becoming who she wanted to be.

The fact was that Pippa was still too scared to leave her fosterling all by herself in the garden. There was always a chance she could become the prey of a hawk, an eagle, a snake, a wild cat, a stray dog or the wicked mongoose.

"Oh com'on! She's big enough now." MadMax reassured her. "She's got what it takes. Let her go!"

"I'm not going to; I've learned my lesson, remember? I won't let anything like that happen again, ever."

But the truth of the matter was that a lot had happened over the past weeks; much more than Pippa was aware of!

Even a blind shrew would agree that Piu Piu had outgrown her temporary home and could easily fly over her enclosure. She loved to sit on elevated places like the coffee table, from where she could look out of the window and watch the forever changing world she so desperately wanted to dive into and be part of herself. Despite the fact that she had never seen herself in a mirror, she was instinctively drawn to the other members of her species. Sometimes, she heard them rumbling and honking on the roof above her. Then they landed on the lawn – to graze, to court or to fight. And, when their friends called from the meadows in the valley, they just spread their wings and took off with enviable ease.

"I want to be like them!" Piu Piu's heart sank a little deeper each time she watched them disappear. But the clearer she made her yearning known, the more Pippa confined her. What had seemed like a funny game in the beginning, grew into a stifling tension between them. Piu Piu loved Pippa and her home; she had no intention of leaving. She just felt an overwhelming longing to spread her wings and experience a world without boundaries that she knew existed – even for her.

Flight was what she longed for.

"It's not for you!" Pippa shouted categorically, building the wall a little higher each day, until Piu Piu, depressed, sat in a corner and wept. *Not for you! Not for you! What's for me then?*

Just when she was at the end of her tether, a flash of inspiration changed it all: "Perhaps I shouldn't look that far?" she wondered. "Maybe there's something I've missed, close-by?"

As she scanned the area just around her, she realized she was not alone. There was a whole colony of 'Daddy Longlegs' who had woven fine, tangled webs between the wall and the desk, where they were undisturbed by insidious brooms, mops and hoovers. They had to be at least a thousand years old!

Piu Piu watched as these spider-like killer machines strode past on their long, skinny legs the moment a moth, a fly, or a mosquito got caught. Their mad struggles for their lives made the insects get even more entangled in the trap of sticky threads, embalming themselves in shapes like hot dogs and roulades. Once Daddy Longlegs arrived, the game was over. Their life juices were sucked out mercilessly and they died. If they were lucky, it was the other way around.

Used to getting her food served on little plates and dishes, Piu Piu was appalled. She got goose pimples at the mere thought that the long-legged uglies could be stepping over her while she had a snooze. Yukk!

One day, when she discovered that this was indeed the case, she snapped at one of those legs and held firmly on to it.

First, Daddy Longlegs pulled hard to get his leg back, but Piu Piu was determined not to let it go. Suddenly it went 'Snap!' and he simply released it from its joint and moved on like nothing had happened at all. He had enough legs at his disposal and, eventually, a new one would grow. The arrogant monster ignored her completely!

Piu Piu spat the leg out. But the moment it hit the floor it moved frantically, opening and closing in its joint like an army knife. Completely taken by surprise, Piu Piu hopped into the air a few times to get out of the way.

"Vicioussss nobodiessss!" a lizard hissed contemptuously. It was looking down from the wall with its forked tongue flicking to ensure it was not missing out on any major event; especially, if there was something to be gained. Daddy Longlegs' limb was still twitching and, despite the leg coming off a very old fart, it remained incredibly attractive. The sleek reptile could not resist the temptation to slip a little further down the wall, which brought it within dangerous reach of the naïve yet unpredictable gosling.

"Jussst nobody! Looksssss!" the lizard sighed seductively. "Looksss . . . ssso delicioussss!"

While Piu Piu looked at the leg, it disappeared like magic before her eyes! The cunning thief had just snatched it from her with a sticky tongue-tip. After slipping back up the wall with her prey, the lizard devoured it with obvious delight. "Sssssss," it moaned ecstatically, "delicioussss! Deliciousssssss!"

Piu Piu was speechless.

While the lizard munched and the long leg disappeared bit by bit in her big triangular mouth, Piu Piu was numbed by an eruption of feelings she had never experienced before. They were a mix of helplessness, ignorance of other species and plain outrage. Something hot welled up deep within her guts as she eyed the enemy beyond her reach. Her body broke into a furious honk, but all that came out was a piteous chirp.

How embarrassing!

"More legsssss," the lizard hissed enticingly, flicking her forked tongue. "Ssssssso many more legssss! Delicioussss nobodies!"

Mesmerized by the reptile's suave persuasion, Piu Piu looked around and spotted another big fellow with confusingly many legs. This time she would not let herself be fooled. But when she waddled up to her target, it suddenly turned into one rapidly spinning blur. Piu Piu could not even see the legs! Head, body, legs – everything was in a whir! Was 'nobody' making fun of her as well?

"Delicioussss!" the reptile spurred her on at the top of its voice.

Piu Piu cringed. By now, her frustration was impossible to bear. Fiercely determined not to expose herself to ridicule again, she closed her eyes and then hacked blindly into the spinning swirl. She hacked and hacked and hacked until nothing swirled anymore and all went still. Dead still.

For some moments, she did not dare open her eyes, but then something hit her on the tail. She jerked open her wings and jumped up and down to evade the chaos of legs twitching and kicking and snapping around her. They were everywhere!

On top of it all, the lizard's jeering squeal drove her insane! Just as she flung herself in the air another time, something happened to her. The moment she landed on the floor, she stood up tall and flapped her wings. Taking a deep breath, she stamped her webbed foot onto the fidgeting limbs – 'smack!' First the one, then the other. 'Smack!' And some more: 'smack!' 'smack!' 'smack!' After that she waited. Soon it tickled her so much that she started to giggle and paddled with her wings to keep her balance, but after a while Daddy Longlegs' legs kicked no more. Slowly, they stretched out and relaxed in a rather appetizing manner; like crab sticks on a platter.

"Sssseesss! Deliciousss legsss and kneeessss!" the lizard hissed beseechingly with juices of gluttony dropping from her mouth.

"Not for you!" Piu Piu snapped boldly, "keep your mouth shut."

The lizard gulped and no longer made the slightest attempt to leave her safe position. At least not for now.

Although Piu Piu was not convinced she'd even like the creepy stuff, merely knowing who was watching gave her no choice but to have a go at the meal. Starting with the largest limb, she gobbled up one leg after the other, munching and crunching with relish – they were delicious indeed!

"Ssseeesss!" the lizard sizzled, hardly able to resist the gravitational pull.

"Not for you!" Piu Piu whistled, sending the lizard back into hiding. Just as she finished the last bit, she suddenly noticed that there were Daddy Longlegs everywhere, staring at her, as though they were paralyzed. She could hardly see where one ended and the next began. "Booo!" she trumpeted and flung herself towards them. "Booo! Boo!"

They spurted off for cover in all directions, leaving a cloud of dust behind. From that moment onwards, Piu Piu was absolutely sure that no Daddy Longlegs would walk over her again, not ever! But then she saw that the sneaky lizard had seized the moment her lack of attention had presented, and had pinched a foot and some toes. Piu Piu whirled around in the way she had just learned from Daddy Longlegs, and came to rest on the beast's sticky tongue.

The lizard barked in surprise and tried to pull it back, but the gosling was firmly glued to her. The more the lizard tried to get away from her, the closer she came. Slowly, she was pulled up the wall backwards and upside down. It was so funny that Piu Piu started to giggle and she rowed in the air with her wings. Eventually, she did what geese do and liberated herself by releasing a massive pancake. While she glided gently back to the ground and remained there flat on her back, convulsed with laughter, the lizard disappeared, never to be seen again.

That's how Piu Piu had learned her first big lesson, and a strategy she would never forget. At least, now she knew how to feed herself. Oh, wasn't that great!

But there was something else she only thought of once her muscles and nerves relaxed. It was that exhilarating feeling when her wings had lifted her off the ground. It had happened so fast – and had surprised her – during her attempts to escape those snapping legs. She closed her eyes and recalled it again. There it was . . . oh, how she'd loved it . . . the thrill of letting go of the ground and escaping into the lightness above. Although her movements were clumsy and she was shocked by her own heaviness when she plopped down, those brief moments up in the air triggered a profound sensation that would never leave her again. "That felt like . . . breathing!" she whispered. "I have to do it again! Yes, I will!"

It was dark when she was woken by an unusual vibration around her; like many little feet marching. When she opened her eyes she saw a long line of ants carrying the tiny remains of the Daddy Longlegs' massacre away.

"Take away! Take away . . . clearing the leftovers of the day!" They chanted to the rhythm of their shuffling feet, paying no attention to her.

Piu Piu stood tall and flapped her wings, faster and faster. "Thank you!" she exclaimed, "you all taught me a lot today."

From that fateful day onwards – and only when no one was watching – Piu Piu stood as tall as she could and flapped her wings. Sometimes her efforts lifted her slightly off the ground, but it was not at all what she had experienced or what she felt it should be. "Hang in there!" she told herself, and each time her heart hopped a little higher from excitement. Whenever she fell over on the floor, she just got up and tried one more time.

One more time became her silent mantra and she knew without the slightest shadow of a doubt that – sooner or later – it would lead her to success. "One more time!" she chirped as soon as Pippa had left and the room was hers. *One more time!*

One sunny morning while practicing, she created such a draft with her wings a fat green caterpillar was swept off the edge of the desk. The camouflaged larva landed right in front of Piu Piu's feet, a little numbed and curled up tightly. "Oooops!" Piu Piu said, glancing down at the weird creature without making head or tail of it. The fact that she saw no legs at all made her extremely suspicious.

"Hey!" she hissed, giving it a gentle push with the tip of her beak. "Show me your legsss."

"Wha ha ha ha!" the caterpillar giggled in a gay lisp, rolling over a few times.

"Ooo hooo hoops!" Piu Piu opened her wings, hopping backwards from surprise. Highly intrigued, she stretched her neck and turned her head to look at it from a safe distance – just in case! Now that one was a strange fellow. The unknown intruder recovered amazingly quickly from his steep fall, stretching and fine-tuning his many abdominal segments into horizontal order. When the tiny curving spine had popped up like a hook at the rear end – which Piu Piu observed with great amusement – the smooth shiny creature lifted its front end up to skim the area. Spotting the tempting salad leaves on Piu Piu's plate, it headed straight for them, sashaying across the tiled floor. Once its strong mandibles got to work, there was no stopping this voracious eating machine.

Piu Piu watched how the little fellow ate his way right through the greens. Everything disappeared at lightning speed.

"Another take-away freak," she thought and, suddenly, her mouth was watering and a bold idea hit her: "Hmm, should I try this tasty salad-wrap . . . "

"Hey, roller!" She lowered her head just above the soft-bodied creature, which was clad in what looked like trendy pajamas. It immediately went into the 'sphinx pose', with the front end raised and the head tucked under. "Hey!" Piu Piu repeated more accommodatingly, "you could say hello."

"Hello," the caterpillar answered meekly, sticking its head out a little and seeing itself reflected in Piu Piu's inquisitive eye. "I will never forget what you will do for me," it said solemnly.

"Hello?" Piu Piu pulled her head away. Did the roller have all his marbles?

"Have we met?" Piu Piu was perplexed, but instead of receiving an answer the caterpillar responded with a request that puzzled her even more: "Help me find a place to hang!"

"You want to hang yourself?"

"That's right." The answers came like bullets.

"Here?"

"That's right!"

"Now?"

"That's right!"

Piu Piu snorted incredulously, blowing out air from all ends. It sent the caterpillar dancing out of control for a few instants, paddling with its ridiculous stubs for something to hold on to. Piu Piu was too confused to laugh. Was it another trick? "Why?" she asked. "You'll die!"

"That's right," the caterpillar said matter-of-factly. "One's gotta move on."

"That's right," Piu Piu said, bewildered.

"Quickly! Quickly!" The caterpillar sounded stressed. "Gotta hang!"

Although Piu Piu felt slightly indignant at being pressurized by the sassy lunatic on her plate, she was just too intrigued – and so she looked up and around. The wooden underside of Pippa's desk looked quite neat to hang on to. But how on earth would the creepy-crawlie get up there? Perhaps by holding on to her nose? "Need a lift, quickly, quickly?" she asked with a genuine intention to assist. As there was no answer, she looked down – but now the caterpillar had disappeared!

"Hey roller, are you taking me for a ride?"

Getting increasingly annoyed, Piu Piu swung her neck up and around, and hissed. The fact that the roller had disappeared right under her nose put her into a state of extreme irritation. She glanced at the makeshift walls that enclosed her. She had inspected them over and over again.

There was no way out!

"How can everyone come and go – and I have to stay?" Piu Piu had a feeling she had been duped again and her mood darkened. She was getting a bit despondent; all this neither helped her achieve her ambition to fly nor find out who she was.

"Who am I?" she asked herself over and over again. There was nobody she could identify with – neither a lizard, nor Daddy Longlegs, and even less this bizarre creature that wanted to hang itself to move on!

"Where do I fit in? Am I like . . .?" she wondered, thinking about the cat. "Furry legs, furry tail, furry ears and fur in the face – plus those preposterous puffy pads with spikes! No! Definitely not!"

The one she loved and related to most was Pippa, despite the fact that their relationship was strained. She had heard MadMax say that Pippa was born with wings too, but ones you couldn't normally see.

Could I be like Pippa one day?

She loved the idea. It calmed her. Puffing up her feathers, she sat in the sunshine that filtered in through the open window. Just as she was dozing off, a butterfly flitted past and the draft carried it outside. "Oh, to be able to do just that." This was something Piu Piu could relate to, although it was still nothing more than a vague concept in her imagination. A deep longing brought tears into her eyes, and silent sobs shook her chest.

"I know how you feel!" A tender voice lisped from underneath the desk, just above her head. "Know all that! Worn those pajamas! But our time to fly will come! Quickly! Quickly!"

Piu Piu gasped. Her 'salad-wrap' was hanging vertically underneath Pippa's desk; she would never have recognized it by its voice. But now her beak was salivating uncontrollably and she felt her taste buds explode. Oh, happy day – her delicacy from heaven was just a snap away!

"Soon you will be a big beautiful goose – free to spread your wings and fly, no matter what others say!" the 'salad-wrap' added, brushing Piu Piu's devious desire away. Before her stunned eyes, the being started to wriggle and twitch while producing a green sheath that, gradually, it pulled over itself, bottom to top, until it was completely enveloped. Now it looked like a green pod hanging from the desk: the chrysalis.

"Is this your new pajama top?" Piu Piu asked a little disappointed, and puzzled at the same time. It no longer had an appetizing appeal. There was no answer either. It seemed that the voice could no longer get through. Fascinated, Piu Piu kept watching. At times, the pod moved slightly; then it remained completely still.

"Keep an eye on me over the next two weeks, will ya?" Piu Piu heard, mentally.

"Sure," she responded spontaneously, but then she added: "Hey! Why should I do this for you?"

"I will teach you my secret."

"I see." Piu Piu replied, unfazed. "But thank you, no. Not another book!"

"Book?" came the answer. "No, no . . . I will fly!"

"You will fly!" Piu Piu almost fell over, laughing.

"I'm on my way," came the answer. "Quickly . . . qui . . ." Then there was silence.

Piu Piu thought about the caterpillar for a long time. She would have swallowed it without hesitation had it not said the one thing Piu Piu desperately needed to hear: that she would become a goose – free to fly! These words literally ignited her imagination. A GOOSE! While it was just another word that had no meaning for her – at least not at this stage – she found it electrifying. Combined with the image of flying, it filled her with joy and confidence. Each morning she looked at the chrysalis and felt inspired.

"Hey, you," she quacked a little more boldly each day. "Com'on, fly! Quickly! Quickly!"

Each day she stood up a slightly taller, flapping her wings faster and – with this 'quickly! quickly!' firing her up in her mind – she even started to run to get some lift. And then it just happened: she rose into the air and flew over the 'wall'! Just like that! No one was more surprised than Piu Piu herself.

"Too bad no one is watching," she thought.

After recovering from her shock, she tried it again and landed back in her prison. She flew out and back in again until she could do it whenever she wanted. Oh, this was exhilarating! "Hey, roller," she shouted, "did you see? I'm quicker than you!"

Soon, however, in and out was getting boring – so she tried up and down. This was even more fun, although a much bigger challenge especially as she never knew where she would be landing. But this was part of the thrill, and soon there was hardly a spot she had not visited, leaving pancakes behind everywhere.

The world had not changed, but Piu Piu had: now she believed in herself!

"I can fly!" she exclaimed at the top of her voice, making sure the computer got it, the banana trees and the 'wall' but, in her spark of grandeur, she bumped into the glass door and dropped flat onto the floor. She flew up instantly and hacked against the glass, honking: "Get out of the way! Don't you see? I fly!"

While the stupid door refused to move, she heard a voice from outside: "Hey cool! I can fly, too!"

Piu Piu looked up and saw a fluffy little sunbird sitting on the deck chair outside. Its parents were in a frantic state, stimulating it to fly further and feeding it in between flights.

"Look!" it chirped, almost losing its balance. But then it flew into the bottlebrush tree, where it was praised and treated to a scrumptious wormburger.

"Nobody rewards me," Piu Piu sulked. Honking a defiant: "Not for you! Not for you!" from the bottom of her lungs, she took off towards the opposite side of the room. In need of a landing place, she slithered across the coffee table and came to a halt in front of the windowpane. As she stumbled back to her feet, the garden opened before her eyes and she saw two magnificent beings looking at her from the lawn. Although she had seen them before from afar, today she felt an immediate bond and an irresistible urge to join them. She stood tall and flapped her wings, ready to fling herself through the window – when a familiar voice stopped her in her tracks.

"Don't be silly, stupid!" MadMax said, curled up in a corner of the sofa. "You'll only hurt yourself."

Piu Piu stared at him, nonplussed: "What are you doing here? You were banned!"

"Really?"

"Pippa was loud and clear! You made her cry all night! Because of you she lost her only –"

"Watch – " MadMax interrupted but Piu Piu didn't let him off the hook just yet: " – it was the last one! She's looking for it everywhere. She's in a bad mood all the time. How could you be so mean!"

" – You've got visitors," MadMax said, unfazed, gazing at the pair of inquisitive geese outside.

"Who are they?" Piu Piu whispered, staring as they came closer, stretching their necks towards her.

"Well, you should know!" he replied.

They were just a few meters away, turning their heads slightly so Piu Piu could see their orange-brown eyes. The smaller one was emitting incessant raucous quacks without taking her eyes off Piu Piu.

"One day, you'll be like them," MadMax mentioned casually. "A noisy Egyptian goose."

The geese outside spread their wings and honked. Moments later they launched themselves into the air and flew off towards the valley. Piu Piu's eyes followed them until they were gone. "Now I know who I am," she said to herself, "I'm a GOOSE! I'm meant to fly and be free. Free!"

She stopped and listened inside. Strangely enough, Dad's inviting mantra: *'Just do it!'* suddenly resonated. "He flies, too. Surely he understands?"

Deep down, Piu Piu knew all too well who held her back – and knew that she did this with her best intentions.

"One day," Pippa kept saying day after day, "when you are big and strong and I no longer have to worry about you!"

One day . . . one day! Why not now?

Piu Piu began to suffer. She felt suffocated and deprived. Eventually, she saw no other way to make herself understood than by messing up Pippa's room. Their relationship became increasingly tense, until that day when the shit literally hit the fan and neither could take any more.

"What a mess!" Pippa groaned, wringing out the cloth and pushing the bucket to the next blotch on the floor. "It stinks. I can't handle this anymore."

"Relax," MadMax said, sitting outside the open door with the afternoon sun warming his back. "Here are your choices: either you ditch school or you spend all your pocket money on Pampers . . ."

Pippa was far too upset to laugh at the idea of Piu Piu waddling around in Pampers.

"Or," he added, "you just let her go!"

Pippa continued to wash the floor, tight-lipped.

"Wouldn't that be the normal thing to do?"

Pippa scrubbed, quietly.

"Did you rescue her to lock her up?"

"Soon," Pippa sighed while changing the water and readjusting Mom's yellow plastic gloves. "Once she's strong enough."

"Once she's strong enough. Don't you see? She's ready now!"

Pippa shot him a wary look. Did he want the goose out of the way?

"Jealousy was never *my* thing," he replied quietly, "you should remember that."

"Self-control neither," she wanted to snap, but held her tongue. Despite her rage and disappointment about the terrible disaster he'd caused, that wouldn't be fair.

He stared into space. Since that other night, things were no longer the same. If only he could turn back the hands of time.

"Well," she eventually broke the silence, "I'm not a goose. I can't teach her the ropes."

"Other geese will."

"That I saw! They came crashing down on her!"

"She needs to learn to stand her ground."

"How can she? With a crooked wing?"

"It's *her* wing," he replied. "Let *her* deal with it."

"All I know is that I have to deal with all her mess right now! It's not the only mess as you know!" Pippa went on her knees and continued the clean-up. "I *hate* this!" she sobbed, "I've never been so unhappy in my life!"

MadMax cringed at each word. He had to admit that Piu Piu had pushed things a bit far. Incidentally, there had not been a single sound from her, not the slightest chirp.

"Where is the brat?" Pippa did not see her in her enclosure. "Miss Pancakes, where are you?"

Most remarkably, there was no response.

"Oh dear, even my cushion is soaked!" Pippa threw it straight out of the door, past the tomcat's head. He ducked in a quick reflex and was puzzled that Pippa could not see the goose; she was hiding only a few meters away.

How blind could a human be?

"I can't believe you're doing this to me!" Pippa gave a hic-coughing sob.

Her words struck right into Piu Piu's heart. Pippa's voice was always a clear indicator of her mood and, since the traumatic incident the other night, she was definitely in a bad temper. She would tell her to stop her irritating chatter as it kept her from concentrating on her homework. Yet, chattering was Piu Piu's natural way of expressing her attachment to and fondness for the most important being in her life: her surrogate mom! She was painfully aware that Pippa often pulled her foot away, com-plaining that she had become too big, too heavy, too everything anyway now. How could she not know that body contact was vital for a gosling – any gosling – not only an orphan like her? Pippa's foot was all she could reach and touch or hold on to. She only did what goslings do, so Pippa's rough reactions left her scared and confused.

She does not love me anymore.

Sadness welled up in her heart. Just when she thought she'd found a way to ensure that Pippa could never leave her, she felt more isolated than ever and, to make things worse, in the way.

But then she remembered the roller under the desk – who had in the meantime turned into an amazing moth that could fly – and realized she was fed up with being locked up. She had to get out – the whole world was waiting for her!

"Just do it!" she quacked, and this time her voice burst from the depth of her lungs, louder and more confident than ever, surprising everyone; most of all herself: "Here comes the goose!"

Pippa stared incredulously at her bed, covered with a white duvet. But too late: at that moment Piu Piu came out of hiding. Without any hesitation, just a loud and determined "Piupidoo!", she took off, leaving a trail of fluffy down and Pippa's staggered face behind her as she sailed through the open door, right past the tomcat's head.

"Wow!" MadMax exclaimed as he ducked. He watched with disbelief how Piu Piu soared into the air, higher and higher. "Knock me down with a feather if that ain't a real goose . . . !"

"I can fly! I can fly!" Piu Piu honked as the fresh cold air flooded her lungs. She was beside herself with joy! She stretched her wings to their fullest, gliding through the sunshine. It was so smooth, so easy! She looked down. The world had shrunk and expanded at the same time. Ripples of awe ran through her.

Oh, to be up here finally . . . to fly . . . to be free!

She let herself be carried towards the white clouds that sailed above the mountain range to the north. A thermal gave her a boisterous lift and, within seconds, she found herself right within them! Billions of tiny water droplets and ice crystals were floating in the air and danced around her, reflecting in rainbow colors. They beaded over her feathers as she rose higher and higher, borne aloft by her ecstasy.

"Oh my God," Pippa cried out, "she's flying away! I can't see her anymore!"

"Relax," MadMax said. "She'll be back."

Piu Piu made a wide turn towards the sandy beach, passing Chapman's Peak on her right. The Atlantic Ocean was calm and shimmering in various shades and hues – from a sparkling turquoise near the shore to a dark midnight blue at the distant horizon. Just for devilment, she caught another thermal that took her lower where she was soon joined by some Cape gulls that rose and sank in synch with her, peering at her with blatant curiosity, occasionally opening their hooked bills to emit a gluttonous squawk. Soon they lost interest and just hovered in the air, waiting for the perfect moment to plummet like arrows into the waves to follow their prey.

Piu Piu no longer thought about flying; it was her second nature. It was like breathing to her. At last, she was her true natural self: a goose!

"Thank you," she whispered, as gratitude poured through her veins. "Thank you, I do remember. Now I know who I am!"

The surge swept her out over the sea where two large shadowy masses were sailing in the water, elevating their flukes to catch the wind. From time to time, they dived into the unfathomable depths of the ocean followed by swarms of sardines, their patterns dancing and dissolving with the rhythm of the sea. "You are so beautiful!" She reached out to them with all her heart.

As they rose back towards the surface blowing a fountain of vaporized water high up into the air, they showered her with love: "You are so beautiful, too!"

Piu Piu laughed and flapped her wings a few times to take her down, and deeper down, until she could feel the heat of their breath. A ripple of joy ran through her: *Oh! To be alive . . . and truly living!*

Intoxicated with joy, she surrendered to the whim of the breeze that swept her higher again, and now she discovered her own shadow gliding across the glittering crests. It followed her back towards the white beach, past the dunes and the quivering wetlands. She flew a low round over the meadows of the Commons, from where a gathering of Egyptian geese greeted her with wide open wings, honking in her direction.

"Hey Piu Piu! Join us for drinks!" they invited her.

"Thank you!" Piu Piu honked happily, "I'll be back! Piupidoo!"

Thank you, thank you! At last, she was one of them. She no longer felt like an alien, isolated and alone. She was tempted to land right away, but then tightened up on the surge that took her back upwards to her home on the mountain. The sun's warm afternoon rays caressed her plumes as she let herself be lifted and carried along, higher and higher.

"There she is!" Pippa exclaimed. "She's coming home!"

Piu Piu circled slowly down towards the garden, looking for the best place to land. Far down, she saw Pippa gesticulating frantically, alone in the middle of the lawn. For a split second, the image shifted and it was not Pippa she saw, but a goose. The gander's wings were stretched wide open. He was looking up at her from lush papyrus marshes, honking as only he did.

"Eiji . . ." she whispered as a tidal wave of love completely consumed her. "Oh, that feeling . . . to be welcomed back, welcomed home!" Her eyes were moist as she recognized the lawn.

"Com'on, Piu Piu!" She encouraged herself to perform the daunting task of landing. "Just do it . . . like on the coffee table! Quickly! Quickly!"

"You see?" Pippa whispered, observing Piu Piu's movements very closely. The right wing was definitely less developed and weaker, giving her an unbalanced slant. "She must have damaged her wing when she fell from her nest. This doesn't look good at all."

"She can fly!" MadMax assured her. "You don't need to worry anymore."

"I'm not so sure," Pippa said doubtfully, watching the rather plump maneuvers of the goose. "First she's got to come down."

"She will," he said, watching Piu Piu. "Trust her!"

"Trust gravity," she snapped, her mind racing. Piu Piu was still young and not fully grown. The handicap could only get worse. Perhaps even render her flightless? What would the implications be for her life? Would she have a mate and babies? Or would she remain an outcast for life? Could she become a target for vicious attacks, both on the ground and in the air?

"She'll be OK," MadMax insisted. "Believe in her. Let go."

"Watch out, here she comes!" Pippa jumped out of the way as Piu Piu came down towards them and ended her adventurous excursion with a less than heroic pancake landing on the lawn.

"Well done!" Pippa applauded exuberantly, drowning the squirrels who laughed gleefully from the oak.

Piu Piu got up and dashed straight to her red bath. She hopped in and splashed water all over herself. "Piupidoo!" she trumpeted, "I did it! I did it!"

Life was wonderful!

"What's up?" Mom and Dad shouted from the terrace.

"Piu Piu can fly!" Pippa exclaimed. "She just did her first round across the valley."

"About time," Dad commented, watching the jolly goose. "Great stuff! That solves all problems in one go. From now on the house is taboo. Miss Pancakes will look after herself in the garden. She will make herself useful by watching the house and providing early warnings in case there's a fire – as a good goose should!"

Pippa wanted to object, but quickly bit her tongue.

"Good girl," MadMax purred.

"Pippa, why don't you call your sweetheart and we'll show her the dam?" Mom suggested, while watching the juvenile goose plunging and diving in her rather small baby bath. "Don't you think she deserves more than a tiny spittoon? She's grown so fast; it's not even been a year."

"Brilliant idea," Dad agreed, turned and took the lead. "Let's do this right away."

As Piu Piu made no effort to follow, Pippa shot a sharp "Com'on!" in her direction. "She's becoming quite a handful, worse than a teenager," she thought. "Com'on, quickly! "

But Piu Piu hesitated. Only when she saw MadMax disappearing as well, she left her bath and came running, too.

There it was: the dam. It had a small island with towering strelitzias and a big red bottlebrush tree in the middle. The water reflected the creamy colors of the blossoming acacias that sheltered it on the opposite shore.

As the small group arrived, a number of frogs jumped into the water, one after the other – splash! splash! splash! A blue dragonfly buzzed by to inspect them, looking the perplexed goose straight in the eye. But before Piu Piu could react, the ethereal being had turned and flown off into the papyrus.

"Go juice, my girl!" Dad ordered in aviation lingo.

Piu Piu approached the new terrain with a mix of caution and curiosity, turning her head left and right while inspecting it from a distance. She recognized it from one brief excursion when she was still a gosling. That day had suddenly ended in total chaos with Pippa catching her just when it had got exciting. *Humans were unpredictable! What did they want from her now?*

"No worries!" MadMax spoke contentedly under his breath. "By now you're too big for the owl."

Piu Piu looked at him blankly.

"You're banned," he purred, enjoying his revenge, and the stupefied look on her face.

"Dad said it loud and clear. Your turn, Miss Pancakes!"

"I can't be banned!" Her mind was screaming and her head started to spin. "I have to go back. I have to! Otherwise, I will never be able to . . . " She fell silent, shaking like a leaf.

"What's wrong with you?" MadMax was intrigued by her weird reaction. "You got what you wanted. I wish I were you. A night at the dam is far more fun than being locked up in a room."

"Damn!" Dad swore like a trooper. Piu Piu shrieked and leapt into the air, while Dad looked under his shoe; he had just crushed two fat snails!

"Yikes!" Mom pulled a face and Pippa did the same.

"Damn snails!" he ranted. "They're everywhere this year! We should get some ducks or – hey! What's going on?"

Dad stopped abruptly and stared: the moment Piu Piu had spotted the snails she'd gone for them like a flash of lightning and gobbled them all up. Then she looked at Dad with expectant eyes clearly demanding more! It had happened so fast that they all stood with their mouths wide open; even the laid-back tomcat was flabbergasted.

"Greedy girl!" Dad grinned. "Wait a minute!" He plucked another snail from a leaf and offered it to her. Piu Piu took it gently from his hand and promptly dropped it. It rolled all the way down into the water. She looked up at Dad and quacked.

"That won't work, my girl," he said and crushed another snail to demonstrate how to get to the juicy content.

Piu Piu jumped on the tasty tidbit and gobbled it up, honking enthusiastically for more.

"She likes escargots sans shells," Mom laughed. "Not bad!"

"That's it, Tiger! Slice, shoot, and smash!" Dad joked.

"Quickly! Quickly!" Piu Piu chirped. After her big flight adventure she was hungry. She started to trample the ground, turning around in circles a few times and then looking up expectantly at Dad again. She did it again and again until Dad laughed so hard that he had tears in his eyes. It was contagious. Mom and Pippa could not stop laughing, either.

Now that she had everybody's attention, Piu Piu continued to trample and turn until Dad complied with her demand by leading her to an aloe that was covered in soft-shelled baby snails. This is how Piu Piu finally learned how to hunt for snails on her own. She devoured them; she couldn't get enough of them. She completely forgot about the rest of the world.

"There you go, my girl," Dad turned to Pippa. "Did you notice her razor-sharp focus? Amazing. . . how they go after anything they want, these beasts! So, what's the lesson here? If you want gooseberries this year, get your snail cracker on fire!"

"Why do you call her Tiger, Dad?" she wanted to know.

"Aviation lingo for a courageous pilot. That's what she needs to be if she wants to survive in the wild with an angel wing. Tiger is good," he winked, "fits your boots!"

Pippa smiled, gazing down at her pink 'Put-a-tiger-in-your-tank' boots, but when she looked up again she was taken aback by the expression on his face. It was the way he was scrutinizing the goose, like saying: "Get fat and juicy, my girl . . . get some meat on the bones!" She wasn't sure she heard what she heard, but a cold shiver ran down her spine.

Later, when the sun was sinking, Piu Piu woke up. She had fallen asleep at the dam, standing on one leg as geese do. She turned her head in all directions and tried to get used to the fact that she was all by herself. She peered cautiously at the water. It was brownish and rather still; nothing compared to the crystal clarity of the sea, but it had lots of delicacies drifting on the surface – like a liquid salad bowl. There was a kaleidoscope of colors, reflections and shadows to be investigated and, in their midst, the mysterious island. Intrigued, she walked into the water, drank a few sips, and enjoyed her first swim. She ducked and dived and flapped her wings, creating a lot of noise.

"Would you mind getting out of my light?" A croaky voice startled the juvenile goose and ended her delirium of joy. She peered around. Was she not alone? She swam to the island and climbed up the embankment. Here she felt safe and had a better view across the dam. Suddenly, she saw him, well hidden amongst the reeds, and motionless.

"Oh no!" Pippa exclaimed. "The heron! I think he's spotted Piu Piu!" She was watching the scene from the kitchen window while setting the table for dinner.

MadMax was lazing on his cushion, looking bored. He already missed the chick and, as always, sensed Pippa's thoughts.

"Don't worry, he's after fish, insects and frogs. He won't go after a goose."

"But he's so big! Just look at that bill. He must be over a meter." The heron held his long slender neck in an S-shape. The head was white topped with a black stripe. The grey plumage and strong yellow bill glistened in the evening light.

Mom joined them at the window, drying her hands.

"His wingspan may well be two meters. I see him quite often here. He wades through the shallow water for a while and then just stands there. Engaged and detached at the same time. Completely free from the self . . . So much to learn . . . "

"You mean like in . . . meditation?" Pippa asked without taking her eyes off the bird.

Mom nodded. The clock on the oven was ticking away. "Restful awareness, personified," Mom said. "Animals enjoy a state of Oneness with creation wherever they are while we always keep searching. We feel separate from the rest . . . We're prisoners of our minds."

The heron's bill suddenly shot into the water and speared a fish. He swung it up into the air, snapped a few times to position it, and then swallowed it whole.

All the way from head to tail.

"Wow!" Piu Piu was impressed. She watched with interest how the fish passed through the long, slender neck. A few more snaps, gulps and burps, and the fish was gone. After wading a few steps, the heron postured again.

"I thought you'd never move," Piu Piu said.

"I don't. It moves. It moves around me. It passes by. I only observe." Having said that, the solitary bird stood completely still again. A few ripples rolled out in concentric circles; then the water was still.

Too still for Piu Piu. She still felt her feathers vibrating and her heart brimmed with life. When a couple of guinea fowl intoned their evening concerto, she stood up tall and flapped her wings, absorbing the warmth of the sun's last rays as they tinted the garden with a magic glow. She honked a few times, taking control of her new space and making her presence known.

"Whoo-hoo!" answered the spotted eagle owl on top of the strelitzia. She looked down at the new arrival in her territory, evaluating it with glaring eyes.

Piu Piu hardly noticed her. Once again, she stretched her wings embracing the fascinating world of growing shadows, tantalizing scents and new sensations. At last, she would spend the night under the stars like a real goose – free!

A soft wind rustled through the leaves and plucked at her feathers, reminding her that she had lost her childhood home. Piu Piu gave a hiccoughing sob and nestled deeper into the grass, putting her head under her wing.

"Whoo-hoo!" said the owl as darkness turned into a dream that would forever change the life of Piu Piu . . .

CHAPTER SIX

Meeting the Shadow

How small the passing landscape of parched desert plains speckled with occasional baobab trees and mountain ridges looked under the soft light of the moon!

Piu Piu breathed in deeply, filling her lungs with fresh, cold air as she led a big flock of geese northwards in a graceful V-shaped formation.

She was a strong goose and loved the feeling of being at the helm, generating the dynamic upwash for the flock. She was fully aware that everyone depended on her instinct and wise guidance during their migration to marshlands and pastures. Although she had been the lead goose for more years than any of her predecessors, she still welcomed each opportunity to prove her superiority to anyone who had the courage or audacity to challenge her. Her reputation was legendary throughout the entire Egyptian goose community on the African continent, and she was feared by those within her own flock who either chose not to, or were simply unable to, follow the high standards of discipline she applied to herself. It was something she failed to understand, never mind, accept. Her total focus on her purpose as a leader had made her merciless, demanding that everyone obey her commands unquestioningly.

Strict laws of nature required that only the strongest female could take the lead position and Piu Piu loved the thrill of confronting the elements. She was perfectly aware that each of her followers was positioned to get the optimal benefit from the initial lift she provided at the front.

Suddenly, she noticed a steep increase in wind resistance. Her powerful wings ploughed rhythmically through the darkness, creating the primary airstream that allowed the geese, flying on either side of her and behind her wing tips, to take advantage of one another's up-lift and to time their wing beats perfectly. This saved precious energy, as the geese were able to glide more often during the long journey, thus lowering their heart rates. They all trusted Piu Piu, knowing her total commitment.

In those days, Piu Piu spent most of her time foraging on the ground with Eiji, her beloved mate for life, but on an occasion like this they all came together as a big family. The flock included several generations of their offspring. Flying over long distances, sometimes several thousand kilometers, could be fun when Piu Piu was at the helm and a safe arrival in a new land of milk and honey for goose taste buds was almost guaranteed. Nevertheless, it was a great responsibility and only those few who had been at the front themselves knew what it entailed.

"Mind over matter!" Piu Piu reprimanded herself, pushing forward forcefully. She ignored the throbbing pain in her chest which had grabbed her all of a sudden and then released her after a while. "Don't be such a lame duck!"

For a few seconds, she lost herself in the memory of Eiji's concerned look when they had said good-bye a few weeks ago. He had grown too old and fragile for long flights, but she could always read his soul when looking into his eyes. This time he was imploring her to stay, knowing all too well she would ignore his plea. So he said nothing. She just noticed that his characteristically upright posture, with a slight backward slant of his grey head, appeared strangely out of balance. His golden eyes followed her as she soared high into the sky and it seemed to her that they had never left her since.

They had been through so much together as a strong, united couple that only now, through the pounding pain that had meanwhile spread into her head, it suddenly occurred to her that she might never see Eiji again. She did not recall ever having had such a sobering thought.

Separating from love – true, unconditional love – was that at all possible?

It seemed absurd, but Piu Piu definitely noticed an instant weakening effect from merely imagining that possibility – so she quickly banished the image from her mind. The idea of scar-

city, never mind loss, had no place in a life filled with abundance! She closed her eyes and took a deep breath through the
pain in her lungs. Then she focused again on her task.

Silently, they flew through the starry night until the first fiery hues of the rising sun crept over the horizon towards the
right. The landscape below changed dramatically. Piu Piu gave
off an elated quack of excitement and relief when she recognized the intricate network of waterways, lakes, islands and
swamps, glittering like jewels in the moonlight below her: the
Okavango Delta, one of Africa's largest inland deltas and, definitely, her favorite spot on earth.

Having made it this close to their destination gave her a
boost. Her heart started to race in anticipation of the crystal-
clear streams lined with lush papyrus, the profuse vegetation
and the nutrient-rich grazing grounds that awaited them. The
trumpeting call of elephants. Waterbucks wading through the
marshes. Laughing hyenas and lions roaring at night. Many of
the geese following her had never been here before, including
her favorite daughter, Emma, who never left her side and was
flying behind her on the right. She observed all her mother's
maneuvers very attentively and Piu Piu instinctively knew that
– one day – she would hand the reins over to her. It was a somewhat comforting thought.

She pulled herself together and picked up speed; there was
no time for sentimentality or distractions. The difficulty now
was to bring everyone safely onto the ground. She had been
here a number of times, but the liquid labyrinth far below them
changed each year, depending on the influx of water, which
was based on seasonal rainfall. Spreading through the various
channels, it created a cycle of rising and falling water levels
throughout the swamps. An island, which might have been an
ideal landing strip a year or two ago, could well be flooded now
or even have completely disappeared. It was always a bit of a
gamble that added to the suspense of the journey.

But Piu Piu had an extraordinary sense of direction. She
beamed with pride when the silhouettes of the tall palms, indicating Chief's Island, emerged out of the white pillows of cumu-

lus cloud that obscured the shadowlands further down. It was the exact spot she had foreseen for their landing! She passed the good news back through the two long lines of followers behind her, each goose sending the motivating message on to the next. A sudden jubilation filled the air and with it came the additional flow of energy needed for the final task: the descent and landing.

Piu Piu also had a deep inner knowledge of her altitude, speed and direction in relation to the prevailing wind currents. However, it was not easy to descend and land in an area where much evaporation and condensation created differences in atmospheric pressure, resulting in sudden updrafts and downdrafts, bubbles of warm air rising like hot-air balloons, thermals and vortices, turbulences and whirlwinds. Sometimes even heavy thunderstorms seemed to appear out of nowhere. These were always a possibility, due to scorching daytime temperatures and high humidity levels.

While Piu Piu tried to minimize the risk by planning their descent during the cooler morning hours, clouds were temperamental and it demanded presence of mind and skill to navigate through them without missing that clearly defined, yet narrow, landing strip. She also knew that the juveniles were exhausted after spending many hours on the wing; they urgently needed a rest.

Normally, she looked forward to her dance with the clouds, diving through the sky and then gliding down onto the island, pulling the flock behind her on the sheer momentum of her passion. But today, she felt Eiji's golden glance on her all the time. Deep down, she knew – after leading the flock once again over vast distances to their promised destination – that her own life hung on nothing more than a silver thread.

This was not what she had expected! She was not ready!

Now she was locked in an iron grip of agony, and her consciousness was shifting. A solemn acceptance washed through her veins and the pain lifted. The labor of flying was transformed into a serene lightness of being where she was no longer aware whether she was going fast or slow or up or down, as everything seemed to be flowing into the other. There were no limits, just oneness. There was nothing . . . nothing but this blissful energy!

She heard her daughter's concerned voice drifting towards her as if from far away. "Mom? Are you okay, Mom?"

As if pulled by some merciless string, she snapped back into time, into her task, her duty, and the jaws of that excruciating pain. As the dominant bird, she would never allow herself any weakness, nor admit tiredness, nor change position to benefit from someone else's slipstream instead of providing it herself. Her purpose was to lead – not to complain. Failure was not an option.

But her fiercest battle, now, was the one with herself. A fire was burning her up from inside, imploring her to surrender. Though conscious that she was losing control over her balance and motion, she gave all she had to hold the course. She knew it was impossible for her to prevent her endurance levels from collapsing. A deafening throb battered her from inside. And then, while she still grimly resisted the torture and gasped for air, she was caught in a downward spiral that literally swept her away.

"Mom?" she heard her daughter's terrified voice; this time it came loud and clear. But too late: a bright light exploded before Piu Piu's eyes and she released her soul in a final breath of surrender. The sky, the horizon, the earth – the whole universe started to spin, faster and faster until it all became one. It expanded. It became light. It became pure energy. It became peace. And it all was permeated by this incredible music that she had heard so many times before.

"I am . . ." Piu Piu whispered.

"I love you," Eiji's voice was close by. "I've been waiting. We're going home!"

Two experienced geese had separated immediately from the flock and come to Piu Piu's assistance. But there was nothing they could do; Piu Piu's feathered body had become the plaything of the elements and was whirling unstoppably through space.

"I'm fine, dear ones," they heard her say, mentally.

They glanced at one another in surprise: was that her? The commander?

"Follow Emma!" Her voice was fluid, flowing and gentle, touching their souls. So they turned back immediately and followed Piu Piu's final command.

Torn between her duty and her love for her mother, Emma hesitated only a split second before she took over the lead position. She knew this was what her mother wanted her to do. The geese immediately fell in line behind her to keep their wingtips in the upwash within the energy-saving V-formation. Those at the back hardly noticed the change; they were far too excited by their imminent descent.

With her heart grieving and tears ripped from her eyes by the wind, Piu Piu's daughter proved her own leadership and acrobatic skill as she guided the geese safely through the mushrooming clouds, down onto the promised land.

Piu Piu woke up suddenly; to darkness resounding with nocturnal voices. Where am I? There was the monotonous concert of frogs, the hymn of a fiery-necked nightjar, the eerie hooting of the spotted eagle owl. A cool night breeze was rustling through the leaves, exposing the cloudy sky before closing the curtain of obscurity again.

"Oh," she sighed, with a tinge of disenchantment. "I'm back here. With that pathetic imitation of me."

Piu Piu would have slipped back into dreamland had her instinct not alerted her to the very real possibility that she was in danger. Big danger! Suddenly, her senses were alert. She noticed a sweet pungent smell in the air that somehow triggered a vague memory; it added to a foreboding that she was no longer alone.

Somebody out there was watching her!

She got up and scanned her immediate surroundings: the dark leaves above her, the vertical lines of reeds and papyrus, the tranquil water shimmering like black ink under a sealed sky. She heaved a sigh of relief as she remembered the place; at least she was on her island! This encouraged her to look further across the water and towards the embankment where sugar-bushes and bottlebrush trees sheltered the dam.

There!

Her heart missed a beat when she saw them: a pair of striking blue eyes, the black pupils contracted to pinpricks, glaring directly at her. Their eyes locked and remained that way for what seemed like an eternity, suspended in a space from which Piu Piu emerged with a strong feeling that this encounter was no coincidence. These chilling eyes: she had seen them before, long, long ago, long before this life, in a different disguise. She shivered. Something deep inside her reminded her that he would always be following her, like a shadow . . . until . . .

"No!" The memory of who she really was flashed through her: strong, determined, a leader! And now she was young!

"I will not surrender!"

Instead of drowning in her fear, she gave herself a mental push and jumped on a wave of clarity instead, to consider her options. She realized that, right now, as they moved out of winter and the dam was full, there was enough water between them. He would not be able to reach her. She was safe.

Relieved, she dared to look more closely, to beyond the magnetic pull of his hypnotic stare. His facial markings and, especially, his typically elongated, black-tufted ears gave him away: a caracal. She couldn't detect much more of his hidden silhouette. He stood absolutely motionless.

"Oh, go away!" Piu Piu honked, swinging her swollen neck defiantly in a demonstration of fearlessness.

"I'll be back," he said, coldly. "You're mine anyway."

"Never!" she hissed boldly, swallowing her rising panic.

"Your noble beau won't protect you this time!" he laughed, "and don't forget: I'm no longer a tramp!"

"No need to remind me . . . I still hate your ruthless mind!"

"This is a ruthless world . . . one has to be ruthless to win the game," he snarled.

She made herself stretch and fold her wings, warding off his evil presence like a shield: "Take your ruthless world and get lost! I don't want you in mine!"

His face broke into a hideous grin. "You can't fool me with your wasted wing, oh, queen of heaven! There will be no escape!"

The moon broke through the clouds for a fleeting moment. She could see him spraying his urine flagrantly on the bushes; then the big red cat leapt up the slope. He stopped at the top and turned his head one more time.

"Happy birthday, Princess," he sneered, his pupils contracting. "I'll eat you before you turn three!"

The shrewd hunter merged into the shadows just as the moon disappeared.

Piu Piu ruffled her feathers. She was highly disturbed. Caracals are masters of concealment. Their hearing is extremely good. That's how they find their prey and then stalk it with remarkable patience. Once close enough they jump, strike and kill. They can snatch birds in flight, leaping over two meters high. Can even catch a few of them at a time!

With a caracal around, a young lone goose like her had to be on her guard day and night.

"If only I weren't so alone! Together, we would . . ." Piu Piu paused abruptly. "I'm confused. There is no we. I'm not sure there will ever be!"

She looked around and listened.

"Where are you?" she whispered, sadly. There was no answer and her eyes flooded. "Why do you abandon me? You were always by my side!"

Briefly, his golden glance shimmered through her tears, resting quietly on her. "My beloved," she heard his mellow voice, deep down in her soul. "I always am. Just feel me. All is as we had wanted it to be. Take heart! Your adventure has just begun!"

She knew he was right. Nevertheless she waited, panting, but there was nothing more to come. She was alone. It was her first winter and the first time since she had gained her freedom, and she was nervous. Highly alert, she turned her head in all directions, thrusting it in the air to pick up any movement. The slightest sound made her cringe.

There!

She gasped: there they were again, those hypnotic eyes. Oh no! Suddenly there were several pairs of them. They were closing in on her. With her heart hammering in her chest she got ready for an emergency take-off; but then realized it was all in her mind. It had tricked her to face what she detested most: HER FEAR.

She gave off a low, heartbreaking quack. Her legs slipped away like rubber and she collapsed into the grass. Her eyes closed from exhaustion and her beak snapped nervously. But her tormenter caught up with her again on the stage of her imagination, forcing her to open her eyes to get rid of his nauseating presence. Getting back on her feet, she peered in all directions. Eventually, she convinced herself that the beast had gone.

Slowly, the moon emerged from behind clouds. She stood quietly for a while, bathing in its soothing light. She felt her tension subside. Her eyes wandered up to the sky where dark clouds heavy with rain drifted past; parting briefly to allow a glimpse of the moon in all its silent splendor, then swallowing it again. She waded into the sparkling water and drank a few sips, bending her head far backwards to let the cool liquid run down her throat.

As she stretched her head forward, with her beak hovering just above the water, she recognized her own reflection. She stared at it dispassionately, without moving a feather. And the longer she looked at herself the more it seemed as if her right wing was becoming heavier and heavier until it dragged her down, deeper and deeper, into a black abyss. She observed herself, sinking, with her spirit numb, as if all this were happening to someone else . . . No, no, this was not her.

But the moment her chest hit the crystal reality of the water, an explosion of rage and frustration brought her back to her feet and she lashed out blindly at her image. It shattered into a million pieces that danced and cringed in luminous ripples and contortions around her.

"Get out of my way, lame duck!" She honked, diving madly into the sparkling fractals of her broken self.

"Who? Me?"

A deep voice responded indignantly, making her spin and stare. At first, she could hardly see him as he was partially submerged: a fat Western leopard toad. Blowing up his throat, he emitted a snoring sound that he repeated every few seconds. He had been there all the time, but Piu Piu was so immersed in her wrath that she only became aware of him now.

As the blanket of cloud tore open and moonlight pervaded the shadows, more and more of these guttural sounds arose. They bounced back and forth, becoming a steady sound wave reminiscent of a revving motorcycle engine.

"He's hot! He's hot!" the toad's enormous mate, sitting in his tight grip right underneath him, rasped in a deep contralto voice, lifting both of them slightly as she, too, inflated her air sac. As if on cue, the entire pond with all its floating vegetation started to vibrate, and chanting in many diverse voices – *"Oh, hold me tight in the heat of the night!"* – accompanied by the motorcycle chorus.

Leopard toads popped up everywhere, old and young, singles and couples, in their mating embrace. The whimsical creatures came in all shapes and sizes, with warty patches from chocolate to reddish-brown glistening on bright yellow skins. They were rising and sinking rhythmically. Some were jumping boisterously into the air. Splashing back into the bubbling water, they created fireworks of twinkling droplets, while a liquid maze of ripples rolled out to the bank.

In the midst of it all, Piu Piu paddled in circles, ducking and diving, as she was carried away by a spiral of joy. There was no more telling where she ended and where everyone else began.

"Happy birthday, Piu Piu!" she trumpeted rapturously, opening her wings wide and fanning up a whirlwind of air.

The dam turned into the most wondrous 'moonlight froguzzi' the garden had ever seen – celebrating life and its creation.

As the music drifted into the valley, two stocky porcupines and their youngster stopped digging for roots and bulbs and sniffed the air.

"Dat's da night, Matilda!" The male snorted and off they were, one after the other, trotting towards the dam. Shaking their black and white quills forwards, backwards and sideways they paraded around the pond. Swinging and rattling the hollow spines on their tails, they provided the rhythmic pulse.

Although Piu Piu was briefly alerted by a few hysterical giggles reaching for her from the dark, she just took a deep breath and ignored them; they were meaningless within an atmosphere brimming with passion and mirth!

The spotted eagle owl glanced across the lavender fields, the wind playing with her feathery ear tufts. Even the mice and moles had left their dens and burrows. They stood huddled together, their eyes raptly lifted towards the pond while they swayed to the music. Somehow, they knew they had nothing to fear. Indeed, the owl hissed softly as her mate landed right next to her. He made a few clicking sounds and she snuggled tenderly against him.

High in the sky, even the clouds picked up on the vibe, flowing into one another and separating, while the wind whirled them across the moon in a jive of shadows and light. Above and below, the feast of vibrant sensations intensified until the moon disappeared and, like a thief, took with it the world below. The garden, mountains, even the sky – gone!

Without any warning, sheets of rain pelted down. A flash of lightning illuminated the pond, followed by crashing thunder. Piu Piu stood on one leg on her island with water running all over her. She had turned away from the light, leaning into the fluid darkness . . .

Pippa was lying awake, listening to nature's unchained elements. "Are you sleeping?" she asked.

"Yes." MadMax replied.

Despite the fact that a year had passed, she never fell asleep without thinking of Piu Piu, especially in winter. She hated to imagine her all alone out there in the rain, exposed to any possible sort of danger – but the goose refused to sleep anywhere else.

"The frogs have stopped," she whispered.

"Toads!" MadMax corrected.

"They were going nuts! Seems they've turned the dam into a breeding pond!"

"You bet! It's that time of the year!"

She listened to the angry storm gusts that shook the house and rattled the windows – and then dropped completely, as if to gather momentum for another assault. It was during these pauses that she could hear it again, the motorcycle chorus, inviting her to hop onto the backseat and be carried away.

She felt the warmth of the tomcat as he snuggled against the back of her knees. His soft yet intense purring vibrated through her being like a timeless caress. It gave her a sense of peace and comfort that passed understanding. Slowly, she let go of the day, abandoning herself to the formless substance of her dreams.

"Do you see it, too?" she whispered, hardly breathing, as a delicate web of ferns fanned out around her, undulating slightly with a tinge of blue.

"It's always there," MadMax purred, his whiskers tickling her skin. "It's part of you . . . of us all."

Enchanted by the shimmering maze of plants and leaves and flowers Pippa finally fell asleep. Above her, the tendrils reached higher and higher into the ceiling until it dissolved, and opened into the star-strewn path of the Milky Way.

"Come!" She heard Piu Piu calling softly. "Spread your wings and fly!" And so Pippa rose from her bed and floated through the floral dome, up, up and away . . .

CHAPTER SEVEN

Heaven is Everywhere

It was a dark, windy night when Pippa lit her candle and pulled the treasure chest from underneath her bed. She could hardly wait for the house to be quiet, to get back to Great-grandfather's book. She had studied the monograph so many times that she knew even the drawings by heart.

Right now, she was excited about an African iris in her plant-press that she expected to be a perfect fit for the corresponding drawing in the book. She leafed slowly through the pages, drawing in their aromatic scents. When she came to the chapter on *Dietes*, under D, she removed the almost transparent flower from the blotting paper and superimposed it on the detailed drawing, taking great care to match each line and fold. When she leant back to contemplate the result, she was fascinated how the original drawing and the pressed plant merged into each other creating something vibrant and new in between the layers of time. Part magic, part real.

In that moment, the candlelight flickered and the pages started to turn. Pippa watched. Shivers ran down her spine and a sense of anticipation captured her mind. Then, suddenly, it reminded her of that fateful moment when MadMax – no! She closed her eyes; took a deep breath. Anything but going back there! The pages kept turning. She knew it was not the slight draft that always sneaked in through the weatherworn windows and doors. No, no . . . it had to be either the book itself or Great-grandad. Or, possibly, herself? No, probably not.

She looked up at MadMax on her bed. His quiet composure always gave her a sense of being grounded in the here-and-now, just that tonight his eyes did not shine. Her fleeting memory of that tragic incident had not escaped him. Her loss was too fresh. He knew how she tried to forgive him; he felt her pain. She never mentioned it but he saw it in her eyes.

Eventually, the flame burned calmly again and the flipping of pages stopped. Pippa turned back to the book. It had opened on another chapter, also under D: *Disa*. There was an array of complex drawings spread over two pages.

"A disa!" she exclaimed, bouncing back into her joy. "The 'Pride of Table Mountain', one of our largest orchids. I wish we had that one in our garden."

After contemplating the intricate drawings for a while, she shook her head: "This just isn't right – it needs color." With her fingertip, she drew over the two horizontal wing-like petals, seeing them perfectly in her mind's eye: "This is red! A deep and daring red . . . with a dash of sunshine in it . . ." She did not even notice how the color flowed from her fingertip, as if from a magic brush, filling the shapes. She continued upwards, over the vertical lip with its delicate network of lines, tracing lightly here and there with her nail, almost not touching the drawing: "These here are crimson . . . almost ruby veins . . . a fine net . . . a web that attracts our winged friend . . . the butterfly, over here."

As the butterfly turned blue, she corrected it quickly: "Ooops, that's wrong . . . that's the one that's always sneaking into my dreams! It must be from another life."

She sat back, smiling. Now it was all in the right colors, including the pollinator of a red disa: the 'Table Mountain Beauty', the butterfly, at the top right corner of the page.

Oh, how I wish I could see all this out there . . .!

"You're making progress, young lady, that's *ausgezeichnet!* Excellent!"

Pippa sat bolt upright as she recognized Great-grandad's voice with his typical German accent. She had not heard it since her memorable lesson on proteas, well over a year ago. In the meantime, she had spent all her spare time studying his work and continuing its expansion and completion in her own intuitive way. As her botanical knowledge grew, so did her desire to learn more about thorough scientific research. She still yearned for a new way of expression that would be more in line with the digital world. Somehow, she had come to an 'in between time', where she had to find a new approach.

But this meant that she would have to reveal her secret.

From the beginning, it had grown like an invisible chasm between her and Mom. Together with her well-founded fear that the book could be taken away from her, was a force within her that allowed no interference. Whatever it was that she was destined to do, it was *her* task – and she would complete it on *her* terms.

She felt she had almost reached that stage; if it weren't for one big mystery she had come across in the book that still kept her tapping in the dark. Nevertheless, she was painfully aware that it was up to her to resolve the sensitive issue with Mom. One day.

She started when she realized Great-grandfather's eyes were resting on her with a loving smile. As she spontaneously smiled back, all her concerns evaporated instantly into thin air. When the tall man with his distinguished upright posture, topped with a tropical helmet, beckoned her to follow, her heart started to pound. In the blink of an eye, she was right behind him as they climbed a rocky path leading out of the scorching February sun into the indigenous forest.

They did not talk on their way up. She had to run and jump to keep up with his long strides. Occasionally, he stopped briefly to point at trees and plants with his elegant walking stick, calling out their names. Sometimes he patted the furrowed trunk of an ancient yellowwood tree, as though recognizing an old mate.

"He's so . . . so different," Pippa thought. "He's not following a predictable timeline – instead, he is giving it direction."

As she paused to catch her breath, and took her eyes off the increasingly spongy and slippery path, she had the strange impression that the thicket opened up in front of him. She turned around quickly and saw how it closed behind them, once they had passed through. She turned again, with an incredulous look on her face, observing how even the gracious old trees bowed and moved aside.

For an instant it reminded her of something but, as she had to follow quickly, she brushed the thought away.

It had to be her imagination!

Soon, however, she noticed how everything was emitting a subtle light. Even Great-grandad! She squeezed her eyes for a clearer vision . . . and yes! It was definitely there: a distinctive yet hardly perceivable glow! Mesmerized, she saw that all these fine glimmering lines were connected, creating an almost invisible web across the ground. And, suddenly, it hit her with crystalline clarity: *How could she be so blind? Great-grandad had to be a holy man!*

As if on cue, the net started to vibrate and tremble and distort as Great-grandad began to laugh. He laughed so hard the ground seemed to undulate in response. "*Mycelium,*" he shouted. "One day I'll show you the secret world underground, not today. Today I have a surprise!" His boisterous voice rolled right down to where she was standing and she saw he was waiting for her to catch up. She could not resist the urge to look back, quickly, over her shoulder. Seeing that the forest had swallowed the path right behind her, she turned and scrambled upwards as fast as she could.

The closer they got to the top of the gorge, the denser the vegetation and the deeper the shade. The path was eroded and overgrown with gnarled intertwined roots. A ray of light was streaming through the canopy of trees and the air dripped with moisture. They stopped when they could hear them: the cascades!

As they listened, a large dark-brown butterfly with yellow spots flitted by, circling around Pippa. Great-grandad observed her thoughtfully with his piercing blue eyes. "Interesting," he murmured, his lips hardly moving underneath his little moustache. "This is indeed very interesting . . . that it should do that. There's more to this than her red dress . . ."

"Weird," she thought, holding his gaze, "now he looks through me like MadMax!"

"So you never saw a disa?" he inquired.

She shook her head.

"Soso . . ." he said, watching the butterfly dance in front of her face. "The little chap is telling you something . . . don't you think?"

She nodded, a big smile lighting up her face. He winked encouragingly. Moments later, she was on her way, following the butterfly. He chuckled to himself, knowing that it would guide her towards the rocks near the stream where she would discover the first clumps of red disas. *Real disas!*

He waited and, promptly, her reaction came: "Oh, Great-grandad!" There they were, those rare red orchids! Their large, majestic flowers were swaying on long stalks against the backdrop of the boulders from where the waters fell, dispersing a light mist.

"Oh, Great-grandad! You made my wish come true!"

And while she absorbed the magic of the moment or, perhaps, it absorbed her, Great-grandad's voice drifted towards her, softly plucking at her destiny's strings:

"Once upon a time, long, long ago, in a country called Sweden, there lived a smart and courageous girl named Disa. It was a happy life as King Freyr bestowed peace and pleasure on his people.

But the times changed like they always do. As the population kept growing and growing, there was less and less food. Soon those who controlled the seeds refused to share them, and a huge famine came over the country."

Pippa's eyelids fluttered like something had touched her inside.

"This is when the King and his advisors decided to kill all the old, the sick and the weak to rid the land of its burden."

He paused a moment, observing Pippa's reaction. While he continued, her unseeing gaze wandered upwards, losing itself beyond the cascades.

"When Disa heard about this cruel plan, she boldly claimed that she had a better solution! The King invited her, but to test her wits he put many obstacles in her way – she was not to travel by foot, or by horse, not in a wagon and not by boat. She was not to appear before him dressed or undressed. She was not to visit within a month or within a year, and neither during day nor at night.

But Disa was a resourceful young woman guided by her heart. She arrived before the King at dusk, wrapped in a fishnet, having met all other challenges to his full satisfaction. So impressed was the King that he made her his wife and the killing was cancelled! Queen Disa ordered a drawing of lots and part of the population was allowed to spread beyond the borders of the country, and each was given a bag of seeds. They found fertile grounds where they grew food for all and built new homes, living happily ever after."

"The forever seeds . . ." Pippa whispered as Great-grandad concluded: *"Praised for her wisdom, Disa became a legend that lives on to this day."*

There was a long pause.

"Is it true?" she eventually asked.

"You tell me!"

She looked up at him: "What do you mean?"

Great-grandad smiled; there was still a butterfly on her shoulder. "Come," he said, heading towards the boulders, "I want you to meet a friend."

They descended along a narrow path that snaked past rugged rock faces and massive stone formations. Although she followed almost blindly, a foreboding pulled at her core. She drew in a few deep breaths to calm her pounding heart, walking as quietly as possible, as if she weren't there.

"Angst?" His commanding voice shook her up. "Not?"

Standing a few steps below her, he was at eye level with her. She gasped; she had never seen him that close. His blue eyes sparkled even in the shade of his helmet. His features softened. "You have her eyes," he said with a low voice, "as green as the forest with a few golden dots . . ."

Pippa saw him look through her and trembled when she heard him sigh. "Great-grandma?" she wanted to ask, but then she didn't.

"She never allowed herself not to shine as light! Never!" He turned and disappeared behind rocks. "Come, we're there!"

Flustered, Pippa approached the place slowly, tentatively. First, she saw the disas. Her heart went out to them and she relaxed, but then she realized that they were erupting within a jungle of ferns which she recognized. As she scanned the fanlike structures, she tumbled back and gasped for, towering above them – some cloaked in shadows, others bathed in light –

were the huge boulders she remembered so well. Overcoming a desperate urge to run away and leave this place as fast as she could, she stood her ground and stared, her entire body trembling. The tree creepers and lichen were still hanging over them like hair and tresses, but they seemed to have grown denser and there were more nests.

She listened, but all she could hear was the brook gurgling past . . . and perhaps a croak in the distance, but she wasn't sure.

She closed her eyes and breathed deeply. This place with its sounds and vibrations had been haunting her – and now she was here. She had come back in a circle!

"How are you, Carl, I thought I might find you here!" she heard Great-grandad say.

"Hermann! It's been a while! But you're right! I can't resist the disas!"

Torn from her thoughts, Pippa glanced around, intrigued to hear another man's voice. Where was he hiding? And where was Great-grandad for that matter?

"Look up, young lady," she heard his sonorous voice from high above her. "Do you recognize my face? Don't be scared, it's just a way for us old farts to hang out in the places we cherish." Pippa took heart and looked closer. She immediately saw his face. "I see you, Great-grandad!"

"Speak up! Speak up!" Great-grandad encouraged her.

"I see you!" she repeated, louder. "Did you escape from the Easter Islands?"

He rolled his eyes and laughed so boisterously that the birds flew from their nests.

"Ohooo! A moai? Am I that monumental?"

The other voice joined in the merriment and now Pippa saw another man's face. He had a receding hairline and his kind eyes were resting on her.

"Professor Thunberg," she heard Great-grandad say, " may I present: this is my grandchild, Pippa!"

Pippa looked dutifully at the ground and made a curtsy. "Good I'm not in my pajamas," she thought to herself, "I can't believe I'm doing this . . . at my age!"

Thunberg bowed slightly in her direction: "Call me Carl. I'm pleased to meet you, Pippa." His voice was pleasant and she noticed his accent; but it wasn't German.

"This, young lady," Great-grandad said solemnly, "is my good old teacher from the Royal Academy of Sciences in Sweden. *The Father of South African Botany!*"

"Aha!" Pippa exclaimed, losing all her shyness, "now I remember. Professor Thunberg came here in the early 1770s. Oh! And later, he inspired you to visit Cape Town . . . and then . . . you never left!"

"Ha," Great-grandad laughed. "I never thought about this. Without him you wouldn't be here today!"

"Brilliant!" Thunberg remarked. "Besides that, I'm most grateful that my valued friend – your ancestor here – continued my work."

Pippa's eyes started to shine: "Yes! And there are the *Thunbergia* vines . . ."

"What a remarkable knowledge!" Thunberg exclaimed.

"Oh," Pippa laughed, "it's all in Great-grandad's book."

Bubbling with excitement, she moved a few steps forward. "Professor, are there any disas in Sweden?"

The faces above her looked at one another and started to laugh so hard, that the rocks trembled and transformed their looks in ways that made Pippa laugh, too.

"I must say, Hermann," Thunberg said, collecting himself, "your grandchild is . . ." and he whispered something Pippa could not understand.

"Funny, you should mention this," Great-grandad nodded. Yes! Pippa saw that he really nodded. A bit of gravel trickled from the inner corner of his eye.

Oh this was hilarious! MadMax wouldn't believe this; she wished he were here!

"You're absolutely right, young lady!" she heard him call from the top, his voice a little hoarse from the dust. "I should be peeved though . . ." he grumbled and she suddenly got scared – but then she relaxed as he added more seriously: "Be open to all, but never take anything for granted – *jawohl?*"

She nodded. She had to shield her eyes with her hands against the sun, which now blazed above the huge rock.

"Good! Then let me answer your question: it was Professor Thunberg . . . my good old friend here . . . who discovered the red orchid and who gave it its name."

"After the wise Queen Disa?" she whispered in awe.

"After a smart and courageous girl," Thunberg said, smiling, "just like you!"

"Professor . . ." Pippa started out to ask her burning question, but – suddenly – there was only the candlelight.

"Shhh!" MadMax hushed her. "But thank you." He grinned.

"Shucks!" Pippa was terribly disappointed. "Just when I wanted to ask . . ." She stretched. "How long was I gone?"

"Barely five minutes," MadMax shrugged. "It seems you were in lettered company?"

"Oh! I've got loads to check on the net." She yawned, closed the book and put it back. "Funny," she said, pensively. "That place gave me the creeps – and just now I didn't want to leave! I have so many questions."

"Right." MadMax was yawning, too. "You're now here. Better get some sleep."

"Sleep," she said, pushing her treasure chest back under the bed. "I hope that's what it's gonna be."

Then she blew out the light.

Hardly back from school the very next day, Pippa checked the Internet, with MadMax sitting next to the keyboard, grooming himself.

"It's all true," she said, looking at the photo of a red disa on the screen, ". . . here they even mention that . . . *Botanist Carl Peter Thunberg named the Disa genus of orchids based on the Disa legend. The dorsal sepal of some Disa orchids has a net-like appearance reminiscent of the fishnet in which Disa appeared before King Freyr.*" She smiled. "That he did not mention in his book, but it's all here. I love this photo . . . the light!"

"There may be more missing than that blank page?" MadMax reasoned, while licking his paw.

"It's a double page," she corrected, while she clicked back to the article on Wikipedia, reading: *The orchid genus Disa consists of 169 terrestrial orchid species . . . primarily from South Africa. . .* blah blah blah . . . Click . . . look at all the species!"

She scrolled down through the species and randomly checked a few links, until – by sheer 'accident' – she landed on the stunning picture of a blue disa. "A *blue* disa!" she exclaimed, flabbergasted, "that's not in Great-grandad's book!"

"See, it needs an update," MadMax purred, with his whiskers almost in her face. She put her left arm around him and caressed his head without taking her eyes off the screen. "A blue disa," she mumbled, "hmmm . . . I didn't know that existed. Are you thinking what I think?"

"Uhum, it's not that difficult to divine, young lady!" he imitated Great-grandad. Pippa giggled and nudged him; then shook her head. "It won't work. The seeds are different. The one I lost looked exactly like a poppy seed."

Pippa paused. "Poppy seeds! Wait a minute!" She felt her blood shoot into her face. Almost feverishly, she typed it into Google: 'blue poppy'.

Never take anything for granted . . .

Once the website was open it displayed a striking blue poppy.

"*The blue flower!*" Pippa whispered. "It really exists."

"Himalayan Blue Poppy," MadMax read out the name.

She flew over parts of the description. "Here's something: *Meconopsis . . . was first described by French botanist Louis Guillaume Alexandre Viguier in 1814 . . .* "

She turned towards MadMax: "That's Great-grandad's time!"

"The Himalayas . . ." MadMax shook his head doubtfully. "Did he go that far?" Pippa shrugged while reading. "I see it was brought to England in the 1920s."

"Hmm, bit late for him, no?"

Pippa scrolled down to find something on propagation and cultivation: ". . . *difficult to grow from seed, but when germinating new plants, using fresh seeds will help.* Fresh seeds . . . well," she sighed, "that explains why the two other seeds never took."

"One," he said, gently, "as you burnt the second."

"I did not burn it. I had it go through fire. That's different."

"Oh."

"Yes, of course. Great-grandfather was very clear on that. Here, further on it says: *Germination is always very slow and erratic.*"

He was grooming his long white belly fluff, trying to track a flea. Was she not aware that she had ingested the seed with Mom's pie? He wondered.

"It seems one can also divide the plants – provided there is one to start with . . ." Suddenly, her voice broke. Tears welled up in her eyes and she leant her head against his.

"There's been no peace for me, since that night. I've been looking for it everywhere. But . . ."

"I know," he said compassionately, grooming her hair, too.

"Last night, when I was with Great-grandad, I wanted to ask. But then 'puff!' I was back here."

She returned to the blue poppy on her screen, scrolling through pages of photos, shaking her head with disbelief from time to time.

"They come in so many shades. Perhaps it will just 'puff' up one day amongst our poppies here?"

"Like magic?" Pippa said, sadly. "Yeah, wouldn't that be nice."

"Magic!" He sat up and flipped an imaginary wand in his paw. "Why not?"

"Wow!" Pippa was impressed. "I like that!"

"If you want magic, you have to believe in yourself!"

Pippa stared at him. He hissed so fiercely it took her by surprise, but before she could get a fright, his face turned into a broad grin – a trick that always got her laughing.

He was very pleased with himself.

"You're right, my wonderful wizard of Noordhoek," she smiled. "I'd better keep an eye on the poppies; they're about to bloom."

"Ask Dad to take you to the Himalayas," he suggested, listening intently, with his ears pricked up and twitching.

"Never! He'd make me fly on my head."

"Pippa! Come quickly," Mom called through the atrium, "I think it's Dad."

Pippa jumped up from her desk and ran out onto the lawn, joining her. They looked up, scanning the bright afternoon sky in all directions.

"Hmm," Mom said after a while, visibly disappointed. "I could have sworn . . ." There was a noise behind them and they both turned. Piu Piu stood on the terrace, stretching to her full size. She opened her wings widely and released her typical welcome battle cry: "Piupidooooo!"

"There he is!" Pippa exclaimed, pointing across the wetlands towards Kommetjie. "In his Slick 360. Look! He's doing his dare-devil loops . . . Can you hear him?"

"Of course," Mom laughed, "how could I not?"

Pippa could hear the thrill in her voice. Dad's acrobatic maneuvers in the sky drew many gasps from the onlookers on the lawn – and probably not only from them.

"Look! A barrel roll . . . spinning left . . . gooood! Left rudder . . . no rudder . . . yes! And corkscrew!" Mom knew them all by heart. "Ughhhhhh, vertical dive now . . . "

"Uhgggggggggg!" Pippa screamed while Piu Piu honked enthusiastically.

"Whoa!" Mom sighed, "this one always sets my stomach flipping."

"I'm glad I'm not up there!"

"Watch! He keeps them coming . . . rolling . . . one after the . . . whoa! I wish he did these with smoke! Real smoke. I hate that other stuff when they call him out!"

"What do you mean?" Pippa looked at her from the side. But Mom smiled, lost in memories. She remembered his love letters in the sky at a free-style event; but she could not deny that his racy stunts made her a little anxious, too. He was a highly skilled pilot and, despite the fact that he was already forty, he continued to push his limits.

"He needs the thrill," Pippa shouted.

"And the risk," Mom nodded. "He loves to be hanging between life and death."

"That's when he feels alive!"

"That's when he feels alive! Flying is in his blood. His dad, granddad – they all did it."

"What about your side of the family, Mom?"

Mom shook her head, without taking her eyes off the sky. "No, no, my folks had their feet firmly on the ground. At least until I broke rank." They watched a while in silence.

Pippa weighed her next words carefully. "And Great-grandad? Did he ever fly to the – Himalayas?"

"The Himalayas?" Mom was clearly taken by surprise. "Certainly not! The first aircraft was invented well after his time. No. I don't remember him having any affinity with the Far East. Ohhhh! That was neat!" She sighed, completely taken by Dad's risky escapades in the sky.

"But he traveled quite a bit, didn't he?" Pippa asked cautiously.

"Well, yes . . . He was one of Europe's most eminent land-scape gardeners. He spent many years in England, Italy, Greece, even Egypt, but – oh, look!" She held her breath as Dad thundered across the beach with the wingtips perpendicular to the ground.

"Wow!" Pippa applauded, now clearly distracted by her thoughts.

Mom glanced at her from the side. "You're still in your school uniform."

"Oh," Pippa said, "I forgot."

"Why do you ask?"

Pippa shrugged, squinting against the sun as Dad pulled the machine all the way into the sky, higher and higher. "I was just wondering." They watched as Dad stalled the machine before going into a vertical dive.

Then Mom dropped the bomb. "Well, I went there."

"Where?"

"India, Nepal . . . Actually, we went there several times."

Pippa stared at her, gobsmacked.

Mom laughed. "Those trips are pretty normal these days."

Tight-lipped and aloof, Pippa watched as Dad's plane plummeted.

"She's still my little girl," Mom thought. She saw her standing all alone, a meter away. So close and yet so far. "What is it, sweetheart?" she asked softly, turning towards her.

Pippa stood like a pillar of salt, hearing her heart pounding. The plane emerged beyond the dunes; it was climbing again.

"This distance between us has been here for a while," she heard Mom say, like from far away. "It makes me so sad."

Pippa's eyes filled with tears. She gulped. "I'm sorry, Mom."

"It's OK."

"I lost it," she started and broke off, biting her lip.

"Please, God," Mom pleaded silently, "don't take her from me just yet."

"I mean . . . it was the last one I had."

"The last what?"

"Seed."

"A seed, OK – can we not get a new one somewhere?"

"It's not just any seed, Mom!" Pippa burst out, "it was from the Blue Flower!"

Pippa's last words were swallowed by Mom's shriek as Dad went into one of his spectacular vertical dives that sometimes freaked her out beyond her control. Startled, Pippa screamed, too: "Mom, are you OK?"

Mom had gone blank. She glued her eyes to the sky, as if she were holding onto it. It turned into a deeper blue . . . the blue above the snowcapped Himalayas. Her senses sank into the rich aromas rising from the hot and humid valleys, she was borne aloft on the sound of cymbals, drums and bells and the Tingsha chimes. Monks were chanting mantras and prayer flags waved in the wind.

Then there was that noise . . . a deep menacing sound she'd never forget. The whole mountain was trembling. An avalanche eclipsed the sky . . .

"Mom?"

Mom's eyes followed the plane.

"*Through time shifting . . . a dream was drifting . . . to meet with destiny's course . . .*" she whispered. "Somehow, I knew it all the time."

The plane was droning towards them at low altitude.

Pippa could no longer resist. She slipped into her mother's arms as she used to do as a little girl. She buried her head against her breast, weeping quietly, while Mom stroked her hair.

"It's a secret." Pippa said.

"Yes, it is." Mom held her tight and waved with one arm as Dad flew a circle above them, waving good-bye with the wings.

"Bye, Dad!" Pippa waved, too. The noise of the plane disappeared beyond the mountains. Arm in arm, they walked into the house.

Finally, the day Pippa had been waiting for so eagerly, arrived. "Whew, MadMax! Come quickly" she called. "They're out. Hold on to your socks!"

"I'm here," the fastidious tomcat replied, "now I know where all those seeds went." Together, they scanned the field of poppies that had exploded into full bloom overnight.

"Red is the color of love and passion," she beamed. "I want it to shine everywhere! And besides," she announced boldly, "I'm skipping school today."

"I did not hear that," he replied.

"I'm having a rendezvous," she laughed, running her fingertips over some flowers.

"Hey, I watch you!" He jumped off the wall and followed her as she waded through the shrubs, some reaching up to her shoulders. But when they heard Dad going to the garage to leave for work they ducked and went into hiding.

"Shhh! I don't want Mr I-told-you to see me," she whispered, "He thinks Mom took me through."

"Tut-tut-tut," MadMax imitated Great-grandfather, "I must say –"

"Hey look! With special convoy!" Pippa giggled.

"Shhhh!" Keeping flat on the ground, they imploded with laughter as the car passed – with Piu Piu flying a few meters above the ground behind it. Once the sound faded into the distance, Piu Piu returned. Circling a few clumsy rounds above them, she went into landing mode with her pink webbed feet stretched forward. The field just swallowed her, leaving Pippa somewhat perplexed.

How does she do this? She always knows where I am?

"It must be the view from the top," she thought and an idea crossed her mind: "I always wanted to fly. I should ask her to teach me." But she quickly shook her head, adding: "I'm silly. I don't even have wings!"

"No need for that," MadMax purred, "you do it all the time. Stretch your wings and fly, no matter what others say!"

"Just do as I do!" Piu Piu joined them with an adventurous glint in her eyes. "Let's go high, Piupidoo!"

"Your rendezvous, My Lady!" MadMax was smiling secretively as he pointed upwards with his paw. The goose spread her wings and honked, creating such a draft that poppies were blown sideways. "The sky is waiting, let's take a tour!"

"For sure!" Pippa rolled her eyes and turned her attention back to the flowers. Like papery flames, each petal faded into white at the base where dewdrops reflected the light.

It was not just any color. It was light . . . infatuated with life!

MadMax gazed at the symphony of red above his head, speckled with dashes of a blue sky like windows to heaven. "Were you not looking for the blue flower?" he asked, his voice somewhat monotone.

He had Pippa's attention immediately.

"How badly do you want it? Do you really, really want to know?" His intensity took her by surprise. She stared at him, unable to say a word.

"How far are you willing to go?"

Seeing her eyes fill with tears, he asked softly: "Can you let go of the shore to explore the Unknown?"

She nodded spontaneously. She loved it when he took her to the movies in her mind, although he seemed different today.

"Okay, My Lady," she heard him say, "just listen and align your breathing. Remember: what you are the vibration of, appears. Relax. Be still. Allow the unexpected to happen . . . get your mind out of the way!" His words vaguely rang a bell in her but her eyes already closed . . .

What she noticed first was a pair of black eagles circling high in the sky, their strong cries echoing through the valley. And clouds of tiny green white-eyes were sweeping from bush to bush, black pupils on white, glittering like beads. Permeating all was the consistent swell of the breeze: a long inhale . . . a gently piping exhale . . . the gap of silence in between.

She hardly realized how she herself tuned in to it. Her breathing slowed down while her awareness expanded. As the frequency of her vibration changed, the orchestration of wholeness around her permeated her being. A new reality arose.

It seemed perfectly natural when a butterfly appeared just when she saw it on the canvas of her mind. Fluttering from flower to flower, its presence grew as it came closer, until it hovered right above her. She sensed the flapping of wings, the faint swirl of air each wingtip stirred. As the coolness of the shadow glided over her face, her whole being seemed to expand. Time stood still when the graceful creature touched the inner corner of her eye to savor the sweetness of a tear.

You are not who you think you are.

A profound peace came over her. The more she aligned herself with Nature the more it appeared to glow. It was an energy beyond color, a vibrational web that reached out in all directions. Tracing each plant and stone and creature, it stretched right through her and beyond, connecting everything, including MadMax and Piu Piu. When she turned around herself, laughing with wonder, the whole field oscillated in response.

"Listen!" MadMax reminded her. "Pay close attention!"

Swinging on long hairy stalks, their petals teased and torn by the wind, the poppies were singing:

Today! Today! We fly away! We all fly away . . . today!

The poppies were trembling with excitement: this was their big annual finale! They would all come together from far and nearby to show off their splendor, one last time, on the fleeting catwalk of the sky. *Today!*

Suddenly, Pippa's heart jumped: what if a blue poppy were amongst them? Would she finally find the elusive blue flower she had been seeking for so long?

"Voilà," MadMax declared solemnly, "your rendezvous is pending!"

"He still knows me so well," Pippa thought. "Maybe, it's all happening today!"

"Let there be magic!" he intoned with a sweeping gesture, and – for a few instants – Pippa thought she saw a wand in his paw. The Cape storm began to roar and deafened the poppy chorus just as it achieved a jubilant high. Dark clouds cascaded over the mountain, sending a menacing grumble down its flanks. The old stone pine groaned as a gust whipped through its crown, ripping off cones, needles and branches. Then it hurtled downwards, sending shock waves through the field of poppies.

Before she knew it, Pippa was swept off the ground and lifted into the air. Bewildered, she looked onto the garden below her; it was becoming smaller and smaller until it was just a tiny dot. Tossed along a surge of air she was amazed how light – if not weightless – she felt, but when she tried to reach out with her hands and feet it seemed they were no longer there.

"My hair!" she cried, reeling, "where is my hair?" The world below her turned and turned as it came closer again, faster and faster. Her stomach dropped. She opened her mouth to scream, expecting to hit rock bottom at any moment. But then her vision dissolved within a blinding blaze of petals spiraling back up into the sky. She gasped when she caught a glimpse of the field far down below her: the poppies had gone . . . yet it glowed! Dissected, separated, torn apart, the petals were in the air, undulating in rhythmic patterns like glittering fish.

"Oh, Great-grandad," she whispered, "who am I now?"

There was no answer; there was only a frenzied turbulence that she seemed to be part of.

Who or what was it? Where did it take her?

"Remember!" She felt the tomcat's voice in her heart and – as her plummeting, tumbling and numbing confusion brought her to the brink of panic – a familiar voice honked close-by: "You can fly! You can fly!" An instant stream of energy infused her. With Piu Piu at her side, it felt so natural, so simple to let go and glide, to follow the waltz of *Today!*, blithely rising and sinking in waves and twirls and tunnels, painting rhythms of color into the sky.

Millions of petals were gathering from all directions. Together, they dived down into vortices which made her head spin – although it seemed she no longer had one, which bewildered her more. But within the turmoil were interludes of peace, where she no longer worried who she was or where her thoughts and memories came from.

"Piupidoo! I am me – I am you!" There was no mistaking the thrill in Piu Piu's voice. She bumped cheerfully into Pippa to ignite her, she snapped into the howling wind. Glued together like twins, she pulled her petal pal along, gliding away, floating, and deliriously eager to give something back.

Some petals missed the upward surge and tumbled back down. Once they touched the ground, they were blown away by the wind; they zoomed across the earth, the grass, the pathways, enjoying the ride even then.

What was there to be afraid of anyway?

"If you want magic, you've got to believe in yourself!"

MadMax had mentioned it to her before but only now, as she abandoned herself to the ecstasy around her, did she begin to remember. All she could see were colors infused with light: shades of red, pink and orange; yellows and whites; and a dark mauve.

And the blue?

Although she did not spot a single petal that was blue, she felt its presence all around her as she followed the flow, moving with and through the others within one breath. There was expansion without pressure. There was trust and no fear. The dancer was becoming the dance. In the ephemerality of time, all that existed was *Today!*

"Who made this happen?" she asked MadMax. "Was it the wizard . . . you?"

"No, no, no!" he laughed. "The wizard is you!"

"Me?" She was sure he teased her again. "What about me anyway?"

"You? You're blue!"

"No, no, I mean, where am I now?"

"Oh! Your ladyship is still down there, I guess."

"Down there?" Pippa was incredulous. "Am I not here?"

"There!" PiuPiu nudged her. "I'm always here!"

"So I'm dreaming?"

"You're waking up."

"What do you mean?"

"You walk in and out of dreams every night."

"But then I wake up and – "

"– you're still in your bed!"

"– not me!" Piu Piu disagreed. "Not me!"

"No?" Pippa was confused. "Where are you?"

"On Dad's dinner plate!" Piu Piu exploded with laughter, pulling them along. "Looking down Dad's throat!" she added boisterously.

"Oh, stop it!" Pippa squirmed.

"She'll go down smoked!"

"You're terrible!" Pippa laughed.

"He'll let you have my feathers and bones!" Piu Piu honked.

"Not for me!" MadMax squirmed.

"All for you!" Piu Piu somersaulted in the air.

"Listen, you monsters," Pippa shouted after them, "How do we get back?" She tried to catch up with them.

"I don't know where I am! I can't see myself anymore!"

"Who cares?" MadMax said, waiting for her, "you are here now." When she'd caught up with him, he indicated a cluster of petals floating in the air above them. "Look closely . . . as they're drifting by."

Pippa observed them for a moment. Then she saw them: each petal had a fine string attached to it. "The silver cords," she exclaimed in awe, "everything is connected."

"We are beings of light," MadMax said as she watched how the movements of petals formed a bouquet in the sky, their luminous filaments uniting into a single stem, reaching down into the garden. "Our vibration radiates. We're bubbles of energy . . . communicating from our hearts by sending out electromagnetic spherical bubbles at the speed of light. Always sending and receiving, always changing and creating. Yes, everything is connected. What affects one, affects all."

Pippa hardly listened. Spellbound, she gazed across the endless sky. "The blue . . . " she whispered. "I can see it now! I remember. Heaven is everywhere."

After what seemed like a timeless moment, she became aware of his attentive look. "So how do I get back?" she asked quickly. "Slither down along my life line?"

"The same way you came!"

She stared at him. Why couldn't he just answer?

"Simple," he succumbed with a sleek grin, "act on your intention!"

"Piupidoo!" Piu Piu honked, "do as I do!"

"Right! Hold on to me, Piu Piu!" Pippa shouted, slightly irritated. She focused, imagining herself back in the garden and, indeed, when she opened her eyes she found herself sitting in the frazzled poppy field. It felt as though she had never left.

"That was quick!" She tapped her head, patted her arms and looked at her hands and down at her feet: she was still there. And so was Piu Piu!

"Instant." MadMax was stretching his back. "We shift. Actually, we keep shifting all the time." He stopped and scratched his ear as he encountered one of Pippa's edgy stares. Some forlorn petals sailed past in the wind.

Pippa glanced at the sky, but there were only dark clouds. "Up there, it seemed like an eternity!"

"Up there, time does not exist."

"Piupidoo!" Piu Piu trumpeted, flapping her wings. "Time for a swim!"

"I didn't notice it was so cold!" Pippa got up and stretched.

"Lunch!" MadMax was striding straight towards the house with razor-sharp focus, his tail high up in the air. "I didn't notice I was so hungry!"

"Right on!" Pippa laughed, "let's shift into the kitchen!" But instead of following the others she paused and glanced across the field. Even now that it was almost bare, with not a single flower left, it was still glowing. *How could that be?*

She wiggled her toes as a vibration penetrated her soles. The tingling sensation spread all the way up through her legs and into her spine, providing a singular balance to her whole being. She felt so good!

"You're glowing," she heard MadMax telling her from the kitchen where he was waiting in front of an empty bowl. Bored, he projected his favorite foods into it . . . but then wasn't able to choose.

"Still the same beloved gourmand!" Pippa thought but then heard the car and quickly jumped up to go.

"Thank you," she said to the field and the sky, "thank you for today!"

She smiled as a light ripple ran through it all like a tender embrace. Elated, she turned and skipped off; her hair flying in the wind.

"These weeds must go!"

Dad came down the staircase and scanned what the storm had left of the field. It was getting dark and the wind was still blowing. "Yesterday here, today gone!" He shook his head. "A complete waste. Useless. Besides, they spread more each year. No, no, no . . . I will see to it that we really get to the roots and clean this out. Let's plant something useful. Agapanthus! Agapanthus always works. What does the boss say?"

"Fine with me, darling," Mom replied, pulling her woolen shawl around her. "Maybe . . . if we could just wait until they're dry? I need them for my flower arrangements . . . and the table decorations for Christmas . . . you know?"

"Brilliant," he ranted, "spread them even more!"

He pulled out a long stem from the ground and shook the soil from its roots. It already carried a few round pods that looked mature. He broke off a dry pod and shook it close to his ear. "Nope. Not yet. All it needs are a few warm days. There will be millions of them . . ."

"Brilliant!" Mom laughed.

His jaw dropped; his temper flared up in his temples. "You're not making fun of me, are you?"

"Hmmm," she hummed, "actually . . . I was thinking that I should try that delicious German Poppy Seed Cake recipe? You know . . . the one I found on the Internet the other day?"

He looked up as if stung by an adder. "Hmmmm! Now you're talking!"

"Crispy cookie crust, poppy seed filling and a baked sour cream topping," she added triumphantly. "Oranges, lemons, eggs and poppy seeds straight from the garden. With a strong, fragrant coffee. Not from my garden – yet!"

"You wicked witch!" He dropped the plant and shook the soil from his hands.

"My personal mix, of course," she added.

"Of course!" he smiled, joining her on the staircase, where he pulled her close and kissed her tenderly. "I love your personal mix . . ."

Arm in arm, they continued towards the house.

Pippa woke up and listened to the silence of the night. She was still enchanted by the mysterious realm she had explored as a petal in the sky. Moonlight filtered through the windows. It glided over her desk, which overflowed with glasses and plates filled with freshly harvested flower heads, pods and seeds in different sizes and shapes. Now she noticed a glow around them that connected directly with her. Her eyes wandered across the hand-carved Balinese banana trees that were casting jungle-like shadows over her bed, creeping up the wall and across the ceiling. Pippa loved to watch these abstract shapes come alive as if being pulled by invisible strings. This usually happened when the wind came up and began to shake the shrubs and plants growing outside her windows.

"Remember," MadMax had said, looking at her with an intensity that still puzzled her, although something had opened up inside her and had started to unfold. She could not yet entirely understand her insight, but knew she had carried it within her all the time – like a reflection of the endless blue sky.

She had slept like a log after her magical journey, and wondered why she had woken up? Drifting deliciously between worlds, her realities transcended, interchanged and shifted, while she remained the silent observer.

Were those shadows playing on her ceiling real? Could she touch them? What if what her senses told her was wrong?

MadMax loved to catch them, jumping almost two meters high up the wall. All she did was manipulate a light source with her hands to direct the projection. He could never get enough of this game and made her laugh at his tremulous crouches, his tail moving eagerly from side to side, until he exploded into acrobatic sprints and daring pirouettes. Not all landings were soft. Sometimes he growled and licked his paw, but as soon as the next target appeared and tickled his hunting spirit, nothing could hold him back.

Suddenly, she clenched her jaw, remembering that fateful night and that he had not done it ever since then.

"It's just an illusion anyway," she thought, looking at his dark silhouette. He sat on the edge of her bed, half listening, half asleep.

Suddenly, he turned his head and listened in the direction of the dam. He gave off a low growl that went right through her. His whole appearance changed instantly; each and every hair on his body seemed to be standing on end and the tip of his tail was twitching.

Piu Piu!

A sense of foreboding shot right through her. That's what woke her up; her bond with the goose was so close that she instinctively knew there was danger.

She leapt out of her bed and grabbed a torch on her way to the door. Barefoot, she slipped into the moonlit atrium and darted into the kitchen.

From the kitchen window she looked at the dam. Everything seemed quiet and peaceful. The summer heat had diminished the water level considerably. She knew exactly where Piu Piu slept on the island. Usually, the goose immediately picked up her presence and responded to it. But tonight nothing moved. She could not detect even the slightest glimpse of her golden plumage.

"Piu Piu," Pippa whispered, "where are you? Piu Piu?"

She switched the torch on. With her heart beating in her throat, she directed the beam towards the dark, shadowy areas on the island. She almost dropped it when, suddenly, a pair of feline eyes flared up, reflecting in the light.

The beast! It was on the island! How did it get there?

Where was Piu Piu?

Now it disappeared behind the strelitzias. Moments later she could see, clearly, the silhouette of the big cat with its tufted ears jumping up the embankment on the other side of the dam. It stopped under the bottlebrush tree and stood still, gazing back to the island. Slowly, it turned its head to face the lightbeam, sending arrows of ice down her spine. Then the beast was gone.

Fighting back a terrible apprehension, Pippa directed the light lower . . . onto a few feathers floating on the mirrorlike surface of the pond. Her hand started to tremble. Then her back hunched over with convulsive sobbing and she switched off the light: Piu Piu, her beloved goose, was no more.

She was cold, she was miserable, and she did not know for how long she had cried when Mom suddenly folded her into her arms. "Sweetheart, what are you doing out here at this time?" She felt the heat on Pippa's forehead, the wetness of her face. "What's going on?"

When she noticed the torch she had her answer. She took her daughter's face into her hands, stroked her hair away and looked lovingly into her wet eyes. "Come, I want to show you something." Putting her arm around Pippa's narrow shoulders, she guided the distraught girl out of the kitchen and across the atrium, towards her room.

Pippa's eyes were almost closed from exhaustion; a feeling of complete lethargy overcame her. All she wanted was to drift away . . . away . . .

"Look," she heard Mom say from far away. She was disorientated. Somehow they came to a halt, but there was no bed for her to drop into and cover her grief. *Where was she?*

"Open your eyes," her mother whispered, holding her tight. "Just a wee bit."

Pippa barely opened one eye. She figured out that they were in the atrium, at the large terrace door facing the sea. But then she gasped and her eyes popped open with disbelief; out there, right in front of the terrace door, stood Piu Piu!

Was it really Piu Piu or just an illusion?

The goose stood with her back towards the house, facing the garden. Her golden plumage glistened in the moonlight. She immediately noticed them watching her and gave off a few happy chirps.

Pippa was about to rush out but Mom put her finger to her lips to indicate it was not the time for a noisy surge of emotions that would wake up the whole house, meaning Dad.

"But . . . the caracal. . ." Pippa whispered, gobsmacked.

"What caracal?" Mom shook her head. "We haven't seen one since the big fire . . . That's long ago. You weren't even born! You must have been dreaming. Look, all is well. Piu Piu is watching over you!"

Pippa could no longer resist; she freed herself and Mom helped to open the door. The child flew out onto the stairs. The wild goose opened her wings and Pippa flung her arms around her. PiuPiu nibbled her ear fondly and chirped away, softly, only for Pippa to hear.

From that night onwards, come rain or thunderstorm, Piu Piu stood guard on the terrace, under the Milky Way. As the water level in the dam had been sinking for a while, she had chosen a much safer place from where she could watch the movements within the house as well as in the garden. Nothing escaped her vigilant eyes; not even a shooting star!

Besides, she loved it when the whole world turned around her. Once the house had calmed down and there were no more lights, she usually gave off a contented quack and tucked one leg under her damaged wing, standing in perfect balance. The wing protruded slightly to the right, it looked as if she were carrying a sword.

Of Being and Becoming

"This is amazing! My blog post *Merry Christmas from Piu Piu* got a real avalanche of 'likes', new 'friends' and tons of new 'followers' on Facebook. Piu Piu will be happy!" Pippa was very upbeat about the overwhelming response her journal, called *Life of Piu Piu*, received. Mom had set up a simple blog for her on the Internet. This was her first step towards her big goal: to bring Great-grandfather's oeuvre to the world.

What she did not know at that stage was that the astonishing way Piu Piu's life was to enfold, and how it was entangled with hers, would prompt her to share so much more.

All that she would find out one day.

As a professional web developer, Mom had linked Pippa's blog to a category *'Life of Piu Piu'* on her own media website, from where all posts were syndicated to her social media accounts. Everything Pippa published on her blog automatically appeared on Mom's Facebook, where it could be shared by family and friends. This was how Pippa could tell her fascinating stories as they happened, and respond to the growing interest of her followers. With her inquisitive mind and Mom's expert guidance, Pippa learned pretty fast how to find her way around the web. She loved having the whole world at her virtual doorstep while living in the wild. The only thing she really hated was the slow internet connection. "This is so boring," she moaned.

"You can't have it all, my girl!" Dad commented.

"They keep asking if we have elephants on the lines!"

"Well, there's a price for everything!"

Was there, really?

Meanwhile, the life and adventures of the wild Egyptian goose from Noordhoek had become a real buzz on the web, creating a lot of friendly interaction between people from all walks of life, from all around the world. Some of them sent links to their own stories, with photos or videos of geese, some of which Pippa showed to Piu Piu, like the one from Maria from LA.

Once Piu Piu got over her initial shock of 'meeting' with Maria, the wild Toulouse goose from Los Angeles, right at home in 'her territory' – meaning on Pippa's computer screen – she was ecstatic! Of course, she was skeptical and not sure it wasn't some kind of trick or hocus-pocus. What if Maria were hiding in this dubious black box? To this day, she hadn't figured out how even Pippa could be in two places at the same time.

A frenzy broke loose on the web when Mom loaded a video of Piu Piu doing her typical welcome greeting onto YouTube. Within hours, there were loads of video responses featuring all sorts of wild geese, from Canada, the USA, Holland, France, Germany, Sweden, Russia, the UK and even Japan – greeting back. There was one video, however, that just did it for Piu Piu. Of all countries, it came from Japan.

"Do you understand this goose from Kyoto?" Pippa asked incredulously.

"*Hai*," Piu Piu retorted, "*moshi moshi*."

Pippa stared at her in disbelief: "What does she say?"

"*Chotto matte kudasai*," Piu Piu chattered cheerfully, and pirouetted. Then she bowed her head: "Please play it again."

Pippa had to play the video of the big Greylag goose from Kyoto over and over again. What impressed her most were the pretty pink cherry blossoms with snow-covered Mount Fuji in the background. "Like in a fairy tale," she thought, "it reminds me of one of Mom's old flicks . . . *Dreams* by Akira Kurosawa." She looked expectantly at the enchanted goose. "Well?"

"He says *daisuki desu*," Piu Piu breathed, her voice trembling. "He?"

Piu Piu nodded, blushing beyond her beak. "He tells me he likes me very much. He wants to show me the snow-capped holy mountain and the cherry blossoms in spring, and then –"

Even when the video stopped, Piu Piu kept staring at it, listening, as if the magic music continued.

His voice . . . she would always recognize it!

Pippa smiled. "I see you're already there. You shifted."

But Piu Piu did not hear her; she was far, far away.

"It's the same in my dreams," Pippa pondered, "language is no barrier. One just understands."

To keep up with her fanmail, Piu Piu normally checked in regularly, but this was not the case today.

"I'm missing her," Pippa thought, "somehow, we've drifted apart. Anyway, the terrace is too hot; she's probably at the dam. Well, what remained of it."

Her eyes meandered over the jars with seeds, flowerheads, poppy pods and grasses . . . and up the wall across the gallery of pressed flower art. It did not matter how long she stared at the pictures; to her they remained distant, dusty and dull.

Heaving a sigh of discontent, she turned back to the screen. She pulled up some of the very same images and compared them with those on the wall. While the colors had mostly faded by now, their fine vegetal structures were identical. And yet – on her screen they appeared dramatically different. They were vibrating. They were so light. There was this incredible luminosity – as if another layer of energy or even a new dimension had been added that breathed back some life.

"I can only work with colors on paper or canvas," she said, "but the computer paints with light. It doesn't matter whether I look at it here or on Dad's iphone or any other electronic device." Musing, she went silent for a while. Then she promised herself: "I will bring all of Great-grandad's work into the frequency of this living light!"

It was not the first time she had thought about it in a certain way – as a vague idea, a possibility, a dream. But now she could see it clearly in her mind. Writing about her goose was a pleasant pastime and certainly a lot of fun, but now that she was familiar with the medium, she yearned for something more demanding. The concept of finding a better way to present, update, continue and spread Great-grandad's oeuvre via the web had started to possess her, with a consuming passion. In fact, her desire for creative expression had been ignited the moment she had opened the monograph and that spark had been sizzling beneath the surface ever since. She woke up with it and it was in her dreams; it was always on her mind. She was relieved to have come to such clarity early in her life, but also cautious not to burn the steps on the way.

"Ooops," she chuckled, "here I'm day-dreaming again. Not the way to get my article on the way. Where was I? Ah, Piu Piu and her kin. Just as she started to write, a noise shook her up. Unwilling to interrupt the flow of her thoughts, she turned her head to glance at the open door, right behind her, "Piu Piu?"

She wasn't too sure it was the goose; the noise sounded more like a lizard or a tortoise rummaging through dry leaves. While it did not alarm her enough to make her get up and inspect the possible cause, it made her alert. It was so hot. The earth was consumed by the sun. An eerie cracking in the pines made her anxious; she had no idea why. Time was ticking away, lethargically, almost sneaking out of existence.

She became conscious of the fact that no one else was at home. Normally, it did not bother her. She never felt alone. But today she tried to ignore a vague sense of abandonment, an occasional shiver when her hair stood up at the back of her neck. Her room was on the sunny side of the house so there were no signs of MadMax or Piu Piu. It was quiet. Just a cicada disrupted the silence, its metallic sound approaching like an alien flying machine. The small monster zoomed past and disappeared in the stagnant afternoon air; summer was at its peak.

Pippa turned back to her screen and continued typing: *You need to know that this area is a Cape cobra and puffadder breeding ground. During the hot summer months they are everywhere. As with most animals, the cobra avoids close encounters, unless she's cornered or very desperate for water or . . .*

She looked up. An old memory floated into her mind. She must have been five . . . perhaps six? The sun was hot like today; the sound of an aircraft buzzed in her ears. She was walking back from the beach, following Mom's footprints, a blue towel spread over her head and shoulders like a tent. Salt was prickling all over her skin. With each step she took she sank deeper. Sand was seeping into her shoes, making them heavier and heavier until they disappeared and she was sucked in, too. Only her towel remained; and the buzz in her ears.

She was there and not there. Somewhere in between. It did not bother her; she still knew her being had no end.

"Let's take it off now," Mom said to her at the car, but Pippa held fiercely on to it, shaking her head, "It's my flying carpet."

"Your flying carpet. I see." Mom smiled as she undid and emptied her shoes. "Are you catching Daddy again? Oh dear, if it weren't for all this sand . . ."

Over Mom's shoulder, Pippa stared at the dune, squinting against the light. There was not a single footprint. Just the sinuous tracks of snakes . . .

"Hey, dreamer. Little feet in." Pippa pulled her feet up and Mom closed the door. She started the engine and drove off. "Ahhh, the heat . . . it's far too hot today. Nothing beats a cool shower now."

"You want to take it outside?" she asked at the house. Pippa nodded. "Want me to wash your hair?" Pippa shook her head.

"OK, sweetheart. I'll quickly hop under the shower; I'll be with you just now." For some unknown reason she hesitated, unable to let her go.

"Where is your flying carpet taking you now?"

Pippa did not answer, but she clasped her towel a little firmer as she continued along the path.

"There's no more water in the dam, don't let it run for too long," Mom shouted, just to hold onto her a little longer; she didn't know why. "What's wrong with me?" she wondered, glancing up at the merciless sky. The sun was almost chilling. She shuddered with a strange sense of foreboding in her gut, but shook it off and stepped into the house.

"I hope she didn't get too much sun."

Pippa startled up as her screen bleeped and went black. "Wait a moment!" she thought, "Who am I now? I'm me, but I'm Mom, too! I know how she feels; I can read her mind. I'm part of her, part of everything, and I'm also observing it all. Something is happening to me . . ."

She did not even notice that her eyes closed and she slipped back into that empty fullness, the gap between thoughts. "Let's see, do I proceed into the shower now – or onto the lawn?"

The little girl walked away and stepped onto the toasted lawn. The grass crackled under her soles. The water from the hosepipe was so hot she had to wait until she could splash it all over her, washing away the salt, the sand and the sun. As the water got cooler, she dropped onto her knees, letting it run all over her skin. She bent forward over her thighs to wash her hair, groping her way around her scalp, hosepipe in hand. What lovely coolness and instant relief – she could have stayed forever, but she remembered Mom's words and closed the nozzle. Rinsed and clean, she thrust her head and upper body backwards to get rid of the excess moisture. But as she came back up there was . . . a bone-chilling hiss!

Everything in her froze. She could not bring herself to open her eyes. Through the nakedness of her skin she sensed the awe-inspiring presence, hardly a meter away: a Cape cobra!

Furious that the flow of water had stopped, and startled by the sudden movement, the snake had raised herself, in a flash, vertically from the ground. Her hood fully spread, her forked tongue flicking with a wild rage, she was ready to strike and uttered another gruesome hiss. She was determined to drink! No one was to take that birthright from her.

A raw, violent energy shot through her steely muscles, just waiting for her cue. She felt it rising . . . higher and higher . . . flooding her head. This time there would be no mercy; all the accumulated hatred, the humiliation and pain endured by her kin would be released with one ferocious bite.

Paralyzed from shock and surrendering to her fate, Pippa slipped into a merciful state of unconsciousness. She was not even aware that, from the depth of her soul, her birthsong poured over her lips.

As the scum of the earth started to crumble under her gaze, and the lethal venom boiled in her fangs, the cobra suddenly hesitated, noticing a subtle change in the air. A wave of gentle harmonies was drifting towards her, calming and entrancing her like a charm. With the sensitivity of her tongue she tasted the new vibration, absorbing its sweetness from within. There was something she recognized. Her awareness expanded; a tremor ran through her core. Almost imperceptibly, her shimmering scales glided apart. Nothing in her poise indicated the rising flame.

Unwittingly, while she sang and the music echoed in each of her cells, Pippa's eyes opened and locked with those of the snake. Her face was glowing. The tips of her fingers sensed a sizzle in the air and drops like tears running down her skin. The coiled serpent at the base of her spine was awakening and rising: the sacred flame.

Looking into the girl's eyes for the very first time, the cobra recognized herself.

"I am you," the girl whispered.

Spellbound, unable to move, Mom stood at the window and stared: two flames were hovering above the lawn, rising higher and higher. They reached out to each other . . . intertwining . . . uniting and separating . . . higher and higher . . . until they merged into one.

Mom squeezed her eyes; all she saw was the blaze of the sun.

Finally, after what seemed an eternity, the cobra deflated. She retreated without ever taking her gaze from the girl.

"Thank you," was all Pippa could think while the veil of timelessness sank back and blood returned to her veins.

"Did you notice," she added, "I always fill your bowl with water. I do this each day."

The mottled cobra turned around and disappeared, flying horizontally across the lawn . . .

Pippa's eyes watered. She reached for her glass. Mom's words still resonated in her mind, although she wasn't sure she fully understood what she had meant.

"Fundamentally," Mom had said, "we may all be more alike than we think. We come from the same source. We're made of the same molecules. The same molecules as the universe.

Source energy. It flows and expresses itself through all that is –
a tree, a cloud, you, me and the snake. Our environments allow
us to develop into unique beings – each one appearing different
and separate from the other in order to play its particular role
within the big game . . . the big illusion."

"If we knew each other so well, why then did she almost – "
Pippa was confused. Everywhere in mythology and legends –
be it in Egypt, Ancient Greece or India – serpents mirrored the
dichotomy of human existence in dramatic expressions of good
and evil. Like in a classical play.

"I never hurt a snake."

Oh, if only Great-grandad were here to ask!

"The cobra lives from the core of her being," she heard
Great-grandad's voice. "It's what humans must learn. *Insist
on yourself! Never imitate! Seek no opinion but your own*, as our
American sage here so rightly put it, some 200 years ago."

Unconsciously, Pippa had shifted to her favorite place.

It seemed as if she had never left it. The monoliths were still
intimidating and the faces only became visible once they moved.
But, when Great-grandfather twitched his moustache and blew
a few coils of smoke in the air, the lines of his face emerged
from the forms and fissures; and she laughed and relaxed.

"Great-grandad! I can see you!"

Great-grandad's head bowed slightly as he turned towards a
number of tall, narrow stones that had been hidden in the shadows. Now, as a ray of sunshine was gliding over one of them, it
revealed another face. The fine lichen growing all over its well-
defined features gave it a marbled aspect, like veins. Behind the
prominent nose, Pippa was drawn to a pair of kind and intelligent eyes. Small birds were sitting on his eyebrows and pecking
his sideburns.

"Your opinion, Waldo?" she heard Great-grandad say.

"I'm honored, Prince . . ."

"Tut-tut-tut! Just Hermann, please," Great-grandad laughed,
turning back and looking down at Pippa.

"Pippa, meet my friend, the eminent Ralph Waldo Emerson.
Remember this name, you will appreciate his work one day."

"Thank you kindly," Emerson said in a simple, distinguished way. Then he turned slightly and Pippa felt a radiant glance that touched her soul: "Hi, Miss Pippa!"

Her right hand went up all by itself and waved: "Hi, Mr. Emerson!"

As he turned back to follow the conversation, a bird, singing a raucous aria, insisted on sitting on his nose. He tried to blow it away discreetly, but it just lifted into the air and back again, without stopping the singing.

"Oh dear, no pancakes on his noble schnozzle, please," she thought and politely looked away, but she was too tempted to peep up again and their eyes met and smiled.

Meanwhile, Great-grandad addressed the square stone resting horizontally in the shadows next to Thunberg, the one with a wisp of ferns and orchids sprouting on top.

"Jussieu, when did we all meet in Paris? Early 1830s, was it?"

"*Beh, oui, trente-trois je dirais,*" the French botanist answered with a Lyonnais accent. Fountains of water spouted from his colossal nose, now and again splashing over his tragic eyes that were pulled upwards between moss-grown folds.

"*Il n'aimait pas trop, notre jeune ami, si je me rappelle bien!*" He laughed boisterously and the others joined him. This was too much for the bird on Emerson's nose, so it flew away and Pippa laughed, too.

"*Sauf pour la bonne bouffe, bien sur, et les vins! Alors là . . .*" The Frenchman whistled and rocked dangerously, risking his balance, which added to the merriment of the others. When he went on to quote Emerson in 'Frenglish': "*A loud modern New York of a place!*" they seemed to collapse towards one another.

"*Et alors!*" he added innocently just when a frog hopped across his forehead and disappeared into his convoluted ear, "*ça vous fait rire? What's so funny?*"

Pippa felt the earth vibrating under her feet. When she looked back at Great-grandad, she saw a trickle running down from his eye. Oh, this was hilarious!

"Monsieur de Jussieu!" Regaining his composure, Emerson leaned towards the French botanist, waiting for silence.

"Sir," he said, "we all are indebted to you. Of course, I loved Paris . . . but the insight I gained after your invitation to the 'Jardin des Plantes' took me far beyond that. *Plants - the reflection of the mind of man.* What an eye-opener! A true revelation! Seeing with my own eyes the way you organized plants. The countless plant families . . . How they were related and connected, and how they all fitted together within the whole."

Emerson stopped briefly, clearing his throat as his memories came back. "Your methodology," he continued, "your brilliant system of classification . . . all this had an immense impact on my vision. It was one of those pivotal landmarks in my life."

He lowered his voice, speaking with great intensity: "Gentlemen, that's when I saw – in scientific terms – *the interconnectedness of all that is. Spirit met science. Nature as it is.* Superb! Absolutely superb!"

"If I'm not mistaken, mon cher Antoine," Thunberg commented, "you were the first foreign member we elected?"

"Jawohl!" Great-grandad nodded, "and, may I add, the fact that many of the plant families are still attributed to you today, says it all – *nicht wahr?*"

He looked down at Pippa, who had absorbed each word. "Our young lady here knows what I mean!" As he winked at her a snake glided from his flank and slithered towards Pippa.

More than happy to be included again, and dying to speak, she did not notice it. "Yes, it's all in Great-grandad's book! But something is missing. I have a question about the blue –"

"It's all one . . ." she heard Emerson say, his voice fading into the chanting overtones in the air before it broke off abruptly.

Into the silence, Pippa heard the same noise again. Instantly alert, she looked towards the open door. She decided to save her document and rather go and check. It happened when she turned back to the screen, then – from the corner of her right eye – she saw a large snake moving towards her foot on the floor. *Was this a dream or reality?*

In an instant reflex she pulled both feet back. This brisk movement alarmed the snake; she made an extremely fast turn and Pippa heard it a third time, that strange noise. Then she saw her: a Cape cobra curling up in the wastepaper box underneath her desk, where she had just dumped some packaging paper.

"Holy smoke! Not again!"

She was just over a meter away and looking straight at Pippa. She did not seem to feel threatened and looked rather comfortable where she was.

"Keep cool," Pippa said. It wasn't clear whether she meant the snake or herself.

"Thank you, that's why I came," the snake replied.

"She's looking at me as though she wants to hypnotize me," Pippa thought. Her surprise visitor was displaying no aggressive behavior at all, but rather a blend of curiosity and familiarity.

"I think she's a female. I'm sure she is." Pippa knew she had to avoid any sudden movement and respect the reptile's space. Except it was her space that had been invaded and Pippa was not keen on sharing her room with a cobra. "I wonder, did I attract her with my thoughts? Or did she hijack my mind?"

"There was an openness, an intention," the cobra acceded. "Call it a field of attraction. Somehow, I felt welcome."

Pippa suddenly thought of MadMax and Piu Piu. All hell would break loose should they suddenly appear.

"I'm sorry," she burst out, "you can't stay here! Please leave." She waited. As there was no reaction from the snake, she stepped backwards and put on her Wellies. Picking up a broom and balancing it in her hands, she gently enticed the reptile to get back into the garden. "This is my space; you have the garden. Thank you for your visit . . . but, please, get out!" It seemed easy enough; the door was just next to her and wide open. It was the direct route and the most logical thing to do. So Pippa thought.

"Hahaha, this tickles!" the cobra giggled and wriggled. Suddenly, she shot past the door and, in a heartbeat, disappeared under Pippa's bed.

"Oh, what a bummer!" Pippa yelped. Now she would be very difficult to spot. Down on her knees, she peered under her bed. Where was she? "Oh no!" She was invading her sanctum of sanctums!

"Don't touch my treasure chest," she wanted to shout, but a lump in her throat made her cough until her head became hot from the strain. She got up and drank some water, panting. She glanced at her bed. All seemed perfectly peaceful. She closed her eyes.

"It's an illusion," she thought, "it's all in my mind."

Not seeing me doesn't mean I'm not here. Seeing me doesn't mean I am. I've been in this space more often than you will ever know.

Without thinking, Pippa got up and filled a bowl with water for the snake, placing it near the door.

"Thank you," the snake responded, sadly. "You no longer hear me. You no longer know me. But you didn't forget that."

A little undecided, Pippa went back onto her knees with her head on the floor, waiting. The tiles felt hard but refreshing against her cheek. Slowly, the snake's head came forward, tentatively, sensing the ground vibrations. Her tongue was flicking to pick up the scent. She looked at Pippa for a moment and then, very slowly, she began to wind herself around the treasure chest. Pippa's eyelids fluttered while she watched the mesmerizing movement of shiny scales and cryptic patterns until the muscular body came to a halt and the cobra's head appeared on top of the lid.

"Please, don't squeeze it. Don't break it. Just hold it . . . " Pippa swallowed her tears.

Completely immobile, the reptile looked like a bronze sculptured part of the treasure chest, guarding the secret entrance to that other world.

Pippa started to weep.

"Wake up," the snake hissed softly.

"You don't understand," Pippa sobbed.

"We dance between worlds all the time . . ."

"Why don't you just go."

Shaking with scattered thoughts, Pippa closed her eyes and put her forehead on the floor. The ringing in her ears mixed with the sound of overtones. Blood shot into her head.

What you are the vibration of, appears!

Pippa no longer heard her ancestor's voice; as she bobbed up she saw the mottled cobra right before her, ready to strike. In a burst of energy ignited by fear, she flung herself towards the broom. This time she turned it around, using it as a weapon that she pushed with all her might towards the intruder.

The cobra reacted like a bolt of lightning. The broom was ripped from Pippa's hands and shattered into pieces, while she herself was hurled across the floor and glued against the wall. Before her terrified eyes the reptile raised herself above her bed, flaring a massive hood. Its explosive presence sent shock waves through the room, but when Pippa started to shake uncontrollably and then collapsed onto the floor, the snake faded away ... as if she had never been there.

Pippa stared into space for a while, her heart pounding and her throat dry. "It's this heat ... " She tried to get up but her legs felt like jelly.

Insist on yourself! This is no heat ...

She drew in a few deep breaths and managed to get onto her knees, panting.

So this is fear ...

She clenched her teeth and, slowly, crawled back towards the bed. She stopped at a safe distance, from where she tried to peep underneath the bed. She sighed with relief. The chest was still there, but no trace of the snake.

That's when she saw the mongoose, just outside the door, sniffing the ground as she followed the track.

"Go away!" Pippa shouted and stumbled back to her feet to chase her away. The small predator disappeared immediately, but Pippa knew that if she had picked up the enemy's scent she wouldn't go far. Either the snake left her room really fast to avoid a lethal confrontation with the mongoose, or she would have to shut the door to protect her. And this without even thinking of MadMax and Piu Piu. The fact that neither of them had turned up yet was rather alarming. A killing frenzy in her room was just what she needed!

That the mongoose might have come to her rescue never crossed her mind.

Where was the snake now anyway? Most probably she'd disappeared through a narrow space between the sliding doors of her cupboard. Her heart sank, for in there were tons of partitions filled with books, files, boxes and glasses with seeds – meaning a million places to hide. While this was anything but ideal, at least Pippa knew where she was. This was her chance to get MadMax out of the way.

She found him sleeping on the kitchen bench, arguably the coolest place in the house. From here he could overlook the dam, or rather what remained of it under the scorching sun. She heard a faint quack and saw Piu Piu perched on the garage. She had spotted her immediately, but seemed too lethargic to move.

"Are you snoozing away?" Pippa whispered, sweet as candy. "You just relax."

What did she say? *Relax?*

His eyes opened wide and he saw her sneaking away. All his alarm bells went off; something had to be wrong! He jumped down and followed her swiftly, but too late; she closed the door in his face. And she locked it.

Things had definitely changed.

"Don't worry," she chanted, moving away fast. "I'll be back soon." She knew well enough that he saw through her; his growls made it clear. But she had to be cruel to be kind. In a situation like this his hunting spirit would carry him away – and, probably, the cobra, too. Plus a mongoose – have mercy, no!

Once back in her room, she slumped on her chair, trying to collect her thoughts. Everything was quiet. Just the soporific sound of cicadas, but even they suddenly went still.

What if it was all a movie in her mind?

Was she creating a problem where there was none? Disharmony where there was nature's balance? It was impossible that they did not know one another, so maybe she was wrong? Should she do as everyone else did on an extremely hot day: relax?

With a cobra in her room?

And so her mind remained in overdrive. She wondered who she could call as her parents were out of reach. She knew what she'd be told: "Get out of the room and leave the serpent alone. Dad will deal with it once he's back!"

Her head felt heavy. She had to do something. Or perhaps not? Where was that 'core of her being'? Her inner guidance? Deep down she knew she had nothing to fear. Perhaps the cobra just wanted to give birth in a cool, safe place?

"The most natural thing to do is to help her create new life," whispered her heart.

"And put everyone in danger? Snakes will be lurking everywhere," reasoned her mind.

In what direction should she lean?

Right now there was nothing to panic about. In the worst case scenario the local vet was fifteen minutes away. The symptoms usually started about twenty minutes after the strike.

"We always have antivenom here. It covers the most common snake bites in the area, excluding boomslang," she had heard the vet tell Mom. "So far we never had a case with a boomslang."

Pippa had encountered the very reclusive boomslang (tree snake) in the flowering gum tree, just outside her room. The slick green reptile almost flew up through the branches. It disappeared within no time from her view; Pippa could still recall its large dark eyes. She remembered reading about it in *Harry Potter and the Chamber of Secrets,* where pieces of its shredded skin were used to make the Polyjuice Potion. It allowed the drinker to assume the form of another person. This sparked her interest initially, but since it would not turn her into a bird like Piu Piu, free to fly wherever she wanted, she did not pursue the matter further.

The strange feeling of being watched made her look up and peep through a slit in the blinds.

There she was, in the blazing light of the sun, pushing herself up from the ground and peering through the window: the mongoose! This time, Pippa just looked at her unfazed: "We're even, wicked!"

As the little devil moved her snout even closer, Pippa yelled "Booooo!" The mongoose fell over backwards and tumbled down the terrace. "I won't let you have her!" Pippa shouted and got up, wondering where the snake was. Carefully, she opened one cupboard door after the other, sliding them open just a tiny wee bit, enough for her to peep in and close quickly if necessary. Actually, her intuition told her where the animal was and that's exactly where she discovered her; the cobra had found a cool place near the water pipe under the basin. Pippa saw her in a split second in that place, quickly closing the sliding door before she could possibly attack or escape – a few seconds later, when she checked again, she was gone!

Once again, she had disappeared into thin air!

But she had to be somewhere! Then Pippa opened the empty cupboard. A large open space yawned at her, waiting for Dad to build in some shelves. As there was nothing but a soft cushion lying on the floor, she almost closed the door but – obeying a sudden impulse – lifted the cushion slightly with a stick. Lo and behold: there she was, curled up underneath it! She was perfectly at peace, looking at Pippa in quiet awareness.

Pippa let the cushion gently fall back to cover her and closed the cupboard door. She knew the snake wouldn't move from there anytime soon.

They planned to have dinner outside on the terrace. At that time of the year, the fireball of the sun melted into the sea right in front of them, beyond the silhouettes of yukkas, palms and flowering gums. The sky was feathered in reds and the mountains had started to glow, appearing closer, almost touchable. The sun's fading light shimmered through the graceful tufts of papyrus, igniting strelitzias like flames in its path and showing itself in millions of droplets that sprinklers spewed up into the air. Amongst it all, a young girl and a goose danced with abandon, releasing the day.

After the heat, nature eagerly absorbed the bursts of coolness rising from the valley. Embracing the night, clamoring voices of hadedas reverberated through the amphitheater where the shadows grew longer. As if on cue, competing groups of 'wheel barrows' screeched their noisy nocturne.

On the terrace, the fragrances from the garden mixed with the enticing aroma of a roasted lamb seasoned with fresh rosemary and garlic. "The lamb's just right . . . so tender . . . as is the asparagus. And the salad's divine," Dad said, chewing with relish and enjoying lots of wine. "From our garden?" he asked as he helped himself to another serving.

"Yes!" Mom smiled, not without pride, covertly hiding the bottle of wine. "The grilled beetroot is from our neighbors because the porcupines finished mine. They wanted sunflower seeds in return. Rosemary, garlic, honey, lemons . . . all our own. The asparagus and feta are from the valley . . . I believe you got the meat from the Karoo?"

Dad searched for and found the wine, pouring himself some more. "Cheers, my angel," he breathed with a goofy grin, thrusting his arms in the air like he were flying over a cuckoo's nest, bottle in hand: "It's Christmas! Let's celebrate and be merry!"

Stuffing more salad into his mouth, he closed his eyes with rapt admiration. "That mix of fresh herbs and seeds, the tangy taste of nasturtium . . . hmmm . . . divine. And next year, guess what we'll have? It will be . . . a roasted goose!"

"Pete!" Mom screamed with disgust.

Tickled pink, he rattled his knife and fork.

"And these are our own eggs!" Pippa added fiercely, brushing away her wet hair and a wave of anger. "I collected them today," she said, her eyes shooting daggers at Dad.

"And our own eggs," Mom repeated, tonelessly. "I suspect the mongoose stole a few – as usual."

"And our own eggs," he laughed out loud, highly amused. "As long as the little devil leaves the chicks alone." With his 'girls' trying so hard to keep cool, he could not resist bullying them a little more: "Who cares about chickens anyway? All I want is –" and he pointed his knife at Piu Piu, who shrieked and escaped into the garden.

Pippa's heart missed a beat and she glared at her father, who watched her with delight in between sardonic bursts of laughter, but then her Mom's daring reaction completely blew her out of the water.

"Stop this now!" Mom commanded and held his gaze, contemptuous of his surprised glare.

"Pete . . . this is Christmas! You've had too much wine –"

"So! Are you giving the orders?" he sneered.

"– that's no good in this heat!" Mom's heart was racing. She was on dangerous ground and tensions were high. She had to navigate slyly. Interrupting him was already a sin; backtalk brought on an adrenaline rush that could make him unpredictable.

She quickly changed the topic: "How do you like my cranberry jelly? I did it differently; do you like it, Pippa?"

Pippa nodded, tongue-tied, feeling a knot in her stomach.

Mom arched her brows and sighed, turning back to Dad. "You did a great job today," she continued in a more agreeable tone. "I'm sure that beast can no longer get into the chicken house. Not the way you fixed it."

Seeing him relax and return to his plate, she added mischievously: "It makes sense to have a man about the house."

Dad listened with a subdued grin and worked his roast. "You're right," he said and Pippa was delighted to see Piu Piu coming cautiously back. "You always are," he continued in between bites of lamb. "It's all your fault, anyway."

"Excuse me?"

"All your fault," he nodded. "You do it on purpose." He licked his fingers, one after the other, with laughter lines sneaking back around his eyes. "It's common knowledge that a delicious . . . a scrumptious . . . meal turns any man into something completely . . . corruptible. A beast. Don't forget, it all started with an apple!"

As mother and daughter seemed to calm down, he added: "Even worse, you teach your brood!"

"*My* brood?" Mom retorted. "If I remember correctly, you were sort of . . ."

"Sort of . . . " Dad was turning the bottle upside-down to ensure there was not a drop left. "That's . . . if I remember correctly."

"Uhmm." Mom observed his shifty eyes. "You don't?"

"Uhmm," Dad muttered, chewing with gusto and feeling his way back into the driver's seat. "I guess there was a certain *je ne sais quoi* in the air!"

Without waiting for Mom's reaction he turned to Pippa. "Listen, I prepared a solid board. About 80 cm high. You insert it in the door, from the bottom up. It'll keep snakes out – as well as your boyfriends."

"The brood thanks you obediently, sir," Pippa retorted, too smart to take the bait. Mom smiled.

Piu Piu wiggled her tail and gave a quacking comment. Perching on the warm tiles of the terrace, she watched attentively and seemed to follow the conversation. But she always kept her distance when Dad was around.

"It's that greedy glint in his eyes when he looks at her," Pippa thought to herself. "Get fat, my girl, I want some meat on the bones!" Could he really be that mean? Perhaps he's only joking?

MadMax was lazing next to her and ignoring the subliminal bullying game. He was much more interested in the voices out there in the obscurity of the garden.

"That one can easily get over it," Dad said, indicating the cat, "but I don't want a repetition of what happened today. You don't fool around with a damn cobra."

Pippa remained silent, nodding obediently, while trying to spear a slippery asparagus with her fork.

When Mom and Dad started to discuss some boring business matters, Pippa's thoughts drifted back to the snake.

With some determined action from Dad the reptile had eventually moved in the right direction and, finally, left her room. But instead of slithering into the lush shady garden, the cobra had shot onto a building site full of stones and rubble – rather rough for slick snake bellies.

Pippa had watched with bated breath as she flew along in full size, her smooth brown scales glistening in the late afternoon sun. Propelling herself forward in horizontal S-curves along the walls, she was overcoming each obstacle with spectacular elegance and ease, sometimes rearing up vertically with one third of her length off the ground, her head standing motionless in the air. Mom was capturing some of these moments with her camera, when she suddenly lost her.

Once again, she had disappeared!

Much later, Dad discovered that she had slipped into a cavity in the wall on the shadow side of the house. Pippa had looked at her mother, knowing what was going through her mind.

Behind everything there is a vibration.

Once everybody had finished eating, Mom got up and collected the plates. Pippa jumped up to help. That's when she took a peek at Mom's golden armlet and saw that it had the form of a snake.

"Amazing," Mom sighed, glancing up at the vast vault, "it's already dark! Time to step into the Unknown ..."

Kommetjie lighthouse was flashing rhythmically in the far distance and strings of lights were glittering beyond the wetlands, where the low mountain chain ran southwards.

"The unusual for you?" Grace smiled at her man and gave him a kiss, lips sweet as damask roses.

His eyes narrowed, signaling 'you bitch', while he said with a smoky timbre: "Pure, lemon, and ice."

"On the way! Come Pippa! Go, quickly change!"

Mother and daughter disappeared in the house.

"I'd better turn the sprinklers off." Dad got up and staggered into the darkness, soliloquizing: "Damn . . . damn darkness, damn, she was right . . ."

As soon as everyone had left, Piu Piu rose to her feet and gobbled up a few greens that Pippa had slipped under the table. MadMax watched her closely. Normally, she'd never miss a chance to hiss a spiteful 'Not for you!' at him. Not today. Was it because of Dad? Clearly, Miss Pancakes was not her usual self.

"I liked that," Pippa mentioned in the kitchen while giving Mom a hand.

"What do you mean, sweetheart?"

"You were not so . . . " Pippa bit her lip.

"So . . .? Speak out!"

"Well . . . so submissive. You always smile."

A little taken aback, Mom glanced at her child. Then she bent down and looked into Pippa's eyes, whispering: "It's only an impression; I never am!"

Pippa held her gaze with big eyes.

Mom laughed: "Little secrets, just between you and me. Finding love is one thing; keeping it fresh and alive is more trouble than meets the eye."

As she prepared Dad's drink, she observed Pippa staring at the bracelet on her arm. "You like it?"

Pippa nodded.

"It's very special," Mom said.

"It's from her," Pippa whispered.

"How did you know?"

As Pippa remained silent, she added: "It will be yours one day. You have her eyes." Then she winked: "Get changed, get the milk, let's go!"

Mom came back carrying a tray with Dad's drink and a bowl filled with fresh strawberries. Pippa, now in shorts and a T-shirt, put down a saucer with milk for MadMax.

He licked up every drop, piously, then jumped onto her lap and kneaded himself into a trancelike state of bliss.

No one even noticed when Piu Piu, quietly, sneaked away.

"Where the heck is that stupid torch?" Dad snorted as he came back. "Haven't seen the bloody thing in ages. Damn, it's so dark . . ."

"You're right, I've been looking for it as well. It must be somewhere . . . Pete, can you get another deck chair from the other side, please. With cushions . . ."

Mom turned to her daughter, keeping her voice down. "Do you have any idea, sweetheart?"

Snuggled into a green deckchair and stuffing strawberries into her mouth, Pippa was gazing into the night sky.

"Pippa! Did you see the big torch?"

"Uhmmmm," Pippa mumbled, absent-mindedly, "Could still be in the shed. I guess."

"The shed?" Mom sounded incredulous.

"There!" Pippa exclaimed, pointing towards a constellation of five bright stars just above the dark silhouette of Chapman's Peak. "I can see it. Look! I can see the two pointer stars as well."

"The Southern Cross!" Dad arrived with a deckchair. "Well spotted, my girl!"

Mom gave him his glass of water with lemon, ice and a smile.

He shook it like a glass of Scotch and kissed her tenderly. "Cheers to the most beautiful stars – those in your eyes!"

Pippa watched her parents quietly. Since she had shared her secret with Mom, Pippa had gained a new perspective on how Mom and Dad had met and instantly fallen in love. It had happened when he rescued her in an avalanche in the Himalayas. "It's true," she thought, "she has incredible eyes. Almond-shaped and sparkling . . . just like Great-grandad's. Just like –"

"My blue flower," Dad whispered, only for Mom to hear, but Pippa picked it up.

The elusive blue flower.

Now she knew that the three magic seeds had come from a pristine valley hidden away in the Himalayas. Mom, too, had been intrigued by the missing pages in an otherwise perfect book. Pippa was eager to resolve this mystery, but whenever she made an attempt to get an answer 'in that other world', she promptly woke up. Each time. It was so frustrating that – just by thinking of it – she suddenly teared up.

Oh Great-grandad, I have so much to learn.

"This isn't the kind of knowledge you learn in books, my dear young lady," she heard his voice again, and it seemed to her that a slight tremor was running across Chapman's Peak. "It's a much deeper knowing you tune into over time."

She held her breath and waited, but that was all he said. Raising her watery eyes towards that vast, velvet, vault of infinite possibilities, she wondered how long 'over time' could be?

Little did she know how her world would be shaken – and her perceptions changed – much sooner than she thought.

CHAPTER NINE

The Voice of the Infinite

Piu Piu stood like a statue, looking upwards with one eye. It was not the first time she had observed the airplane with the unique sensitivity of a goose and a certain sense of curiosity and surprise. It flew, like a silver bird, in a straight line across the cloudless sky, far beyond Chapman's Peak above the sea. At some point, it ejected thick white smoke that followed it, like a mushrooming wisp of a trail, over a vast distance. It stopped abruptly, but the aircraft continued and disappeared. The broad horizontal puff of a cloud remained right there, in the air.

Intrigued, Piu Piu waited for something to happen. Out there. Her neck quivered lightly. She was not too sure what she was expecting to see – but why not a billowing mirage? A flock of migrating geese carved in smoke by an invisible hand? She saw them vividly before her eyes, strong and magnificent, heading north towards those greenest of pastures, the magical swamps from her dreams. She felt elated and, spontaneously, spread her wings and lifted into the air to follow them – but after a few ridiculous strokes she dropped back onto the lawn, plump and lame. Embarrassed and hurt, she ran to the dam to hide her rage, to be alone and fall apart amongst the reeds. "Not for you," she wailed in a turmoil of emotions that shook her to the core.

Without Pippa's love, she would never be able to fly again.

She gave off a distressed hiss. Hardly a day passed without some form of cruel reminder that she was, and would always be, handicapped. But deep down inside her she knew there was more. Since that fateful night everything had changed. Something was eclipsing the sun. Words could not express how much she yearned to soar high up into the sky, to fly wherever the wind and her sense of destination carried her . . . just to find it . . . to bring it back again.

Slowly, the mysterious formation drifted towards the coast on the early onshore wind.

Less than an hour later, puffy wisps of cloud criss-crossed the morning sky. As the sun rose behind the mountains, they spread into a diffuse and layered cover, scattering the light. It stretched as far as Piu Piu could see.

Peering upwards, she turned her head to the left and then to the right, while perching at the helm of Mom's yoga mat on the lawn. The golden glow on Chapman's Peak seemed paler than usual. Even the shadows were imbued with a dizzy hue.

Was this real or her imagination?

Did Mr Know-it-all notice it, too?

MadMax had snuggled up in Pippa's lap. Grateful that she accepted him again, he avoided any movement that could disturb her during her meditation and risk his being sent away. He could not imagine anything closer to this bliss. With his tail tip over his face, he was happily purring away.

Sensing her beak go green with envy, she glanced at Pippa.

The young girl sat upright with her legs crossed in the lotus position, her hands resting lightly on her knees. Her eyes were closed. Now and then her eyelids fluttered, revealing the fleeting presence of a memory or a reminder of mundane tasks drifting into her mind. She breathed deeper, mentally repeating the mantra of the day, observing her thoughts and letting them go. The deep vibrating sound emanating from the tomcat calmed and reassured her on her path to connecting deeper with Source. She was acutely aware of Mom's powerful presence at her side, like a river of light flowing towards the sea.

A picture of that happy world beyond her reach.

Piu Piu could no longer bear it. She got back on her feet and stretched her neck forward, quivering madly. Beating her head up and down, she was barely able to resist disrupting the tranquil morning routine. Her tail feathers twitched as she looked at the boiling sky, with a terrible sense of foreboding.

Could no one else feel it, out there?

Or was it within her? Was it . . . her shame? Her guilt?

She saw it coming down, almost imperceptibly: a fine shower of acid particles. First it reached the tree tops, sending tremors through their crowns, their trunks and branches, which instantly contracted under the toxic assault. Unstoppable, the invisible substance filtered through the bushes, the plants, the flowers and grasses. Unseen, it penetrated the soil.

Honey bees, which had swarmed out early to look for nectar and pollen, returned to their hives in a hurry, performing a 'danger dance'. The same alarming signal came from everywhere: "Close off hive! Don't go out! Wait till the sun is back!"

Two little frogs tried to escape, squeezing their tiny bodies deep into a lily. They hugged each other and closed their eyes, listening to toads' warning calls from all directions, their voices reaching an almost hysterical pitch.

A black spider urgently left her web and took refuge underneath leaves. She gasped when the elaborate structure she had patiently spun became twisted and warped and was eventually torn apart as shock waves ran through the earth. Roots trembled and contracted as the toxic substance hit them.

Terrified and disoriented, mice and moles scurried through tunnels and burrows. Earthworms and scorpions dug deeper, their frantic pace fuelled by a raw instinct to survive. Seeds ached with pain and burst. All growing and germination stopped. Finally, the poison oozed into the groundwater. It hissed, steamed and exploded.

Then there was silence.

Stupefied with horror, shaking, Piu Piu stood and stared until an endlessly sorrowful realization poured out from her heart: "What have I done?"

Dad stood on the terrace with a mug of steaming coffee in his hand. Pulling on his cigarette, he stared at the false weather bank pushing rapidly up the mountain. He blew out tense puffs of smoke. He hated to see it glaring so blatantly in his face. He knew. He had been out there himself. Following orders blindly, did that make him guilty, too?

Was there any escape?

Torn, he turned away. His face softened at the sight of his 'two graces' doing their morning meditation. He was very protective of them but, somewhere deep down, he harbored a resentment – even a jealous streak – at their ease of slipping away from it all, untouchable.

"In God's hand . . ."

This image hit him suddenly, it was exceptional for him and rather surprising. He gnawed fiercely at his cigarette butt, drawing the final drag of nicotine deep into his lungs . . . anything, not to be overwhelmed by that 'woo-woo-stuff'.

He coughed profusely while putting the stub out. Nonetheless, he could not shake off a feeling of being left behind.

"Blowing more smoke in the air won't get you there." As usual, Mom had hit the nail on the head.

"My angel, my demon," he grunted, promptly striking a match and lighting one more.

"But, Mom," he remembered Pippa saying, "they don't spray this stuff down here?"

"It doesn't matter where," Mom had replied to save his face, but not without shooting an accusing look in his direction – at least, that's how he perceived it. "We all share the same air, the same atmosphere, the same water. Whatever happens in one part of the world will eventually affect all of us. Even here."

"Like if one person suffers, we all do?"

"Exactly," Mom nodded. "We and the world are one. Just think of yourself and Piu Piu."

"That's not the same, Mom. She's a bird."

"So?" Mom was surprised; Pippa had never seen any difference before. "There's nothing more sensitive than a goose! She's even sensitive to fire! Much more than we are. Animals quickly pick up on vibrations and see to it that they remain in harmony with nature. They don't fake. And don't forget plants. If they suffer – in one way or another, we'll get to feel it, too."

He sighed. It wasn't all that easy – but he loved her magic. There had been magic between them from the moment he'd first looked into her eyes, willing her life stream to trickle back along a fine invisible cord.

They had dug her out from under the snow, literally on the roof of the world. "Her eye is hazy, Pete. She's gone," he heard the Sherpa say. But all he saw and continued to see, with everything else blanked out in his mind – was that incredible blue reflecting the sky – and he saw when it began to sparkle again. "You . . ." she whispered, just that. As her eyes closed, she smiled: "I thought I'd never find you."

It all seemed like it happened just yesterday . . .

The sky was now covered by cloud. He shivered. The dark front that had been looming at the horizon had disappeared behind a breaker of billowing mist rolling in from the sea. It had already swallowed the valley and closed in on the mountain slopes. He loved to see the world disappear below him; that feeling of supremacy, of floating above it all.

Today, however, the fog did not stop where it usually did; it pulled a hood right over his world.

"There's something disturbing out there," Mom noted later, when she prepared the breakfast smoothies: purified water, some pieces of fresh fruit – banana, pineapple and papaya – plus two scoops of her 'magic mix'. And, of course, seeds.

Pippa nodded: "It gives me the creeps." She hated the noise the blender made, but it only took a minute and the result was delicious. "Piu Piu is nervous, too."

"Hmm, is she? I guess winter is on its way. One can feel the change."

Dressed in her dark-blue winter school uniform, with her hair tamed into a neat ponytail, Pippa sat at the kitchen table. As she looked through the fogged window her heart sank. She desperately needed good lighting conditions today, but the mist was so thick and dark she could hardly see the dam. Now and then Piu Piu emerged from it, looking inquisitively towards the kitchen window before gliding back into the cottonwool jungle again.

"Dad will drop you off at school and fetch you later," Mom said, handing Pippa her breakfast shake. "Do you have everything in your bag that you need for the day?"

Pippa nodded. The more she looked at the daunting darkness outside, the more depressed she became.

"The geese are gone."

"Well, that's normal, isn't it? At this time of the year. . ."

"I hate winter!"

"Great! You just attracted more of it."

"I'm looking forward to spring!"

"Really, sweetheart, watch what you think! Each season plays its role in the rhythm of life – isn't that in his book?"

A smile flashed across Pippa's face and her back straightened. *How could she forget?* "Remember, Mom?" she said, sipping her smoothie. "I will need your cam."

"Is it today?"

Pippa nodded. "I only have the afternoon."

"Oh dear. OK, I will load the batteries and leave it on your desk." Looking out the window, Mom had her doubts, too. She knew how her child felt. The photo competition was important for Pippa, and it was restricted to taking the photos on one particular day. That day was today. "The fog will lift," she said with confidence. "Miracles do happen if you ask and –?"

"– and have faith!" Pippa added, feeling a little something move in her veins.

"Do you?" Mom asked, embracing her from behind.

Pippa nodded, leaning into her warmth,

"Really? Do you see it clearly in your mind?"

Pippa nodded and closed her eyes, putting her small hands into Mom's, who folded them into hers.

"Do you really . . . really feel it inside?" Mom whispered. "The warmth of the sun as it glides over your face . . . the scent of flowers releasing their fragrance . . . the tangy taste of dew? Do you hear the insects buzzing around your head . . . feel the weight of the camera in your hand . . . and then the quick 'click', 'click', 'click'? Imagine those gorgeous pictures. They're already out there, waiting for you. They're waiting for you today."

"Click! Click! Click!" Pippa chanted, energized and smiling. She jumped up and gave her mother a kiss.

"I love you, Mom. I really really love you."

"Click! Click! Click!" she chanted as she skipped away with her ponytail swinging. Then she was gone.

Enveloped in her own sadness, Piu Piu was intrigued by the grey emptiness around her; it had stolen her familiar sights and muted all sound. She snapped a few times at the bubbles wafting around her feet, and shook the late autumn chill from her feathers. While the rains had filled the dam to the rim, the cryptic absence of distractions was confusing. Now, even her own reflection was elusive – had she become a ghost?

Silently, she glided into the water and swam a few strokes, assuring herself that she, indeed, still existed. She quacked with relief when the vertical lines of reeds and papyrus gracefully emerged, like an archaic guard at her side. As she paddled in circles, she glanced at seeds and rust-colored leaves floating along the ripples she drew behind her. Bit by bit, she extended her trusted space, too watchful to be afraid.

Suddenly, she gave off a startled quack. Over time, she had become so used to his discreet presence that she completely forgot him: the blue heron. He stood unmoving while the fleecy mist drifted past, a statue of quiet awareness. Embarrassed, she apologized and changed direction, without being convinced the large wading bird had even noticed her.

But as she swam towards the dim light that filtered, like flowing beads, from the kitchen window, it seemed she heard his voice, trembling slightly as he drew in a breath: "My outer world reflects my inner world . . ."

Conscience-stricken, she quickly left the water and waddled up the embankment towards the house. When she looked back, she gasped: the dam had disappeared. It was eerie! This grey and hostile world without shape and shadows was getting to her and, as she stood in front of the kitchen with only a vague light shimmering through the window, but no one looking out for her or calling her name, an intense loneliness came over her. There were no tasty bread crumbs waiting for her on the ground as there used to be – before her crime. No crunchy salad leaves either; not even a slick and slimy snail sneaking up the sweating wall. Nothing! And as things looked, nothing exciting would be happening in the near future either – because nobody was around.

"Piu Piu alone at home!" she wailed, turning in circles. As the curtain of murky mist did not open and produce the beloved being she most needed right now, she reconciled herself to her fate and stalked all around the house, her wings folded backwards and her head down, occasionally uttering a squawk of discontent.

Suddenly, she stopped in her tracks. Had she not wished for an occasion like this, where no one would prevent her from doing what she needed to do?

The one big task that remained?

How could she forget? Today could well be the only chance she'd ever get.

"Com'on, Piu Piu!"

With her heart hammering in her throat and her legs shaking, she hopped up the steps onto the main terrace . . . and up a few more towards her surveillance spot in front of the terrace door, where she usually stood guard. This was where her world ended, beyond was the forbidden realm.

But today, something extraordinary happened in the life of Piu Piu. Noticing that the door was not fully closed, she ignored Dad's taboo. With a defiant quack and her head held high, she walked straight into the atrium; that happy space which had been her 'home' almost three years ago.

"Piupidoo!"

Finally, she was inside! Oh, this wide and open space without a trace of fog! Taking a deep breath, she shook off the suffocating clasp that had strangled her whole being. Here, there was light! Filtering through canopies of exotic plants, it glided past African sculptures and candles, ancient furniture with silk cushions, and a peacock chair. She saw it flowing across the coffee table and the bouquet, illuminating amethysts, rose quartz, fossils, books and magazines, until it lost itself on the floor.

A pleasant warmth rose through her feet and up her legs as she slipped along the smooth ceramic tiles. She had to be mindful of her steps to keep her balance. This floor was tricky for goose soles as she could easily do the splits and end up on her bum, as had happened in the past. While it had made everybody laugh, she had felt embarrassed at the time, and then Dad banned her from the house. Nothing could change his mind: Miss Pancakes had to stay outside.

Boooo! Now she was back within!

"Not for you!" she quacked boisterously. "Not for you!"

"For you!" Her voice echoed through the atrium. "For you!"

Surprised, Piu Piu looked up and around, intrigued by the resounding response, wondering whether she heard what she heard? What a contrast to the muting mist outside that had swallowed even her breath! She repeated it a few more times, starting off timidly but soon getting the best from her voice. She listened with disbelief and awe as the sound cascades reverberated everywhere – even off Mom's precious crystal glasses on a shelf. Oh, how she liked the invisible chorus . . . the sense of support! Inspired, she raised her voice, adding her name a few times. When she stopped to catch her breath, a sound wave set everything moving and dancing, sweeping the goose off the floor. This was fun! Her spirits lifted and then she heard it clearly from everywhere: "For Piu Piu! For Piu Piu!"

Relieved, she promptly released a colossal goose puddle. Shocked by her outrageous negligence, she skidded a few meters, promptly landing on her feathered bum. As she came to a halt, sitting in her own juices and wanting to laugh, she began to choke. Suddenly, it all resurged in her mind: that old, buried, perhaps forgiven yet never forgotten, devastating moment when Dad had separated her from Pippa – and her home.

"Enough! I will no longer tolerate this stench," he had yelled.

"But Dad," Pippa had pleaded, "she's just –"

"She's just a goose! You're right!"

He shouted so loudly the glasses clinked: "Geese stay outside!" Then there was silence. She could still hear it today.

"Just a goose? Excuse me!" Piu Piu jumped up and flapped her wings, her nostrils dilating with indignation. The painful memory brought tears to her eyes; she stood up tall and honked:

I'm not just a goose! I'm the wind and the rain!
I'm the sunshine!
I'm a petal in the sky and a kiss on your ear –
I'm Piu Piu of Noordhoek; I'll always be here!

"Piu Piu!" It echoed back from everywhere, sounding like 'good' and 'free' and 'fun'.

"Thank you!" she answered, and, once she had calmed down: "I'll watch my rear end now." Ooops! Too late . . . another one. But – to her surprise – everyone laughed.

"Excuse me! I can't help being a goose. Now and then shit happens!" She laughed and moved on. Besides, she thought, it wasn't really a problem. Once dry, it would hardly be noticeable and not nearly as toxic as what they carried in each day under their shoes.

What was much more important now was her purpose. She had entered the forbidden space with a clear goal in mind; she'd better get to it before anyone came home and caught her *in flagrante delicto.*

Fired up and excited, she steered straight into Pippa's room. *Oh, to be back again . . .*

Waddling past the coffee table, her head held high and memories connecting with her from all sides, she remembered her first flying efforts almost three years ago. How badly she had wanted to get out then; to fly and to be free! Now that the world outside had become hostile, she was glad to return.

She stopped in her tracks: he was watching her through half-closed eyes from his favorite spot on the sofa – how could she forget the cat? She stared at him for a moment, not sure how to react. But then his eyes closed and she smiled to herself and moved on: "Maybe, I'm not here? Maybe, I never left!"

Nothing much had changed. Just that the number of jars filled with seeds had grown, all neatly placed on white papers with scribbled descriptions and, sometimes, a drawing. And there were more plates and baskets with drying flower heads of poppies, proteas and dill.

Which reminded Piu Piu of her task.

Almost magically, she was drawn to Pippa's desk. The chair was still the same, just a bit more worn, but exuding the same energy, the same fragrance. She could not resist the pull of the past and squeezed herself underneath the desk. All of a sudden, her vision blurred and all she knew was that the world around her was rising and expanding while she became smaller and smaller, and smallest, until she was a little gosling again, settling on Pippa's right foot. She immediately gave off a happy chirp.

Life was bliss!

But her happiness did not last. One day, Dad put a wall around her – "to protect her" he claimed. All she knew was that it reduced her freedom of movement and separated her from the world. And, of course, from Pippa. It happened very subtly; until that day when she realized Pippa herself had slipped away.

She knew why; it was that ominous object under her bed, her 'secret'. From that first moment Pippa had opened the book, she was no longer the same. It became her passion, obsession, her entire focus – there was no more time for Piu Piu. And, as if that wasn't painful enough, she shared it all with the tomcat – never with her. This had been too much for Piu Piu to bear. The fire of possessiveness already consumed her and, as it was cruelly fuelled each night, she only had one burning desire, one hope, one goal: to get Pippa back!

She felt the same rage today, but now there was also her shame. The problem was that she had hidden the stolen treasure so well that she no longer remembered where. To return it to Pippa, she had to retrieve it; that's why she was here. Her heart sank when she realized there was only one way to locate the hiding spot and come clean. And so she gathered all her courage to face up to that dark and hideous night once again.

It had been well after midnight when Piu Piu was woken up by the grinding noise of Pippa pulling the treasure chest from underneath her bed. As had happened so many times before, Piu Piu watched the shadows flicker across the wall and ceiling when Pippa opened the lid and heaved out the book. She placed it on the floor next to the candle and bent over it, brushing her curls from her face. Piu Piu's curiosity made her wide awake and completely still. Listening closely, she was picking up everything that passed between Pippa and the tomcat, whom she envied shamelessly for his privileges. As usual, he sat exactly in her line of vision, blocking the view with his back. If only the tidal wave welling up within her could flush this pompous gigolo away! Being so completely ignored made her feel she did not even exist.

And if that wasn't enough, now Pippa even put her arm around him, their shadows merging into one: "Oh, my Pasharotti, what would I do without you?"

If Pippa had known how the repeated hurt had made Piu Piu boil over with indignation, she could have saved herself a lot of pain. How could it so completely elude her? Whenever she opened Great-grandfather's book she was sucked into a magic bubble where there was no place for Piu Piu.

On the day patience and hope were overturned by rage, Piu Piu became fiercely determined to destroy whatever was stealing the beloved being from her, to get it out of the way. She would have Pippa back – no matter how! Her intention was clear. She had faith that the right opportunity would present itself; she had a hunch it would be tonight.

"Now there's only a single seed left," she heard Pippa wail, "since the rest did not take. What do I do? Plant it and pray – and lose it, too?"

"Maybe it's just in your mind?"

MadMax crouched as Pippa snapped indignantly: "Are you blind?" The candlelight reflected madly in her eyes, when she added: "It's a magic seed!"

"How do you know?"

"It can take us anywhere, achieve anything – if only I could get it to grow!"

That's when Piu Piu's alarm bells rang. She blew up her neck and hissed: "Go!"

"But I'm happy here," MadMax said blankly and, to avoid her irritated response, he quickly raised his voice: "Is there nothing else in the book?"

"Shhh!" Startled, Pippa looked up, "I think I heard something?" There was a moment of silence. Then she shook her head. "The pages are blank."

While she continued to leaf through the book, a big moth peeled from the darkness. Piu Piu's eyes followed it as it took off towards the light. "Perfect, roller," she directed it with her mind, "go for that stupid cat!"

"It shows under contents," Pippa indicated, "here, see? *The Blue Flower*. Page 547. But there's nothing. There's 546 . . . then blank . . . blank . . . until 551. I checked it all. Or someone –"

MadMax growled in a low voice that hardly concealed his excitement. He was distracted by a big moth – or rather its magnified shadow – that danced across the ceiling and the wall.

"They're just blank," Pippa said. "I don't know. Maybe I can't see?"

Piu Piu watched the moth's flight, too. Strung to breaking point, she stood upright and amazingly still – only her tail feathers twitched uncontrollably.

"Anything's possible," Pippa sighed. "He mentions it even in the introduction: my greatest discovery, he wrote." She broke off, shaking her head. From the corner of her eye, she noticed the big moth but did not pay any attention to it. "There's something I'm not getting. And, whenever I make an attempt to ask him, the magic stops. Then I'm back here."

Meanwhile, the moth was turning sedately around the candlelight. MadMax crouched with excitement, his tail twitching madly as the shadow came into his reach on the sliding door. His head was following its movements, up and down, up and down. The sublime moment of ultimate ecstasy . . . of flinging himself forward to catch it . . . was coming closer.

"All I found in here," Pippa spoke almost to herself, "were three seeds, wrapped in this . . ." She unfolded the delicate vegetal paper with care, taking in its exotic aroma with her eyes closed. "It's not from here; it smells like . . . like . . . far away." Fascinated by the thought of its distant origins, she looked down at the tiny black seed. "This is the only one that's left."

It's the last one . . .

She moistened her finger with her tongue and picked up the remaining little seed with her fingertip. She moved closer to the candle to see it in the light.

"It's so tiny. It's like a poppy seed. A little speck of dust! It's my last –"

And then Pippa screamed so loud that Piu Piu jumped up in her kraal. It all happened at once: there was a big BANG! as MadMax crashed against the cupboard door. Pippa shrieked and looked up, making a brisk movement with her free hand to prevent the moth from nose-diving into the candle, thus extinguishing the flame.

"The matches!" she cried, keeping her finger upright while groping in the darkness with her other hand. "Where are my matches?"

Oh, my God, I must not lose it! It's my last chance ...

"Just do it," Piu Piu commanded coldly. "Take it from her – now!"

The large hawk moth hovered just above Pippa's finger. It adjusted the airflow to its wings by pivoting its abdomen steadily up and down, in finely tuned movements, which enabled it to remain airborne in one spot. Equipped with excellent night vision and a long, flexible proboscis, it targeted the tiny seed on Pippa's extended fingertip. It took only the blink of an eye – much faster than sucking nectar from a flower. Then the invisible thief vanished from the scene of the crime.

Piu Piu waited with her heart pounding. A silver shimmer filtered in through the window as the crescent moon appeared from behind clouds. Suddenly, she felt a draft from flapping wings. The hawk moth hovered close to her above the ground. She wanted to say something, but in that moment the candle was lit again. The moth instantly changed the angle of its wings and lifted back into the shadows, leaving the minuscule seed on the floor.

"What have you done?" Pippa sobbed in the background, "it's all your fault!"

Piu Piu looked at the black pip for a while, without paying attention to the hysteria in the background.

Was this it? A seed? Seeds were delicacies for goose palates and she was tempted to swallow it. But the fact that Pippa was so obsessed with it intrigued her; she heard her searching for it in the background. She had even kicked MadMax out of the room; something Piu Piu had never seen happen before.

"About time," she snapped gleefully, pretty content with herself. Nevertheless, it irritated her that Pippa was crying her heart out in her bed. After taking a few sips of water and looking at the seed one more time, she decided to do nothing she might possibly regret. So she picked it up with the tip of her beak and tucked it away in a hidden place under the desk.

"I have my own secret now," she thought. "I can do with it as I please."

But then Dad had banned her from the house and she never returned. *Until today . . .*

Today . . . Piu Piu regained her poise. She was more conscious than ever of the repercussions of her outrageous coup – and the implications for Pippa's future. She felt distraught when she realized Pippa had never got over her loss. Hardly a day passed without her looking for clues to solve the mystery of the Blue Flower. Now she spent most of her spare time investigating each and every plant which bore blue flowers, amassing a wealth of knowledge that stunned specialists in the field.

Instead of bringing them closer, she had lost her even more.

And so Piu Piu held on to her secret – even more so once she was banned from the house. The fact that Pippa got it all wrong and the cat took the blame gave her some satisfaction; for once, the Universe was on her side. But, when the weight of her guilt pulled her down and she felt her transition approach, Piu Piu realized it was time to come clean.

Once again, the Universe conspired to lead her here. Now that she knew where the seed was, she just had to get it. While this was easier said than done, she already felt a sense of relief. The mere idea of returning the seed was lifting a heavy weight from her shoulders.

Oh, to become whole again!

"Too much meat on the bones, my girl," she laughed at herself, squeezing her way underneath the desk to get to the hiding spot. When she thought she had it, it was something else, something sticky when she spat it out, and she was too absorbed to hear the car.

After some searching she finally found the seed and carried it carefully on the tip of her beak, backing out of the narrow cavity rather awkwardly because of her damaged wing.

That's when disaster struck.

Just as she turned around, Mom, rushing into the room, camera in hand, almost bumped into her. She jumped and shrieked and so did Piu Piu – and in that crucial moment the inevitable happened: she swallowed the seed.

Gone!

"Piu Piu!" Mom exclaimed, "what are you doing in here? You scared the heck out of me!"

Piu Piu looked perplexed. She could not utter a word. Had she come all this way to fail once again? Now she would have to live with a terrible guilt, and with only herself to blame.

"Come, Piu Piu, get out. Hurry up, Dad will be here any moment." Mom opened the door to the garden and Piu Piu walked out quietly, sadly, alone . . . back into the fog.

MadMax sat up on his cushion and watched as she waddled around the house, to the dam. Her eyes erupted with tears as she waded into the water and swam into the misty maze to hide her shame.

Here comes the sun!

Pippa heaved a sigh of relief as she gazed towards the magic mountain: "Oh, look! A colorless rainbow, all across the valley. If that ain't a sign!" She had waited for this moment all day. It was indeed a miracle – the asking did help.

The convoluted blanket of murky menacing clouds had suddenly ripped open, releasing a blinding ray of light that beamed across the valley. The tips of leucadendrons in its path turned into flaming spears emerging from a sea of fynbos. Gliding deeper and deeper, the radiant stream penetrated the shadows.

Almost spent at its end, it still transformed the flowering bush into a luminous bouquet. Clouds of delicate white flowers exuded a sweet scent, attracting butterflies and honey bees.

Light!

Pippa loved the Unknown. Contradictory as it seemed, it gave her a sense of direction. At that stage, she had no idea what her impromptu excursion to capture her contribution for 'Life in a Day' would lead to, but in her heart she wanted it to be a tribute to the bee.

Coincidentally, when she glanced at the calendar on her screen, it featured a honey bee for the month of July, accompanied by a quote by Saint John Chrysostom:

'The bee is more honored than other animals, not because she labors, but because she labors for others.'

'Sweet Mother Teresa on Wings' Mom had added, with a smiley. Little did she know what her daughter was up to on that cold and gloomy day.

"Click! Click! Click!" Pippa whistled to cheer herself up as she left the house. With her equipment safely around her neck and MadMax at her heels, Pippa hit the narrow winding trail that descended into an arcane palm and strelitzia forest. She chose her steps with care among the tall slender stems where spiders lurked in sticky webs and serpentine creepers reached out for her like ghastly moray eels.

She pulled the hood of her waterproof rain jacket down to her eyebrows, ignoring the chills running up and down her spine. High above her, fluid accumulated and tumbled, playing the broad leaves below like drums. Soon her steps adapted to their rhythm: drops falling down, down, down, accompanied by staccato clicks of frogs.

After a while the forest ejected them. It happened so suddenly that, before Pippa could even reorient herself, a mystic maze of bushes and branches had already sucked them in. Up to this point, Pippa had found her way with ease. Now, however, the shrouded surroundings had a strange allure. There was no identifiable path; just a labyrinth of choices, each leading who knew where, or stopping after just a few bends. Worst of all, the way back to where she thought she had started was not the same way she had come! *Was someone playing a trick on her?*

"Oh, I have no time for this. We have to move on!"

"Click! Click!" she picked herself up and pushed forward – only to bump into a thorny bush.

"Click!" she snapped the tree and turned, colliding with a protea. The more she got entangled and confused the more the ghostly patterns seemed to be breathing, changing and shifting in the billowing banks of mist. Even the ground had changed; now it was rough, sandy and disconcertingly unpredictable. Hidden stone slabs revealed themselves only just as she stumbled upon them. Weathered stumps and rotting branches, sharp-edged fissures, treacherous holes and burrows, all obstructed her path although by now she neither knew where she was going, nor why she was there. She cringed when rocks seemed to resemble prehistoric monsters looming through the past. Panting, she slumped on a toppled stub, trying to compose her mind.

Where are we?

MadMax sat down next to her, appearing cool and relaxed. He followed her, regardless. He did not seem overly concerned, but rather interested in the phenomenon of fading greys and swirling scents, where anything could reveal itself at any moment. His calm was reassuring. She got up and groped her way down the slope – surely, it led into the valley?

But when she turned around to see nothing but an impenetrable barrier, her throat went dry; all her familiar points of orientation were no longer there. As the wafting vacuum lapped against her and the ground slipped beneath her feet, it struck her: "We're trapped!"

Dad's strict warnings never to venture into the mist in the mountains sounded in her ears. Too late! It had looked so easy from her window; simply down through the forest and into the valley, following the beam of light slanting in from one side. The magical mistbow was so close and enticing.

Only there was not the slightest glimpse of it now.

"Crack, this is boring!" She squared her shoulders and forged forward. "Let's move on!"

Tiny for her age, she had a good sense of direction and thought she knew where they were.

Dad said, there's always a way out!

As they continued their descent, the temperature dropped and so did her courage when she saw a giant cloud crawling towards them. She stared at it, petrified. There was no escape: within seconds, a blanket of freezing fog had wrapped itself around her, driven upwards by a cutting breeze. Solemnly, it piled itself up against the now-invisible mountain, and the silent world drowned in its embrace.

For one passing moment, her confidence faltered, but she quickly picked up the direction of the sea, somewhere out there in the void. Denser than mist, the fog carried a new energy, a capricious dynamic affecting everything it touched. Time itself ebbed away, becoming slower and slower, and slowly the forms started to flow into one another, boundaries feathered out, became fuzzy and blurred and, gradually, disappeared. It was a strange sensation, as if she herself were drifting apart. She looked down at her hands and limbs and wiggled her toes in her Wellies: were they still part of her or dissolving, too?

She noticed the stillness. There was not a sound. But there was always that palpable presence.

"MadMax?" she called meekly, wincing at the loudness of her voice. "Where are you? MadMax?"

There was no answer. Bewildered, she called him again but, while they drummed in her head, her words seemed to be swallowed the moment they left her throat. She gulped and went blank; without him by her side she felt suspended in a remoteness beyond her grasp. It seemed to absorb her memories, her mind, and she began to wonder about that speck of consciousness she called 'I' – had she now lost that, too?

Where am I?

Her soul stretched into the epic silence. Water dripped from her hood; it ran over her face and her lips, leaving a frozen trail.

Nowhere?

Was her existence just another version of an elusive dream?

Everywhere?

Suddenly, she was overcome by an instinctive sense of danger. She wanted to call his name one more time – but too late! Her squishy surroundings trembled and quaked, and a raging gust of wind tossed her onto the ground. She stumbled and slithered until a merciful tree broke her fall into the abyss. Swallowed, blinded by racing whiteness, she held on to the branches and slowly . . . gently . . . she was laid onto the ground. Her fingers and palms patted the sand, groping their way along short tufts of grass into which her tears fell, plentiful and unseen.

Down on her hands and knees she crawled forward, exhausted, hurting, alone, and fiercely determined not to reach that pivotal point of surrender from where there was no return. Lashed by a cacophony of sound that descended on her, she paused. She resigned herself to the now. She listened. Past the raging gale, the rumbling mountain, and the waves crashing on distant shores, she became still.

She only listened.

And, as she listened, a deep emptiness filled her, an emptiness in which her thoughts disappeared. But within this emptiness that enveloped her, she was not alone. It was there. It was more of a vibration than a sound. It was moving on the ground, somewhere ahead of her.

Was it coming towards her or trying to escape?

When she moved, it moved, too. When she stood still, there was nothing. She sensed that it was as lost and as vulnerable as she was, but the liquid fleece that burnt her eyes kept obliterating her view. Spellbound, she waited, expecting nothing, yet listening with an incredible longing to meet that other soul.

Then it arose, not far away, and muffled through layers of mist: *the honking of a goose?*

There! Now she caught a glimpse of it. And really, what she saw was an Egyptian goose! With her wings spread wide open and her head raised towards the sky, she was turning in circles, honking and turning. "Piu Piu?" She called at the top of her lungs. "Piu Piu – is this you?"

The goose kept turning and honking, oblivious to the world around her.

Oh God, this will kill her! She will never be able to fly! She's doomed!

"Piu Piu!" Like a swimmer, she started out towards her through the amorphous soup, but she never got closer.

"Piu Piu . . ."

Undeterred, the goose honked and kept turning and turning as if dancing to an inner tune.

"Oh, Piu Piu," Pippa whispered, with wisps of whiteness wrapping themselves around her. "How could I forget who you are?" At last, she listened to her. She aligned her breathing. She reconnected. She understood. Waves of love flowed from her heart towards that other part of herself.

Piu Piu turned and turned feeling her wholeness emerge. And then the impossible happened: the fog swirled and lifted, revealing a shimmer of light beneath a colorless arch.

"The magical mistbow!"

Pippa watched with bated breath . . . and then, as the fynbos drifted back into form, the goose took off and soared into the air, past barren branches that reached out for the sky – like brushstrokes on wet paper.

"Fly, fly . . ." Pippa's eyes followed her into the otherworldly landscape. "One day I'll meet you there."

"Hey, stranger! Remember life in a day?"

MadMax! It was him, although his voice was distorted. Oh, the joy! She looked back and there he was, floating towards her with his tail high up in the air. She closed her eyes with relief and he rubbed his drenched head and cold nose fondly against her. As his frosted whiskers tickled her nose she clenched her teeth and sobbed: "I thought I'd lost you."

"I've always been here."

"I couldn't see."

"How could you? With this mist."

Before she was able to answer, a melancholy boom permeated the stillness: the foghorn. It brought her back to her feet. She clasped her hands firmly around the camera still safely tucked under her anorak. "Hey! We've got to hurry up and catch the mistbow! I saw it; it's just down there!"

"Right – let's hurry up!" MadMax grinned. He had already moved a few steps ahead and was waiting. Now that he saw her energies flowing again, he was keen to get away; foghorns made him nervous.

Following his lead through the eerie thicket, they continued downwards. As her intent cleared and her confidence grew, her surroundings changed. When she'd been at her most confused, Piu Piu had shown her the way. She knew where she was going again; she saw the light in her mind. She would find that spot – even if she were blindfolded. A joyful anticipation spurred her on to move faster, to breathe deeper. It carried her forward, leaving no room for hesitation or doubt. The fog seemed like balm on her face.

"There it is! The light!" Together, they stepped into it, danced along with it, down, down . . . until it appeared right before them, taking their breath away: *the blooming bush!*

MadMax shook off his mantle of moisture and arched his back, happy they had arrived. He knew from experience that Pippa's photo sessions took time; in this particular instance it would last as long as the light played along. Luckily, the odyssey had not taken as long as it had seemed. Now that Pippa was herself again, she beamed with creativity and her camera clicked in sync with the buzzing bees: this was her world!

Nectar is a sweet liquid bees love to drink, sucking it up with their tubelike tongues. By offering their precious juices to the visiting bee, the flowers expect a gift in exchange. It is just a little pollen grain they want, but not just any grain! It has to be from another flower of the same species. Obeying life's most magnetic attraction, this little grain fuses with the egg cell inside the flower to create a new seed.

Insects – and especially honey bees – fascinated Pippa. Taking great care that none of her movements disturbed them, she got as close to the bees as she could. She breathed in the same fragrance and, sometimes, was tickled by the tiny petals beneath her hands. Dad would get a sneeze attack from so much pollen in the air, but she just tuned into the vibrations around her where the observer and the observed merged into one.

Meanwhile, MadMax was lazing in a sunny spot underneath the flowering bush. With his eyes half-closed, he drifted between daydreaming and watching the scenario from a different angle. His ears twitched a few times as he picked up a hollow sound that disrupted the monotonous humming of the bees. It was gone as quickly as it came. A passionate hunter by nature and bored by the buzzing socialites above, he turned his head slightly and concentrated on a shady area in the bush from where it had emanated.

There! Again . . . and gone! He opened one eye and scanned the fine network of branches and leaves, but nothing moved except for a solitary bee that landed on one of the lower flowers. She immediately scuttled through the jungle of stamens, picking up pollen all over her fluffy body.

There it was again! MadMax sat up with his ears pointed forward and the tip of his tail twitching. This time he saw it immediately, the moment the bee had appeared: a green triangular face with long antennae and two large protruding compound eyes, each with a dark pupil. It spun around in an instant reflex, electrified by the unexpected arrival.

MadMax stretched himself forward, his whiskers vibrating. There! Now he saw her, hidden by the shadows and perfectly camouflaged among the twigs, with her spiked forelimbs folded in a prayer position, she waited patiently for her prey. A praying mantis! Many times the size of a little bee, the powerful mantis could turn her head almost 180 degrees while the rest of her long body remained motionless.

Focusing entirely on her purpose, the bee visited one flower after the other, totally oblivious of the sword of Damocles hanging over her. Soon she stopped to groom herself, enjoying the much-needed warmth and sunshine on a gloomy day.

All her activities were attentively observed by the predator. Mantises are not only carnivorous, preying on anything from insects to frogs to birds and even fish and small rodents, but these 'natural born killers' are also cannibalistic, the female biting off the male's head during or after the mating ritual. That is, if madam is hungry!

While a potential drama unfolded at the bottom of the bush, Pippa marveled at the industrious insects through her lens. The magnified format allowed her to see structural details more clearly. Soon she switched over to the video function to capture movements, atmosphere and sound. She almost stopped breathing when one of the bees, with its monstrous compound eyes, closed in on her. She imagined how each of their many photoreceptor cells sends its respective message to the bee's brain, which instantaneously combines all these individual pieces into one image. Compound eyes pick up all rapid movements, for instance a person swatting or running away, which could immediately set all the bees' alarm bells off and get them into bee community defence mode. Hence, Pippa controlled her movements carefully. Even when a bee crawled inquisitively over her finger as she pressed down the shutter release, she resisted the urge to blow her away. They were not at all disturbed by her presence. Probably they had lost interest altogether after realizing that she provided strictly nothing for discerning bee palates! Besides, they were far too focused on collecting nectar and pollen, and transporting them safely to the hive. Here it was converted into honey to feed the baby bees, and royal jelly to feed the queen to keep her healthy, happy, and producing more baby bees. They stored the rest of the honey in the honeycomb as food for winter.

MadMax turned his head: there was the noise again! In pursuit of her prey, the mantis climbed forward and upward through the branches in slow, mindful movements. As she pulled her long heavy abdomen along, she created a hardly perceptible raspy sound that fine feline ears picked up immediately. The insect's eyes were firmly fixed on the bee while it steadily closed the gap. Once within range, the razorsharp forelegs could lash out at lightning speed, lock the victim in an inescapable grip – and devour it alive!

Was the bee's fate sealed?

Pippa loved the little furry insects with their translucent wings glittering in the sun. They were digging deep into the flowers to get to the nectar, whirling through the stamens and gathering sticky pollen grains all over themselves. From time to time they stopped and scraped the pollen from their abdomens and other parts of their bodies and pressed it into the pollen baskets on their fuzzy hindlegs. As more and more pollen accumulated they looked quite comical, as if they wore thick, golden knickerbockers at a hockey match!

How on earth did they still manage to fly?

As they climbed through the flower maze, diving from one calyx to another, the fine golden dust rubbed off here and there on a flower's stigma and pollinated it. When the flowers withered, they formed fruit or seeds from which new plants sprouted. These, in turn, fed a new generation of bees – it was an eternal cycle of interdependence within the great symphony of life.

Pippa made a mental note not to forget to collect some ripe seeds to grow more of these useful shrubs. Bees were constantly buzzing off to carry nectar and pollen to the hive, while new bees were arriving.

She had read that it took more than 5000 flower visits to make one teaspoon of honey! And what was one teaspoon? It quickly melted on Mom's decadent pancakes or disappeared in a cup of hot milk in winter. Nobody ever thought of all the little bees doing their work diligently behind the scenes; the many trips it took to gather the nectar, by drinking as much as the bee could hold, and take it home into the hive.

There, it was passed on to another female worker bee who poured the precious liquid into one of countless hexagonal cells in the honeycomb. But this was not the end. Now, she spent time whirring her wings to evaporate all the excess moisture, leaving nothing but the most delicious honey behind. While the wind is a significant natural pollinator, blowing the pollen grains from flower to flower, the truth is that human beings owe one in three bites of food to the bees.

Suddenly, it all resonated in her ears, everything she had heard in the news, learned in school and read.

'If honey bees become extinct, human society will follow in four years,' visionary physicist Albert Einstein had warned in his lifetime.

Right now, the world was facing many tragedies in ways never seen before: bee colonies were collapsing and the bees were disappearing in many countries. Scientists were investigating the reason for this alarming situation. What they found was that – in addition to having to cope with the loss of habitat and the exorbitant use of sprays, chemicals and pesticides – the bees were stressed by the extreme changes in weather patterns and rapid temperature fluctuations. This weakened their immune systems. It changed their behavior.

She remembered that Dad had mentioned that – as the southernmost tip of the Cape had the highest average wind speeds throughout the year in South Africa – many queen bees were lost during their nuptial flights . . . and died.

All of a sudden, the camera felt too heavy in her hands. She took her eye from the viewfinder and stopped. She sat up.

Why was she doing this anyway?

Who would be caring about a bee when the whole world was twittering about how to eat, sleep and brush teeth? She shook her head as an annoying bee kept whirring its wings in front of her nose, almost making her sneeze. Then she froze. She closed her eyes and took a few deep breaths, centering herself.

"Oh no. I did it again."

"Never get stuck with what appears to be," Mom had taught her. "Think of what could be! Think of what's possible!"

How could she forget?

All she wanted were happy bees in a happy world – and this she anchored in her mind. She got up and stretched, squinting at the fading light.

"I should have enough material. Hey, Mr. M! I'm hungry!" When the tomcat made no attempt to move, she went back onto her knees, camera at the ready. She hardly believed what she saw: here was a little beauty flirting with flowers while a ferocious beast looked on, blending perfectly into the background. But instead of lashing out with her deadly Swiss army knife forelimbs to catch and kill the sweet prey, the mantis stayed poised in a prayer position, staring at the bee.

I see a happy bee . . .

Pippa zoomed in on the scene. All she had captured earlier appeared banal in comparison with the drama unfolding here.

At this moment, the bee suddenly turned and moved away.

With an expressionless face, the mantis watched her disappear – stretching herself forward noiselessly to keep the target within her field of vision.

Was she going to let the tasty titbit – filled with nectar and dipped in nutritious pollen – slip from her grasp? Containing her burning desire deep within her and never making a mindless move, the 'natural born killer' remained motionless. Waiting.

There was just a slight change in the size of her pupils when the bee flew away.

"Oh, happy bee!" Relieved, Pippa put the camera down. "Those deadly mandibles were already moist with drool, all set to slice and chew her up."

Suddenly, the bee was back! After hovering for a few tantalizing moments directly above the mantis, she landed almost next to her. She buzzed off immediately on her shopping spree, without paying the slightest attention to the killer.

The mantis seemed somewhat stunned by a tactic she frequently used herself: the element of surprise. With her raptorial forelimbs folded, she remained still.

Pippa held her breath, keeping the two actors in focus, not missing any critical moment.

Was the bee aware that she was dangerously suspended between life and death? And if so, did she care?

"She's watching," Pippa heard while she kept filming.

"Not the bee," MadMax added, "she's watching you."

Pippa got goosebumps: only now she realized that the mysterious monster was staring at her! Once behind a camera, she forgot about herself. Slowly, she zoomed in on the insect's face . . . then on one of its big eyes.

"Amazing," she thought as she drifted deeper and deeper into that unknown space where anything was possible.

"Pupils converging . . . She's fascinated by her own image reflecting in my dark gigantic eye." She sensed the energy. The vibration. Then heard it – *'the voice of the infinite in the small'* –

as Mom's ancestors in Namibia used to say when they listened to a mantis. It all fell into place.

Holding her breath, she slowly zoomed out – the eyes, the head, the insect, the whole – feeling a form of communion. It was a dance, a meditation . . . into which the bee came back in a circle!

Unwittingly, in her dedicated search, the bee crawled over the foot of the mantis.

This immediately got the beast's attention! She flipped her head around at lightning speed and –?

No!

She did not lash out at the bee; she watched her. And when the bee decided to leave, she let her go.

Through her glazed eyes, Pippa watched the bee fly away, legs heavy with pollen.

"I hope I got the pictures right," she thought. "It's hard to believe what we witnessed."

As she got up and stretched her back she noticed how the mist was moving in again from the sea, greedily consuming the light. The flowers closed their petals and the magic bush faded into oblivion. All that remained of the day was an eerie void.

Pippa packed up and pulled her hood over her head. "And I thought we got out of the fog. . ."

"We sure did," MadMax replied. "This is nothing compared to what we had this -"

"Phew!" Pippa almost lost her balance as a gust of wind hit her back. "Let's get out of here real fast!"

"Phew!" MadMax echoed. "Not bad for life in a day!"

Anxious to get home fast, he hurried a few steps ahead and waited for Pippa to follow, leading the way back home.

"Piupidoo!" Piu Piu trumpeted from the terrace, welcoming them. "I see you!"

"Oh, Piu Piu!" Pippa replied, "what did you do?"

Flabbergasted, the goose stood with her beak wide open. Her wing slid to the side and hit the ground, just as Pippa and MadMax slipped into the house. Within seconds, the first showers pelted down, right over Piu Piu.

BORN WITH WINGS 167

"Winter's almost here," Dad commented at the dinner table, later that day, glancing at MadMax who was snoring in front of the crackling fireplace.

"I'd better get more wood. And the pine cones, Pippa?"

"I will collect them, Dad. There are lots of them under the big old pine."

"Tomorrow!"

"Yes, Dad, tomorrow!"

"It got so dark," Mom said while she lit her favorite Madagascan vanilla candle. "I love vanilla. Pure, spicy and delicate. This feels much better! There wasn't a single glimpse of light today."

Pippa smiled. The candle, too, was a gift of the bee.

"The old warrior . . . " Dad mumbled, heaving a sigh. "What memories may be . . ."

Pippa shot him a glance. The flames were darting across his craggy face. She wondered why – all of a sudden – her hair stood on end.

CHAPTER TEN

Cape of Flames

"I'm not going there!"

Piu Piu stood like a pillar of salt in the middle of the narrow path that snaked past the big, old, stone pine. The path was carpeted with pine needles and autumn leaves that rustled under Pippa's feet.

"Oh com'on, Piu Piu!" the young girl called, "help me collect pine cones for the fireplace." But she knew that the goose wouldn't move. Whenever they approached the ancient tree it was always the same. "It's just a pine," she wanted to say but then caught herself and, after a moment of reflection, asked: "What do *you* see, Piu Piu?"

Piu Piu did not take her eyes off the dark and daunting coniferous tree. It had to be old, very old, most probably many hundred years older than any other life form in the garden. It was so tall she could not see the top of it, and it had black charcoal scars on its trunk and on its bare, partially broken, lower branches. The pine must have gone through a fire and, for the sensitive goose, it still carried destructive energies. She saw the branches smoldering, glowing at the edges, with clusters of needles crackling as the fire caught. Gooey resin was melting under the heat, mixing with sap on the trunk and dripping down . . . down . . . where pine cones burst open, releasing winged seeds into the toxic air. She sensed an all-consuming force that – once unleashed – would know no boundaries. There was no way she would go near that field. *How could no one else feel it?*

In his typically nonchalant way, MadMax hit his claws into the furrowed bark. He sharpened them, extensively, with an attitude of superiority that normally educed at least an irritated hiss from the goose. Not now. "Sissy!" He sulked and stalked away, his tail stroking the air with a twitch of annoyance.

Piu Piu did not pay any attention to him as her memories came back. This was where it had all begun and – ended. Well, almost. No light penetrated through from the top branches. The higher she looked the denser and darker it got. Once again, she heard the storm howling in the crown and slashing through the branches, deafening her desperate chirps. She balanced on the edge of an empty nest; abandoned, alone, and oblivious of the feral hunter who had picked up her voice from the ground. Trailing his long tail, he moved adeptly from branch to branch, climbing higher and higher, closing in on the nest.

The little gosling looked into the abyss and trembled. Then saw the beast. It was coming directly towards her. Panic-stricken, she gave off a soft little chirp and – just before those deadly claws could grab her and the jaws crushed her neck – she took a leap of faith. Down . . . down she tumbled, into the unknown world. The mere memory of that moment made her shiver. Her legs felt like rubber. She bent her knees and slumped onto a bare patch of soil.

This far, no further.

The wind plucked at her plumage and rustled through the grasses. A golden leaf, blown off a plane tree, sailed past. Silently, it landed on the earth. Incidentally, just as Pippa gave it a glance, a large butterfly settled on it.

"A Table Mountain Beauty!" she exclaimed, her eyes sparkling. "What are you doing down here?" Putting her wattle basket on the ground, she squatted down to admire the rare visitor. "Look at these colors," she whispered, "dark velvet browns, warm yellow bands and large eye-spots with blue dots." She bent lower, her voice reduced to a thought: "Oh, and these delicate feathery scales on a gold thread texture . . . Where do they take you, those marvelous wings?"

The butterfly flapped rhythmically, its long antennae sensing her presence.

"They took me here," the butterfly replied, unable to sit still.

"I see that," Pippa said, a little disappointed. "You like the grass tussocks – or is it the pine?"

"I came to visit my memories."

Perplexed, Pippa glanced at Piu Piu who sat very quietly, listening.

"Your memories?" Pippa turned back to the graceful being. "You mean the past? Backwards in time?"

"Time?" The butterfly whispered, "I don't know time. I dream."

"But . . . when you wake up? What then?"

'Boingg!' A big raindrop splashed onto the leaf and the butterfly flitted away. Pippa's eyes followed its flight upward where it danced with the leaves. One after the other, they lifted off into the sky. Suddenly, the plane trees stood naked and bare. Only now, as she gazed past a riddle of leafless branches, did she see the dark, menacing clouds, towering right above her.

Grabbing her backoto, Pippa dashed for cover underneath the pine. Phew! She made it just in time before the first showers pelted down. Of course, MadMax was already there. He had snuggled into a soft nest with his fluffy tailtip over his eyes. Had he dozed off into a parallel world of milk and mice?

"Are you dreaming?"

"I'm here."

She sat next to him with her back against the woody tissue of the trunk.

"Lost in that other world?"

"No, no – I enjoy where I am."

"Are you sure?" She thought for a moment, then she laughed: "Right now, I'd prefer a hot chocolate with whipped cream and a marshmallow on top!"

"That's wicked!" He wanted to sit up but ducked back again as the north-easterly storm howled down from the saddle between the mountains in the north, driving sheets of rain into the valley. It lashed out at anything in its path but, at the foot of the old stone pine, they were miraculously sheltered from its wrath. Slowly, the light trickled away as water cascaded all around them, closing them in.

But Pippa's thoughts were with Piu Piu, somewhere all alone out there. "Something frightens the hell out of her. What does she see . . . or feel . . . that I don't?"

She ran her hand through the pine needles that had piled up over time, year after year.

"Falling from her nest was certainly traumatic, but this? There has to be more . . ." she thought.

The cold rough bark began to hurt her shoulder blades and she shifted to find a more comfortable position. That's when she became aware of a warm, an almost magnetic attraction between her and the pine. She felt how her spine and the back of her head connected with the inner core of the tree, the steady flow of its juices. This fusion kept her in a gentle yet tight embrace that prevented her body from sliding down. She hardly noticed how her lungs expanded, filling up with fresh air. Her eyes closed and – gradually – the world beyond the liquid motion disappeared. All she sensed was a warm and vibrant lifestream flowing through her, pulling her along. Rising from the furthest tips of its roots anchored deep down in the earth, it pulsated upwards through the vascular system of the tree and its many branches, spiraling higher and higher in a pyramid shape. Upon reaching the crown, it connected with the sun and the sky in a sacred communion, exploding with information and receiving an abundance of source energy in exchange. Fuelled with new inspiration and joy, it continued the eternal circuit in a downward movement, nurturing each cell on its way.

There was no beginning, no end.

Vibrating in close communion with the tree, Pippa ceased to exist as a separate form. All she sensed was a force that pulled her upward, and the higher she rose the further time rolled back. One by one, she recognized the memory triggers of her childhood and beyond: Great-grandad's Book . . . Piu Piu . . . the Garden . . . MadMax . . . Dad . . . Mom . . . the Flames.

Oh, that fire! The key cue!

It was a grueling view: the whole mountain range had turned into a burning inferno with flames over 10 meters high, all the way from Chapman's Peak in the north through Silvermine Nature Reserve and the Cape Peninsula National Park towards Fish Hoek and Kommetjie down to Cape Point. In those hot and fateful days in January 2000, the tranquil Cape Peninsula was transformed into a 'Cape of Flames' of vast expanse and massive destruction.

Midnight had long passed.

Mom was resting with her back against Dad's chest. He was in his camouflage army garb, holding her and the growing life within her as they sat on the Noordhoek Village lawn, together with neighbors and friends. Quietly, each one lost in their own thoughts and sadness, they looked up at the raging fires that had engulfed their homes and their land. Propelled by a fierce wind, the bellowing beast was storming down the hill, towards them.

Occasionally, some exhausted shadows in firefighting garb passed by, dragging their feet along on their way to get water and food. Avoiding the hopeful glances, they nailed their eyes to the ground – or just shook their heads.

Mercilessly, the fire unleashed its red-hot wrath high up into the night, fuelled by gale force winds. At the same time as it burnt traumatic pictures into their minds, they heard the drama unfolding as trees exploded and creatures lost their lives. No one said a word. Not even the frightened pair of Egyptian geese sitting high above them in an old oak.

There was nothing they could do but pray, hope, wait.

Over months the temperatures had been sweltering. For the first time ever, the dam had completely dried out, leaving nothing but scarred, barren earth. Over 120 fires had already been reported in the news when earlier, in the late afternoon, Dad phoned to warn Mom that a new fire had broken out along the road that led directly to their home.

"Be careful, Grace, get out of the way. Don't take risks, not now," he insisted. "It's blowing directly towards us. I'm on my way . . ."

Then the connection broke off.

"He may never get through," Mom completed in her mind, suddenly feeling alone and abandoned. She looked at the sky. It was blue and cloudless, but there was a brooding haze hanging in the air. Despite the fact that the fire was still kilometers away, she was extremely restless, largely due to the incessant honking of the geese. She decided to take their pets and their most important items and valuables – like photo albums, documents, computers, cameras, some pieces of art – into the safety of a friend's house in the valley.

As soon as she had left the house the pair of wild Egyptian geese – as usual high up on their favorite lookout spot on top of the chimney – honked in all directions. Then they spread their wings and followed her down into the valley, flying low along the flamboyant avenue of flowering gums. In full bloom, they had erupted in dazzling shades of reds, pinks, oranges and whites . . .

Many thoughts crossed Mom's mind on her way back home up the mountain.

How understanding the pets were! As if they knew.

What really did matter in moments like these? What was important or not? What could she easily give up? Leave behind? Let go? In fact, there was not much one really needed and, on one's final journey, it would be nothing at all.

Weird she should be thinking of that . . .

How quiet the road was; nobody lingered outside. There were just a few curious squirrels crisscrossing and never quite making up their minds which way they wanted to go. She loved the old shady oaks and the splendid flowering gums against the majestic backdrop of the mountains and the blue sky.

Ironically, it all looked like a perfect day!

She parked the car under a shady palm tree and went down the staircase to her house. The wooden chairs and the table had to go into her studio; it was too dangerous to leave them outside – just in case the fire did come down this far. While this seemed improbable at this stage, she wanted to be prepared and to focus on the essentials – although it was hard to figure out what exactly these were in an always possible, yet never really expected, situation like this.

Water! The first thing that would go was water. Especially here, at the top.

She evaluated the situation. She should stuff the downpipes with newspapers and fill the gutters with water – but for that she needed help which she did not have. That was off the list.

So she went for the hosepipe instead to, at least, water down the roof and walls of the house. As they lived quite high up on the mountain slope the water pressure was always low. During an emergency they'd be the first to have no water at all. She had to act fast. Soon the roof hissed and steamed.

She was totally lost in her work, was dirty and dripping, when she heard a noise on the path along the boundary of her land, slightly above her. It was the British lord of the nearby manor house, who rolled past in a trendy golf cart, raising his eyebrows when he saw her hose down the roof. The famed keeper of gorillas, tigers and casinos sat very tall and upright, all dressed in white with a burgundy necktie and a solar topi on his head. He looked like an apparition against the kinetic backdrop of the pine forest rising behind him on the vacant plot that separated her ground from the mountain reserve.

Up there, the tall slender stems grew next to each other with almost military precision, covering many hectares of land – an army of potential Christmas trees reaching high into the sky. Masses of undergrowth and pine needles had piled up beneath them, over decades. She used to go looking for mushrooms and raspberries there, sometimes disturbing wild antelopes.

Now, however, she saw it from a different perspective and her mouth went dry.

"Well, well, my dear," she heard the aristocrat observe without dropping the amused undertone in his voice, "it should be a bit early for that!"

She strained to hold her tongue, watching the ridiculous white vehicle turn uphill on the fire break, where it was swallowed by the thicket.

She knew the sometimes steep and unpredictable path well. Large rocky outcrops and hidden burrows, fallen tree trunks across deceptive swamps, rotting branches and overgrown piles of wood – he wouldn't get far. The path was edged with majestic and partially broken stone pines that formed a natural border, running from the valley all the way up into the mountain: a landmark in the area.

And what a feast for a fire!

Towards the east, the forest just continued, past isolated dwellings, and became infiltrated with Port Jackson willow, a fast-burning alien tree.

Bewildered, she turned north. There was a dense, continuous, canopy of pines and blue gums as far as her eyes could see. She remembered having seen large patches of Port Jackson underneath them on her mushroom gathering trips into the wild, uninhabited territory. It was this emptiness and space, the silence, and a sense of place that had attracted her and Pete, when the area was not even on the map. Nature's hidden paradise!

A blaze in there would be unstoppable!

She felt nauseous. Shaking off the paralyzing angst, she pulled the hose around the house, despite rising doubts as to how effective it all could be in view of the potential furnace that was painting itself in her mind.

She took some deep breaths and continued; action now would keep her calm, sane and simply alive.

Was there a sudden smack of smoke in the air?

She usually picked it up fast – but no, it had to be her imagination! So, although there was nothing tangible yet, she knew the clock was ticking. There was that brooding stillness, the devious harbinger of a Cape storm. She was all alone and so much had to be done! She had to close all windows to avoid draughts, to stop sparks from jumping into the house and setting it on fire from inside. She should, at least, fill the kettle and perhaps even the bathtub, just in case . . .

And the garden? The lawn had already suffered extensively from the scorching temperatures over the past months. However, fynbos and indigenous vegetation, including many proteas and leucadendrons, that covered most of the ground were a different story. Ironically, fires at regular intervals of every five to twenty years were built into the matrix of their life cycle. It was Nature's way of maintaining biodiversity and clearing the build-up of old plant matter and undergrowth. Fires stimulated the propagation of seeds in the soil, releasing essential nutrients into the earth that, in turn, nurtured new growth. If the fire came down this far, everything would burn! Although she knew that it would re-establish itself over time, the mere thought of the devastation was horrendous.

Fortunately, they had cleared all alien vegetation from their ground, although it kept coming up so fast every year that it was an ongoing task. Most were propagated through both their roots and seeds. These seeds could lie dormant in the soil for decades until a fire literally kissed them to life. Those fires were even fiercer; not only did they bake valuable roots and seeds within the soil, but they damaged it in a way that caused it to repel water and become prone to erosion. Large portions in the mountains were infested with alien vegetation. It meant that a fire would spread much faster, especially if fuelled by strong winds.

No one would be able to control it!

Her eyes wandered across all the newly planted beds, her young palms and the spacious new hen house. She was glad that the big laying hens and her favorite Bantam chickens had not yet arrived. However, a pair of graceful duikers were living in the garden. It was their home and she loved the adorable little buck. The bigger antelopes came down each night to drink at the dam. Sometimes they were standing on the driveway, their eyes glowing in the lights of the car, when she and Pete came home at night. They were in no hurry to leave!

Seeing a caracal with its young the other morning near the big pine had filled her with absolute awe. This reminded her of all the noisy squirrels and birds living in that huge imposing tree, not forgetting the couple of Egyptian geese. She often crossed paths with the mongoose and never a day passed without a tortoise, lizards or frogs, dragonflies and bees. And there were snakes . . .

Would they be able to escape?

Sweat was running down her face, mixing with the dust whirled up by sudden gusts of wind. It was exhausting to pull the heavy hosepipe and untwist its coils. She held the nozzle over her face to cool down but the water was burning hot. Her arms got lame. She had to pause to catch her breath. She put her hands protectively on her belly. She closed her eyes and listened to the growing life, drawing from it new energy and hope.

We've got to be strong, little princess . . . With the wind blowing in our direction and all the dry vegetation in its path, the fire could be here in no time.

A noise made her turn. The golf cart came rattling down, this time in a hurry. The gaunt man at the wheel passed her without a word. It was the last time she saw him; minutes later the smoke billowed over the mountain. She stood and stared, with the hosepipe in her hand, until she realized that the water pressure had dropped. She ran into the house and was just in time to fill up the kettle and some jugs for the fridge before the water stopped completely. Not a drop.

Panting, she hurried from window to window to close them. Each had been designed to offer a clear view of the garden against the backdrop of a unique piece of landscape. While she burnt each picture into her mind, she observed the rapid progress of the fire – with any earlier hopefulness all but erased. On its unstoppable course of destruction, it raged along the top of the mountain range, enclosing the valley like a ring of fire – gruesome and fascinating at the same time.

Her mobile rang; it was her French neighbor and friend.

"Hello Grace! *T'as vu?* It's coming down."

"Yes . . . terrible."

"Comment ça va?"

"I'm fine."

"It will hit us first . . ."

"I hope not."

"Eh bien, we'll have to wait and see. They closed off the mountain road. They say it's one hell of a fire. Constantia is burning, Hout Bay . . . *C'est partout* . . . everywhere!"

"Oh my God, Pete!" she shrieked.

"Il n'est pas avec toi? Is he not with you?"

"He was on his way . . . I've no clue where he is."

"Olala. Ne compte pas sur lui. If Chapman's Peak and the mountain road are closed off his only chance is via Kalk Bay. But he'll be stuck for hours. It's chaos on the roads. *Olala, ma pauvre chérie. Viens chez nous si t'as besoin de quelque chose, d'accord?"*

She suddenly had a lump in her throat.

"We'll be in touch," she heard her friend say. "Good luck for Pete."

She sank onto a chair and tried Pete's number again, but did not even get a signal. She stared vacantly at the floor. She thought of her neighbors on the plot below them; they were far away. And her friend, on the eastern side. Was he in the country? Did he know? She called his number and got him straight on the line.

"I'm here," he said with a low voice, "my house is going to burn like a matchbox."

"Miracles happen," she said softly.

"We can only pray . . ."

Meanwhile, the gale force winds from the south-east had fanned the flames down along the steep rocky mountain slopes, where it eventually reached dense bush and masses of dry vegetation. The flames flared up two or even three times higher than the vegetation that fuelled them, well over ten meters high. Spot firing ignited other areas within seconds, from where the firestorm gathered momentum and spread rapidly until the whole mountain range was burning.

When she went onto her terrace she saw that even Chapman's Peak was ablaze, and the hazy afternoon sky above the sea had turned red and black.

Everything became very still within her. She glanced up at the wooden structure of her roof, the strong white walls, her furniture, the cupboards filled with clothes and linen, not to speak of the books and her indoor plants. It was not really a lot. However, the more she thought about it, the more she realized what she carried along. All that stuff.

Suddenly, the house shook and trembled as the first Oryx helicopter thundered right overhead on its way up into the mountain to release 2000 liters of water, from its huge underslung Bambi bucket, onto the rapidly advancing firefront. It was this thudding sound of rotor blades pounding the air that would accompany her over the next hours. It was a race against time. Once the darkness of the night and loss of visibility set in, the tireless and brave rescue team would call a halt to the operation.

Would their, often heroic, efforts – that demanded experience, concentration and precision and that were never without risk – stop a fire of this magnitude?

Into the cacophony her mobile rang. At last! "Pete," she almost yelled, "where are you?" It was not Pete; it was her friend from down the road.

"Grace! Can you help us . . . please!" She sounded desperate, her voice stuck in her throat. "The horses are panicking! We've got to take them to the *Dunes*!"

"Of course," she shouted back just as the next helicopter thundered past, "am on my way!"

She quickly washed her hands with water from the fridge. Her eyes wandered from the strained face in the mirror to the small bulge under her heart. The fact that she was due within less than a month was well concealed and would come as a surprise to many. Right now, however, she had to push herself as her energy levels were dwindling and her back was painful.

When she opened the front door, an intense heatwave engulfed her; it felt as if a barrage of laser arrows had attacked her scalp. The air was thick and sticky with the acrid smell of smoke. Holding her hand over her nose and mouth, she hurried up the steps to the driveway. Only now she saw the hectic commotion of trucks and fire engines that passed along her driveway and up the firebreak. It was the best way to get through – and they had to act fast. Sirens were blaring in the valley and two helicopters thundered up and down, up and down, relentlessly waterbombing strategic areas. They flew so low she could see the water dripping from the buckets and feel the spray on her face.

Her body tensed when she saw firefighters in protective garb pull massive hosepipes across her land. From volunteers armed with firefighting tools, to farmers from far away who were experienced in fighting farm fires, they were all on their way up into the mountain like some *'Pyroclassic Park'*.

"All hell broke loose up there, let's move!" a man yelled and someone else shouted: "Hoo Boy! This is so cool!"

Bewildered, with feelings fluctuating between reluctance in one moment and gratitude the next, she stared at the throng of strangers streaming past her – nondescript men and women of all ages laughing loudly and waving – like a ghost train slicing through her heart. Even so, she was humbled by the thought that – during times of real danger – one's life may suddenly depend on the selfless service and compassion of total strangers. People we do not know, and probably will never meet, become a part of us and us of them.

Do good; expect nothing in return.

Her heart skipped a beat when she realized that, should they not succeed and the fire came down, it could, very realistically, result in the complete annihilation of everything she and Pete owned, and had built.

She never felt more lost than now.

Just as she climbed into the car, her mobile rang. A hopeful smile lit her face. But no, it was not Pete. The stables at the Dunes were no longer an option as the sparks had just jumped down into the wetlands, too. A fierce firestorm with its own dynamics was racing from the Lakes towards Chapman's Peak, consuming all the reeds and bushes in its way. They were, themselves, preparing for the worst.

"All roads are closed or blocked! We have no place to go!" The connection broke off and her mind went blank.

Trapped!

Slowly, she pulled the door to close it, feeling dizzy. Her head started to spin. A wave of violent pain welled up within her, cutting through her abdomen and driving sweat through her pores. The baby was moving. She focused on her breathing and enveloped her unborn child with light.

The dull ache in her lower back intensified. She knew she had to relax to relieve it, but how could she when it seemed that all her worst nightmares were turning into reality?

Another contraction was coming; she braced her feet against the car. She closed her eyes and tried to breathe deeply, but her body jerked and she collapsed in her seat. With her heart pounding in her ears, a soft velvet darkness embraced her, warm and fluid like a mother's womb. Slowly, she floated away . . .

Damn! Why doesn't she answer her phone!

Heaving a frustrated sigh, Pete put his mobile down and turned up the radio. His face brightened; he liked Cape jazz. Hugh Masekela on a trumpet . . . The many times they had listened to him, live! And yet, he could not bring himself to stop the shambolic onslaught of anxious thoughts, of traumatic projections in his mind. It had to be the heat, the traffic, the intolerable fact of being at the mercy of something he could not control. Hours had passed since he'd last heard her voice and, although he had tried to reach her countless times, he tried one more time. Every few minutes, one more time. It kept him awake and sane as the interminable line of traffic yomped lethargically along the coastal road. Time seemed to slow down by the minute, if it still existed at all.

Kalk Bay. They had to wait for a train at the level crossing. Eventually, the locomotive passed, giving off a high-pitched whistle. There was a rumbling of wheels and he gazed absently at wagon after wagon flashing past – all empty! Not a soul! At least, now he could catch a glimpse of the sea, the wide expanse of the Atlantic. There was an ominous dark front at the horizon, and not one seagull. None. None at all.

Mannenberg – Is Where It's Happening, blared from the radio. Marabi jazz, the vibe of the Cape Flats. Static crackled – he cursed – and then the music continued. He turned it up to maximum volume; windows wide open. Ou B's saxophone always gave him a thrill as it climbed, higher and higher, inspiring him to believe, to trust. To hope!

Moenie worrie nie, alles sal reg kom! Don't worry, all will be fine!

His head moved to the soporific rhythm; his mind abstractly focused on the movements in front and to his side. Everything was slowing down. The queues of cars and vehicles travelling in opposite directions on the narrow road sporadically ground to a halt; but it no longer mattered as everyone seemed to have tuned into the same music, and all those faces passing by – unknown and yet familiar – were swinging, smiling and relating to each other despite the nerve-wracking uncertainty ahead. The raw, the unbreakable spirit of the Cape! Remember Madiba; this was the first music he heard in decades.

Fish Hoek . . . and the monster dragged on, expanding with sudden rush-hour traffic which made it even more excruciatingly slow. For some unknown reason, the music stopped. He closed the windows, put the aircon on. News was coming up in static-filled Afrikaans that was largely unintelligible, except for an underlying pulse of drama and emergency. He turned it down before reaching for his mobile. One more time. Still no answer. Damn.

We all grow up with our own Robben Island . . .

He got more nervous by the minute, having had his last cigarette hours ago. He was dangerously tempted to stop and buy a pack, but it would be sheer madness to leave his spot in the queue. At least the aircon was working, but the stress and strain were weighing everyone down; there was dynamite in the air.

He slammed on the brakes as the car in front stopped abruptly for a skinny black dog. The creature shot across the road out of nowhere, disoriented and scared.

As long as we still stop for a dog . . .

The closer he got to Noordhoek Valley, the darker the incendiary haze, the louder the eerie screech of sirens, ambulances and a continuous cracking and crashing that echoed through the storm. A glance at his watch showed 8:33 p.m. As he came over the hill he felt a chill: a gobsmacking ring of fire was running all along the mountain range, with Chapman's Peak in the distance glowing diabolically. His jaws clenched. *Hell . . . it's there!*

The radio crackled intermittently and went off, then came on again, as he turned onto the Main Road leading to Noordhoek. His fingers drummed nervously on the steering wheel as he watched the choppers drone relentlessly up and down the mountains, picking up water from the lakes. They were flying so low he could hear the blades churning and water splashed onto his windscreen. As he wiped it away he saw the sky above the sea dramatically layered in black and red. He knew the race was on: once darkness set in these heroic rescue operations would end.

What then?

He pushed his sunglasses back on his head and scanned the mountain; somewhere up there was their home, right beneath that torrent of smoke and flames pouring down the crest, powered by ferocious winds. Once again he tried her mobile, again there was no response. He dialed another number. No answer. And another. At last someone took the call!

"Did you see Grace?" he yelled, but all he heard was noise and someone screaming. He wasn't sure whether it was on the phone or outside. Forget it!

Only a few kilometers now and he'd be there and take things into his hands. *She's with friends. She's safe . . . somewhere.*

If only he could believe it himself!

Teeth clenched, eyes on the road, he focused on the last stretch. Why the hell does everyone go to Noordhoek?

He barely noticed when day turned into night, only that the choppers had suddenly stopped. He looked aghast at the dark sky and his throat went dry.

What if I'm too late?

Wake up, Mom. Wake up!

Her eyelids fluttered. Where did this familiar voice, as clear as a bell, come from? Was she dreaming?

She opened her eyes and pushed herself up in her seat, feeling extremely weak. Where was she? Why was it so dark? When her arm bumped into the steering wheel her memories bounced back. But what had happened to the world? Had she lost it?

She vaguely realized that something impenetrable covered the windscreen and shut her in. A glance into the rear mirror showed the same thing. She peered through a small opening in the side window that was protected by an overhanging palm leaf. All she could see from her obscure cocoon were masses of particles floating past like snow flakes in a moonless night. It was so soothing and mesmerizing to watch. Her head slipped into a comfortable position and her eyes closed . . .

"Sorry, sir, we can't let you in!" The uniformed guard stopped him at the entrance gate to the estate.

"You don't understand. I live here! I've got my house up there . . . my wife –"

"I understand, sir," the guard interrupted, "but this area has been closed off. It's an emergency zone. Everybody was evacuated an hour ago. I must ask you to wait with the other residents at the Village. Please, could you move your car, it's in the way."

Pete felt the blood draining from his head and a wild rage constricting his chest. He felt ready to kill.

"Can I help?" A familiar voice asked calmly and a man in fire-fighting garb leant down. "Oh, it's you, Pete! We already wondered where you were. Listen, we're doing our best up there, trust me . . . We've got the marines, the army coming in. Please, for your own safety –"

Grinding a curse between his teeth, Pete reversed past heavy military trucks that stood with their diesel engines running, waiting to be let in through the gate. Damn! The last thing he needed was this! But before driving off he stopped again and shouted: "You sure everyone's out?"

"Relax, man! We won't leave anyone to the flames!"

He drove away with an oppressive feeling that did not go away when he rolled onto the quiet village complex and parked in the darkness under old oaks. He slumped forward on the steering wheel and closed his eyes. His nightmarish journey had come to an end.

Had it . . . really? Or had it just begun?

The sudden calm was confusing and he got out. His legs felt like rubber; after all these hours on the road there was no ignoring the strain in his muscles, his neck and his back. But it was good to have his feet back on the ground.

He stood tall, reaching out and stretching . . . and as he stretched higher he glanced up into the leaves, comforted by a soft rustling and the bluish speckles reflecting from a lonely street light.

I'll find you. I'll always find you!

"Pete! We've been looking for you! Where's Grace?"

Pete immediately recognized the voices of the two men who peeled from the shadows and walked towards him.

"Is she not here?" he asked. "I just arrived."

"You just . . . ?" The taller guy gaped at him. His thick-lensed glasses reflected eerily while he digested what Pete had said.

Pete gave a grim chuckle. "Long story . . ."

"Wanna beer?" The short man with a bald head and a big smile handed him a bottle; Pete opened it with his teeth. "We're all here, you know . . . running around like headless chickens," he added, watching with quiet amazement as Pete drained the bottle in a single gulp.

Jeeez! That guy was thirsty!

"It's the end of the world," the other proclaimed, shaking his beer like a fist.

"To hell with it all . . . as long as there's beer!" The short man jeered and raised his bottle in triumph.

Suddenly, Pete felt himself grabbed by the arm. "You must look for her, now!" the grim guy urged him, his voice lowered to a throaty whisper and his spectacles flashing as a car drove past. "Before it's too late!"

Pete gave him a dumb look, then he shrugged, threw up his hands and walked away. *Why the hell do they think I'm here?*

"Why does he look so worried? Hey, mate! I'm sure she's here. Where else should she . . ."

Pete no longer heard them, but their concern tightened the knot in his gut. Filled with trepidation he started out at Kim's Farmstall – but no, Grace wasn't there. No one had seen her. Mary's restaurant, the camp – all negative. He checked the small groups of people standing around, lost and scared, or huddled together in the darkness on the lawn – but they just shook their heads.

No one has seen her! How could this be?

Suppressing his alarm, he returned to the parking area and searched for her car . . . and, as he did not find it he started all over, this time looking into each car. Nothing. Nothing at all. Not even a sign. Just a dog here and there, too frightened even to bark. Where else could he look? With any earlier hopefulness all but erased, he walked back, staring vacantly on the ground – until he almost collided with his French neighbor.

"Ah Pete! Great you made it! You must be tired; come, have a glass of wine."

He looked up as she passed him a glass: "Grace was so much waiting for you! How is she?"

He held on to the glass as he emptied it; then he shot her a glance of speechless exasperation.

Are you asking me?

"Don't tell me –" She dug into his eyes, searching . . . but all she found was despair. "We spoke in the afternoon," she said, her voice toneless. "She was closing off the house . . . well before it all began. Didn't you call her?"

Something hot edged through his spine and exploded inside his head; he crushed the glass in his hand. Slowly, he turned his head and his eyes narrowed, focusing on the beast up there. Within seconds, his spacial hearing became crystal clear.

We won't leave anyone to the flames!

"She must be somewhere . . . *Elle avait l'air très fatigué.* Maybe she just fell asleep in her car. Did you check?"

Everything in Pete froze. Quietly, he stole away into the darkness, a shade amongst shades. His eyesight adapted to the tenebrous night, watching for movements and changes. From the darkest blacks to blinding whites – nothing escaped his attention. Crouched into the shadows, he was just a stone's throw away from the gates and the chaos, where men like puppets were drifting between headlights and stinking exhausts, yelling orders, directing torches at faces and number plates. No one unapproved would pass! *No chance!*

But he no longer heard the cacophony of vehicles, trucks and tractors, men shouting in between the hum of running engines, blaring sirens, walkie-talkies, and storm gusts shaking the trees.

What he really heard and felt through all his being was the ambient crackling of fire, the continuous sound of explosions destroying his world up there. He sensed how the earth itself reared up in agony and trembled. A feral fury shot through his veins and discharged itself as a bloodcurdling growl. And although the brutish sound was absorbed by the turmoil at the gate, he picked up an intriguing response. His head spun around and his ears pricked up as he scanned an obscure area, further down the road.

"Meow!"

There! Again! The brave little cry came from the other side of the road, beyond the electric fence. It was where the massive old stone pines began their march all the way up into the mountains, forming a natural barrier. Suddenly a wild, an impossible, idea formed itself in his mind and quickly possessed him.

He glanced at the commotion at the entrance area, he counted the guards, observing their behavior, their level of attentiveness. The electricity – was it still on or had they switched it off? It did not make any sense with that fire but then one never knew. He estimated the distance, calculated the risk. He had once been a high-jump record holder for his class, but that was long ago and, in those early days, he didn't smoke. Within his contrasting emotions between bravado and hope, he felt a surge of fear: his mission would require an extraordinary performance. Would it be possible?

Time is running out . . .

Hidden in the shadows of overhanging shrubs and trees, he cautiously followed the road up to the point where the pines started. There he waited and watched, his heart pounding. His peripheral vision picked up a Siamese cat on the other side of the fence; her blue eyes staring straight at him. He found himself drawing comfort from her presence. He was not alone. His tension eased; he was in control again, feeling his energies flow. With his senses acutely alert, he absorbed everything happening around him – each movement; the slightest vibration; the topography; the vegetation; all the shapes and forms; the fence, its height and details, the different strands of electric wire – and encoded it all onto the memory card of his mind.

Then he imagined himself going through his paces. He counted the steps, feeling his feet on the asphalt and tasting its stale smell mixed with the sulphurous murk in the air. He rehearsed the crucial moment to lift himself off the ground into one gigan-

tic jump that would carry him higher and higher – with his gaze
fixed on that bright spot in the distance – and the earth's cracking inferno whistling past his ears. Now the exact moment to let
himself sink, going down in a controlled way, yet carried by an
exhilarating sense of achievement. And, finally, how to hit the
ground safely; knowing he had done it. His chest expanded with
joy; he sensed the sureness and the pleasure – and yes, he knew
he really could do it!

He breathed deeply, collecting himself. His vision was clear.
He optimized his body position. His focus eliminated all extra-
neous form.

*It is possible! Yes, I know it is! Let your mind be a fresh slate for
every step. Slow down to speed up.*

"Meow!" the cat cheered him on. *You are a winner!*

He gave a low hiss. Then his neurons started to fire and his
muscles contracted, ready to push themselves to the limits.
With a few powerful leaps – the perfect repetition of his mental
rehearsal – he flung himself to the other side of the street and
then up high . . . and higher over the fence . . . and then coming
down with control . . . and touching the ground . . . and diving
into the shadows, unseen.

The cat watched him bolt through the woods with shuttle-
blasting speed like a panther, racing against time, up into the
mountain, towards the blaze.

He knew the way well and soon reached the dirt road leading to the plot beneath his land but, as he stepped out of the
pine and eucalyptus forest, he stumbled back, overwhelmed:
the flames were lashing out so high that he could not even see
the rooftop of his house, not a tree or anything else! Spitting
sparks in all directions, the all-consuming heatwave made it impossible to get close to his land, at least not from the south. All
the fynbos was burning!

His world was disappearing, soon to be gone.

He stood and stared, frozen with disbelief. The air was acrid
with smoke, constricting his chest. He gasped for breath like a
fish on land, regurgitating the wine he'd had before. His head
started to throb and his delirious visions returned – merciless

and vivid. Fuming, the beast reared up in his face while he stood stock-still, filled with horror, and with a bizarre fascination, too.

That's when two uniformed men grabbed him, after their urgent calls did not filter through to him. Too shocked to resist, he surrendered to their firm grip. They pushed him forward, running, and then they lifted him onto the truck. He quickly looked back as a violent gust of wind spewed a cloud of ashes and red-hot sparks over the path behind them, where he had stood just a minute before.

"Man, are you mad?" one man barked as the other started the engine. "You wanna kill yourself or what?"

"That's my home!" Pete shouted, wedged between the two large men and suddenly wide awake.

"What?" The sergeant to his left snorted while stealing a last glance at the scene as the truck pulled away. "We're getting you right outta here before you burn your arse! One's gotta believe how freakin' crazy some guys are!"

The driver stopped at the intersection, changing gears to turn downwards, to the left.

"Stop!" Pete shouted, a rush of adrenaline invading his head. "Go right! Right!"

"What the . . ." the sergeant yelled, but Pete insisted: "We must go right, my wife's up there!"

"Bloody nonsense, man! You waste my time! We got'em all out! Turn left!"

Without any warning, Pete grabbed the steering wheel and blocked it with an iron grip. "Go right!" he growled, his level of despair and resolution sending chills down their spines. "You got wives? Kids? Do ya? You'd grill them, yes? My wife is due any moment and I know she's up there! You wanna kill mother and child?"

Bewildered, the driver looked at the sergeant.

What if it's true?

"Get out!" Pete's voice trembled on the brink of insanity. "While you look for your marbles I go it alone!"

"Marbles!" The sergeant cursed, motioning to the right with his head.

Tense beyond description, he suddenly started to giggle, his eyes red from exhaustion and smoke. Marbles!

This coming from him!

Pete released the wheel, perspiration beading all over his face. He heard how the guy to his left, who had just giggled like a madman, drew a threatening breath.

"If the lady ain't up there . . . Man, I'll wrap that shit-eating grin of yours right around your head. Is that clear?"

With his jaws tight, the driver turned right and the truck rumbled upwards, higher and higher, on what seemed to be the straight road to hell.

"Dankie . . . thank you," Pete muttered, his voice ragged with emotion. *Please God, don't let me be too late.*

Something had stirred her awake; but she closed her eyes in response to a pounding headache and, soon, the soothing blackness engulfed her again. Maybe it was a premonition – or her instinct – that made her listen just before she slipped back into comforting numbness: a trembling noise penetrated the muffled silence and shook the car. A generator? An earthquake?

Oh please, not again . . .

She placed her arms around her tummy. The growing life within her moved again; this time without pain. She sighed with gratitude, relaxing back in her seat. Whatever was happening outside – in here they were safe.

Suddenly, she winced. There was a painfully loud scratching noise; it came from the rear window. She squeezed her eyes open and – ever so slowly, with her heart pounding – lifted them towards the rearview mirror. An opening in the blanket of ashes appeared, invading the privacy of her igloo. She watched with disbelief as the hole rapidly grew bigger . . . and then she recognized the shape of a flower. It was their sign! It had to be Pete!

"Pete!" she called through her sore throat, blinded by the glaring light of a torch from the back. Her heart jumped with relief, but then her jaw dropped: the sky behind his silhouette was red. Reality trickled through her foggy recollection.

The fire! It was here!

She unlocked the doors and, within seconds, he was at her side. "Oh, my God, Grace! What are you doing here? I had no clue where you were! You never . . ."

"Sir," someone shouted down at him from a huge truck, with its lights on and the heavy diesel engine running. "You've got to go. We're moving in."

"Sure, Sergeant," Pete answered, as he heaved his wife from her seat.

The man jumped to the ground and came over, shock written all over his face.

"Thank you!" Pete shouted, "hey – sorry for insisting a bit much . . ."

"Damn glad you did," the man mumbled, still staring at Grace. "God alone knows how long this will take. Unless a . . . another miracle happens."

"Such as?" Pete asked, while helping his wife onto the passenger seat and closing the door behind her. She was coughing and struggling to breathe. The South-Easter had strengthened, whipping up new fires and whirling dust and ashes through the air. The firefighter's radio crackled. Communication was intermittent and difficult against the roaring noise of destruction echoing from the mountain. At times it broke off completely.

"Man, it's the wind," the man replied, coughing, as huge flames flared up near the manor house and a cloud of black smoke poured over the top of the pines.

"Unpredictable! Pray that it changes direction . . ."

Pete could not resist taking one last glance at their beautiful white home. It was shimmering innocently in the darkness while the entire mountain range was on fire, from Kommetjie all around to Chapman's Peak. The distant ocean had disappeared into total obscurity. He thought he saw a faint light, far out at sea. Probably a ship or perhaps a fishing boat. What a spectacular view they would have of the whole Cape Peninsula burning!

"Sir?" The sergeant sounded tense.

Pete returned to the car: "On my way." He wiped the sticky layer of ash off the windscreen, jumped behind the wheel and started the engine, lowering the side windows to clear them, too. The heat and smoke greedily invaded the car.

As he reversed, the tall firefighter walked through the light, holding up a hand to stop him. "Is this yours, sir?" he asked, bending down at his window and displaying a mobile phone in his hand. "Picked it up down there."

"My wife's. This explains a lot. Thank you, sir."

The man saluted briefly. "Will do, sir. Go straight down, keep to the left."

"Close call," he thought as the car disappeared in the ghastly landscape. But good to see new life on the way.

His radio crackled. "Ready!" he barked back and gave his orders: "Trucks, engines, oxygen! Tempo!" He switched over. "And gimme my damn cigarettes!"

Which, of course, nobody was supposed to hear . . .

"The wind has changed!"

Pete wasn't sure he had heard correctly. The positive news spread fast to all those assembled outside on the lawn in the farmhouse village area. They were waiting anxiously for the green light to return to their homes – or what was left of them. It all seemed unreal, like a scene one would expect in a movie, but not in real life. Nobody really knew what awaited them. Given the intensity of the fire the worst was assumed. During the past hours there had been nervous breakdowns and heart attacks in response to rumors and speculation as to which houses had already gone up in flames.

Pete tried to keep a clear mind and remain calm; what mattered most in his life was right here in his arms. Nothing . . . nothing could take that away from him! Once again, acting upon his intuition had proved to be the right thing to do. Only this time it wasn't ice but fire! Once again, it was in those crucial moments that their future destiny together was decided; the pendulum could have swung either way. Whatever they had to face during the next hours could be resolved over time. It would not be easy, but it could be done. The fact that the community had come together in amazing ways made the future look less grim for those worst hit. There would be help and support for anyone needing it. Within chaos and despair, a great human spirit prevailed; a sense of who they really were and what they were capable of, if they all stood together as one.

Noordhoek wasn't even on the map when they came – but yes, this was home . . .

He pulled Grace closer. She had dozed off in his arms. At times he could feel the baby move beneath his fingertips; they so much wanted this child! He just had to get them safely through the challenges ahead – and he knew she would not let him struggle alone.

He looked up and saw it had become much darker. The miracle had happened: the wind had turned and, finally, the blaze had abated. He could still see the glowing ring of fire higher in the mountains, but the intense heat waves rolling down into the valley had stopped. In fact, it was getting a little chilly from cool air blowing in from the sea. The morning would soon be dawning; it looked as if the sky had already become a bit lighter above the mountains. *Or was it his imagination?*

Another hour passed in nerve-wracking silence. One after another, stars became visible. Fortunately, the wind had dropped completely and the cool air from the sea was pleasant and refreshing. The sky beyond the mountains towards the east gradually took on a golden hue; this time it definitely was the rising sun. Honking briefly, the geese took off towards the swamps in the meadows.

"You may go up now, sir." Pete recognized the sergeant's voice, speaking softly behind him. The moment of truth had come.

"Let's go home," Grace said quietly yet determinedly, dismissing all possible objections right away.

Pete took the lead in her small car, with their neighbors driving right behind them. The first stretch looked quite normal. About one third of the way up the mountain, the air got thick and black with smoke. Soon the reddish brick road turned into a slippery mess of mud and ashes that had been deposited by the heavy trucks and fire engines. A huge hosepipe still lay on the left-hand side of the road – a reminder of the fiercest battle a whole army of courageous firefighters had possibly fought to date.

Their headlights danced across the road they traveled on daily. With their throats tight, they searched for familiar sights and claimed them back with a sigh.

The higher they climbed, the more brutal the devastation. Many of the old tree trunks along the road were burnt and still glowed, looking like ghosts. Black embers and clumps of charcoal covered the ground. The entire undergrowth had been consumed. Above them, yesterday's flamboyant flowering gums towered in black like widows in mourning. Through the sliding shadows, small isolated flames were gasping for oxygen, lapping like tongues from gurgling swamps and suffocated hotspots. As he navigated around heavy branches that had crashed down onto the road, he could only imagine the difficult task that lay ahead. And it had to be completed before the wind rose again.

It was not over yet.

The car behind them was following closely. Soon they would know. As they took the steep final turn they could hardly see anything ahead; the smoke was so thick they could have cut it with a knife. Eventually, their eyesight adjusted to the eerie landscape. There was an uneasy sense of openness, of space.

"Oh my . . ." Grace gasped: the entire pine forest on the mountain side was gone – right down to the road! It had simply disappeared, leaving a black and barren battlefield. Lifeless stumps and smoldering branches on bare ground revealed a new topography.

Pete drove slowly, trying to detect their neighbors' house to the right. Finally, there it was. The stone walls of the entrance gate were still there and, from what he could recognize from the road, the building, too. The question was: in what shape? They communicated with their cars' indicators and the lights behind them disappeared to the right.

Now it was them, alone.

"I still can't see it!" he thought to himself, getting agitated. The pine forest bordered their property; and as these trees pro-

liferated so profusely they had spread to the surrounding area –
only not as densely. To the left, everything was now reduced to
a field of coals, glowing embers, and minor fires that would die
down sooner or later as there was nothing left to burn.

"Look!" Grace whispered. Pete slammed on the brakes instantly, and she gasped.

"Damn, this stupid car! When will you get a real one!"

She just stared. There it was: slowly, the white entrance to
their property emerged from its ghastly surroundings.

"Damn," he mumbled, "this is unreal!"

"There was a big pine tree, just to the left of it . . ."

He nodded: "There was . . ."

He rolled slowly onto their land. The road was heavily
scarred with deep tracks and completely swamped with mud
and ashes, as if a river had come down. "This is unreal!"

"My palms!" Grace exclaimed as the palm alley appeared in
the spotlights of the car, one tree after the other, standing upright on both sides of the driveway.

It didn't take my palms!

"Holy smoke!" Pete shook his head with disbelief. "The
whole forest burnt down and it didn't touch your palms!"

It was still impossible to see the house. All was enveloped in
mysterious obscurity.

They both shrieked as, suddenly, an entire bush burst into
flame on the neighboring plot, sending sparks in all directions.
It kept exploding like a big fire cracker until it had consumed
itself.

"*Hakea.* Now the seeds will be all over the place." She tried to
pierce the shadows to the right with her eyes. Then she gasped,
raising her hands to stop him.

This time he stopped the car carefully. "Oh . . . that." Now
he saw it, too.

"My gazebo," she whispered, "it's gone!"

He rolled the window down. The smoke flooding in added
more acidity to the moment, so he closed it again.

"My books . . ." she stammered. "How could I have forgotten
them?"

He shot her a mystified look. In a moment like this, how could she think of such trivial stuff? "We've got the Internet; who needs books!"

She felt dizzy. If he knew . . .

Slowly, the reality of what she had lost sunk in: her happy reading space, hers alone . . . and with it her grandfather's botanical work, his notes, his drawings.

All the memories. It was irretrievable.

She gazed in abstraction until the car turned into the parking area. He stopped the engine and switched off the lights.

"Right!" he said tonelessly.

"Right!" She regained her composure and sat up straight, searching for his hand and finding comfort and warmth in it. Together, they stared at the dark forlorn space, where their house should be.

"I feel her heart racing in my hand," he thought. "It's so cold. Her blood pressure must have dropped." He pulled her hand to his lips with both of his and blew warmth onto it. She closed her eyes and felt his breath in her hand. She wanted to hide in those strong, warm hands . . . now that he had rescued her again. How would she ever be able to give back? And he so much wanted a . . .

"Oh boy!" He could not even see the silhouette of the roof, nor a glimpse of the dependable flash of light beaming over from Kommetjie lighthouse. Nothing. The entire landscape had disappeared behind a dark and impenetrable filter. It was just after 5:00 a.m., but the familiar early morning sounds from birds and cicadas were missing. Not even a hadeda's shriek echoing through the valley! Spellbound, they sat in a realm with no light and without sound.

"It's there!" Before he knew what she was doing, she had released his hand and left the car. She stood upright at the top of the outside stairs leading down to the house, her light dress flying in the morning breeze.

"It's there," she insisted, pulling the shawl tightly around her shoulders, while staring into absolute nothingness. She closed her eyes and drew a deep breath. I know it is!

Just before she, too, could disappear before his eyes, he joined her. "Everything's fine," she said firmly as he put his arm around her.

"If you say so . . ."

Together, step by step, they descended into whatever awaited them. The solidity of the stairs beneath their feet was reassuring: this was something real. And then, with each step they took, the familiar views materialized. Solemnly, they walked around the house, claiming it back.

"Look," she whispered, pointing at the sunbird's nest high up in the strelitzias on the terrace, untouched by the flames. "There was a little bird . . ."

"It was still empty," she heard him say as he opened the door. His voice sounded so far away.

He caught her just as her legs slipped away.

"Don't worry, my angel," he said softly, "all this will change!" Then he carried her inside.

The power of their love permeated Pippa's entire being and she felt herself soar with the tree's rising juices. With her heart still heavy from what she had witnessed, she was hardly prepared for this: the earth was scorched and scarred as far as her eyes could see. Charcoal stumps and broken pines protruded from it like petrified limbs from a forsaken sea.

A deafening noise erupted, breaking the silence, as three men armed with chainsaws and clad in protective orange overalls and rubber boots, closed in on the big old pine. They were cutting down burnt trees and removing all the black remains on the path. The ghastly skeletons crashed onto the ground, sending dust and ashes whirling up into the stagnant midday air.

A tall man separated from the others and headed for the pine, chainsaw in hand, leaving dark footprints on the ground.

As he approached, a colossal tremor ran through the old tree. From the tips of its roots through the trunk and up to the crown it took a deep breath. Then it froze.

Pine needles, that had bravely survived the fire, silently sailed down now . . .

Looking up from underneath its widespread branches, the man inspected it from different angles to estimate the damage. When he took his helmet off, Pippa's heart almost stopped.

"Oh Dad," she whispered, feeling his wrath, his determination, but also his pain. "Please not!"

Directing a clean-up of nightmare proportions over the past five days had taken its toll; he looked worn out and stressed and he had grown a beard. He saw that the trunk and the lower branches had been severely burnt, but that the rest had survived. The old warrior had to be close to thirty meters high. It would be a gigantic effort to fell it, not counting the cost in time and petrol. *Was it worth it?*

"Please, Dad!"

The man who never wept stepped into the deepest shadow and leant against the trunk. He wiped the sweat from his face, coughing and struggling for breath. His eyes were closed when, to his surprise, he felt a healing touch on his back. He drew a deep breath, stretching his body with his head high up against the bark. As he lifted his eyes to glance at the branches above him, his chest opened and he felt some relief for the first time in days.

But soon the sound of chainsaws drilled back into his consciousness. His eyes glazed as he looked across the land. The firestorm had burnt everything: all the fynbos and proteas, and almost all trees – but not anything Grace had newly planted. It was one of those things he failed to comprehend, especially seeing that the heat had even exploded rocks, killing anything that lived in cracks and crevices. Trapped tortoises' shells had melted while they were being burnt alive. He had found blackened skeletons everywhere, even of birds.

With winds blowing up to ninety kilometers per hour, the blaze had moved so fast that not even the pair of rapid duikers in their garden could outrun it. The smoke overtook them and led to disorientation and panic when their only escape routes were barred by fences. He found the graceful antelopes in the wire fence, their hooves completely burnt. He buried them quickly and never mentioned them to Grace.

A noise in the old pine tree jolted him out of his reverie. Two Egyptian geese were sitting high up on what remained of their nest, peering down at him hissing sadly. After watching each other for a while, he sighed, picked up his machine and walked away, putting his helmet back on.

Joining the two workers, he indicated that they should continue in another direction.

The old pine sighed with gratitude and recovered from a paralysis burnt into its core for all time. Once its juices had regained momentum, and Pippa emerged from her shock, she was carried higher until she reached the crown.

Oh, the light! This feeling of touching the sky, of expanding into a much wider awareness! Now she could see with her soul!

And as she gazed across the vast burnt land there was a sense of awakening everywhere: fire lilies in bursts of red thrust themselves through the charred crust, leaving the blackness behind. It was not long before the sudden explosion of color attracted the Table Mountain Beauty. Welcoming Nature's way of letting go of the past, the butterfly absorbed life's sweetness from curved perianth tubes.

Then, suddenly, Pippa's vision started to spin, faster and faster, until it all blurred. There was a pushing and pulling that felt familiar and raw at the same time, but before she could give it any further thought, she was ejected from her space of oneness, warmth and bliss, into the adventure of a new life!

"We should call her Phoenix," Dad said, admiring his baby daughter in her mother's arms.

Mom smiled: "She's our African princess."

"I know you like 'Patricia'. How about 'Patricia Phoenix'?"

"That suits her well," she agreed. "Patricia Phoenix it will be!"

"Pippa in short . . . for me," he grinned.

"That's where we all come from anyway," he added with a twinkle. "Just a little pip!"

"A seed!" She kissed her newborn daughter tenderly on her soft warm head.

"It holds the whole universe within it," she whispered and the melody of her birth song started to flow over her lips . . .

"Pippa!" Mom was calling, accompanied by Piu Piu's loud and agitated voice. Pippa shifted instantly back into the here-and-now; the rain and the storm. "I'm here, Mom," she replied, a little disoriented and not overly enthusiastic about being pulled from her journey into the past. She bent forward and stretched her legs. How long had she been here?

Mom appeared underneath the pine, wrapped in her poncho, with an umbrella in her hand. "So here you are! Piu Piu made a big fuss until I followed her. Are you okay?"

"Happy Birthday!" Piu Piu trumpeted from a safe distance, swaying on her toes and doing her best to flap her wings.

"Com'on, Piu Piu, we know it's soon. We won't forget it," Mom reassured her, while MadMax shook off pine needles and arched his back, intrigued by the steam that lingered around his nose and frosty whiskers like a fleeting puff of smoke.

Pippa got up, shivering. She had not felt the freezing air before, but now it suddenly hit her. "I'm fine," she said, her teeth clattering, while Mom rubbed her down.

Satisfied that she was all dry, even her hair, Mom glanced up into the tree, shaking her head with disbelief: "The driveway is a river; it poured in through the roof – and here you sit outside and you didn't even get wet! This pine must be *your* tree, my sweetheart. It really took good care of you!"

As she looked at Pippa, she was puzzled by the silent exchange between the goose and the girl; they hardly listened.

"Com'on," she clapped her hands and spurred them on, "let's get into the house before anyone catches a cold!" She turned and took the lead back home.

Piu Piu followed with a limping gait, much slower than usual.

"What's going on with her?" Pippa waited for Piu Piu to catch up. "How did she know about my birthday? Is she a seer? Are animals psychic?" She watched her closely, feeling her heart ache with sudden sadness. "She's changed. Since that day when we found each other in the mist she's no longer the same."

CHAPTER ELEVEN

Rite of Passage

It was a mild summer's night beneath the twinkling stars of the Milky Way. A shadow sailed past and landed on the flowering strelitzias, high above what had once been an island in a now parched dam.

"Woo-hoo!" Surprised, the owl turned her head and focused her hypnotic glare on the solitary goose below.

Night after night, Piu Piu had been standing guard on the terrace in front of the house. Tonight, however, she had returned to her favorite spot at the dam.

It had been another boiling hot day and she was exhausted. Balancing on one leg, her eyes closed drowsily as she drifted back to some happy memories of being there just after rains. Once again, she absorbed the coolness rising from the bottomless dam, blissfully oblivious of her right wing hanging out to the side much more than ever – a sword that had become too heavy to bear.

She gave off a hoarse quack in response to the owl, neither changing her position nor taking her attention off the movements in the dimly lit kitchen behind her.

Mom was finishing her domestic chores, preparing for the next day. A tempting aroma of freshly baked poppy-seed muffins hung in the air. As she put them aside to cool off overnight, she brushed the crumbs into her hand. When she turned towards the window she paused, astonished to see the familiar silhouette at the dam, and disturbed by her strange behavior: the goose was holding her head just above her usual drinking spot and seemed to be taking a few long sips from where there used to be water. Then she stretched her neck upwards to let the fluid run into her throat. She stood like that for a while, with her eyes closed.

"It moves around me," Piu Piu thought, "it's all one. There's so much light!"

"You're allowing it in," the heron's voice echoed. "Now you're in sync with your animal nature."

"She must be in pain . . ." Mom sighed. "Let's see if she still reacts." The moment Piu Piu heard the noisy sash window, she turned and spread her wings, limping up the small mound to get a bedtime treat.

"You like poppy-seed crumbs, too, don't you!" Mom watched the goose gobbling up the crumbs on the ground. She gave her some more. "Are you watching at the dam tonight?"

Piu Piu quacked a whole long story in response, devouring each crumb.

"Yes, yes, yes . . . I understand," Mom replied, gazing across the empty dam, "the terrace must still be steaming hot from the day."

Piu Piu glanced up at her and started to turn in circles, slanting heavily to one side.

Mom observed it quietly and played the game, giving her another round. She noticed how the light glistened on her feathers and an occasional wisp of wind played in her down. "You are so beautiful, Piu Piu," she told her fondly. "God must have had you deep in his heart to give you silky feathers like these . . . in shades of gold . . . and white . . . and dark . . . and a tender touch of green. So unique. A special gift just for you. Just for you!"

Piu Piu had stopped her pirouettes and listened to Mom's warm voice showering her with love. Her chest vibrated with emotion and her eyes shone.

"Good night, Piu Piu," Mom said softly. Piu Piu wished she could prolong the magical moment. Oh, if Mom could continue to speak to her for just a little while longer, so she could cuddle up in the kindness of her voice!

"Tomorrow will be your special day!"

There was the familiar squeak as Mom pulled the old sash window down.

Piu Piu ruffled her feathers and turned her attention back to the ground, pecking up a few lost crumbs and swallowing her loneliness with them. Then she waddled back to the dam, dragging her wing along.

Hidden in the obscurity of her kitchen, with a growing lump in her throat, Mom watched her go.

Much later, when everybody was fast asleep, the moon emerged from behind the mountains. As its silvery light filtered into the garden, the warbling voice of a fiery-necked nightjar rose, comforting the goose at the dam.

Piu Piu searched in vain for her reflection in the water.

"I must be dreaming," she thought, "I'm not here." Closing her eyes, she raised her head into the soothing moonlight, taking a deep breath. As the cool air entered her lungs, she felt it: that subtle change within. Oh, she remembered it well. With each inhale she tuned in more and aligned with the trusted energy. With each breath out she felt a greater ease of mind. Although the process filled her with a deep sadness, her soul unfurled itself into a graceful state of release.

Lighter than ever, she lifted herself from her body and sensed her way through the house. The walls drifted slightly apart – just enough for her to slip through. She had done this before, hovering above Pippa's bed for a while and watching her stir in her dreams. MadMax usually twitched one ear to acknowledge her presence, knowing that, after a few minutes, she would disappear.

Tonight, however, everything was different.

She landed ever so gently next to the girl and snuggled up to her on her bed. Immersed in the warmth of her space and thought waves, she watched her features, listening to her heart, her breath. In her peaceful slumber, Pippa put her arm around her, with her fingertips touching her angel wing.

A soulful tremor ran through the goose.

"My sweetheart," Pippa whispered, "I see the hourglass is turning upside down. Memories like golden sand are drifting past your timeless mind . . . spiraling into the light . . . up, up and away . . ."

Piu Piu's eyes closed as she listened to Pippa's entrancing voice. Time began to consume itself as the pictures of that other night drifted back before her eyes. The heat, the fire and that unbearable moment when her father honked in despair, spreading his wings to escape the flames . . . and then her mom did the same. Abandoned, alone, she started to tremble, feeling the burning presence of the pine. Frozen with fear, she sat up, suffocating and gasping for air, too eager to escape.

"Remember," Pippa hushed her gently, "you are eternal. We all go through flames."

Unable to move, never mind to fly, Piu Piu's body quaked with tension.

"Do not resist," Pippa continued, reliving it all herself. "Slowly, slowly allow it to flow through you and complete. Observe it, let it go."

Clinging to Pippa's voice like a lifeline, Piu Piu tried to release her pain, but her head jerked violently as she struggled with energies beyond her control.

"Breathe . . . keep breathing . . ."

Despite her inner rebellion, Piu Piu realized that only when her body relaxed, her mind could follow. Only then, gradually, her resistance melted away.

"Feel . . ."

"I betrayed you," Piu Piu whispered, "you who I love."

"Feel the eternal flow . . . "

"I cannot forgive myself."

"Get out of your own way."

"How I wish I could."

"Let go. Remember who you are."

Sobbing softly, Piu Piu settled down and stretched into the energy of Pippa's love, the tip of her beak nestling under her curls, close to her ear. "Who am I now?" she suddenly thought. "Who have I become to feel the desire for life so intensely? What's preventing me from simply taking the path of least resistance? Am I not just a goose?"

Like a river, Pippa's mesmerizing voice carried her onwards: "Do you smell it, the fragrance of the pine?"

Piu Piu sighed. A tear dropped from her eye. *I'm almost there. Only one more thing I desperately need to know . . .*

"See the golden sap dripping from the bark. Hear a gentle murmur lulling you to sleep. Sinking deeper into the comfort of your nest, you feel the sunshine on your back . . . warming you. Nurturing you . . ."

With Pippa's voice reaching deep into her soul, Piu Piu felt a touch that was profoundly familiar, and good. Leaning into this exhilarating sensation, her heart suddenly jumped: from the soft white feathery fluff around her appeared her mother's head, peering down at her tiny gosling with love and pride. It filled Piu Piu with joy and a sense of belonging she thought she had never known.

"Remember," Pippa said in her sleep, "you are deeply loved."

Piu Piu just floated in her acceptance, her trust, her bliss. And when she eventually lifted her head she met the tomcat's mischievous glance. "Nothing beats a warm nest," he purred, putting on the haughty grin that had driven her up the wall at times, but now? She just stretched her head towards him and blew out a kiss of hot air.

Somewhere close by an owl hooted.

Piu Piu got clumsily back on her feet. Her eyes flooded with tears as, one last time, she looked at the beloved being, unable to leave just yet.

"I love you," she said and a smile glided across Pippa's face.

"As do I love you," Pippa replied in her dream, "we all do! We admire you. You've been our teacher for eons of time. Oh, and we love it when you make us laugh. We've been missing that for a while . . ."

"I did not forget," Piu Piu whispered. "You'll see . . ."

Then she rose into the air, spreading her perfect wings.

He had been observing the goose every night as she stood guard on the terrace – confident, unreachable and strong. But tonight she was not there. The big cat sneaked through the shadows, his black tufted ears picking up the slightest sound. Instinctively, he knew where she was.

"Woo-hoohoo!" The owl, greedy for drama, turned and glared down at the covert arrival.

The sly ambusher immediately spotted the goose. There she was, on her favorite spot where once the water's edge had been. Caked, cracked and bristling with bits of rugged rock face and isolated pockets of parched reeds, the dam yawned at him – empty and dry. Instead of scintillating on the mirror surface of the pond, the moonlight crept across the broken earth and jagged structures, succumbing to ennui.

She was just some ten meters away from him, a solitary goose staring onto the ground. He watched her with a mixture of cautiousness and confusion: was she not aware of his presence? Was she not conscious of the imminent danger? What could be hidden in the dust that she so totally ignored him – her ultimate defeater?

Nothing in Piu Piu's withdrawn composure revealed her inner ecstasy: all around her in the dam the wild Egyptian geese were rising! They were lifting themselves from the earth and from the shadows, stretching their heads upwards towards her, honking and cheering. Her entire clan was there!

The caracal stood perfectly still, his pupils contracted to pinpricks. As the wind blew through the vegetation, his reddish-fawn coat gleamed briefly in the light. He hesitated, observing the goose carefully. Somehow she appeared different, both in her structure and presence – or rather, the absence thereof. She seemed ethereal, she lacked substance.

He grinned gleefully and his mouth watered; she would be an easy target and become the feast he had been visualizing for three years! A stream of energy shot through the stealthy muscles of his legs. He stretched his toes and clawed the ground. His short tail twitched in anticipation; finally his patience and perseverance would pay off! From the moment he had seen her, something deep within his entrails knew this day would come. Although he had to admit he was taken aback, if not disappointed, that it would be so easy. He loved the thrill of the kill! Be that as it may, the time had come; there was no escaping him. He would simply launch into the air using his strong hindquarters and limbs, covering the distance between them in a flash and taking her by surprise. He would be so fast she would not be able to take off in time; and even if . . . he would simply pluck her from the air!

However, being so blatantly ignored – and this by a goose – really annoyed him! What was she staring at with empty eyes? His stomach rumbled and saliva ran from his snout, yet still, he hesitated. Something irritated him; that fine haze vibrating in the air, an invisible twist, a whirlwind out of nowhere sweeping up dust.

"Piupidoooo!" Piu Piu's voice cracked right above him, like an invitation to the dance.

He leapt up and ducked into the thicket in an instant reflex. Incredulous, he tried to distinguish the goose amongst the branches of the tree, but all he could see was a vague silhouette. It could be anything.

"Alrrrrrightttt!" Now it came mockingly from the dam.

The ferocious beast spun around and flung himself towards the goose just as she was taking off into the air. Handicapped and slow, she should have been easy prey, but the surge of countless invisible wings synchronistically flapping the air swiftly carried her out of reach.

The caracal howled with anger; how was it possible he had missed that stupid bird? He could not accept it; she had to be there still! With his energies exploding, he spun himself around and up in the air – a warrior on the loose fighting with his shadow.

Gliding calmly through the air, Piu Piu saw a spawn of energy bounce across the dam just as the geese left it, as they receded in rhythmic waves, lifting themselves into the air, rising, and spiraling upwards higher and higher to join her.

Disturbed by the turbulence and dust, the owl flew away, her shadow gliding across the dam. Confused, the caracal stopped in his tracks. Drilling his claws into the ground and uttering a spine-tingling hiss, he turned his head to scan the place where the goose had been. It appeared to him that something of her still hovered there, a fine luminosity, a wisp of presence. He crouched; he was going to have her, every bit of her! But as the dust settled, he realized no one was there.

No one but himself.

Frustrated, he leapt up the embankment and scanned the sky. His stomach rumbled, reminding him that his dinner could not remain in the air forever. Soon he spotted a lone goose flying with apparent difficulty. It had to be her. He licked his snout.

"The game ain't over, yet . . . Princess!"

Piu Piu was floating placidly in the air. The soothing sound of many wings behind her was cradling her.

Oh, the freedom! To touch it again, to sense what it would be!

Intoxicated, she hardly perceived the slumbering landscape that swept past below her. She just let herself be – and she did not know or even care how much she was still part of any physical form at all.

Hidden in the darkness, her killer waited. But the malicious delight on his face changed to that of surprise, if not disbelief, when the goose turned and flew directly towards the big pine.

"Nah . . . You not gonna go back there? Com'on, it scared the hell out of you all your life!"

He growled: was it possible that she'd got away once again? With her, one just never knew! It was not the first time she'd escaped him. Her courage had often amazed him. Keeping close to the bushes, he followed her shadow as it moved across the lawn and the paths.

The veil is getting thinner. Soon, soon I'll be free!

Piu Piu pumped herself up while her heart was racing, and the blood receded in her veins. Her lungs expanded as she invited the cool night air to take all she was. She became lighter and lighter and she rose higher, her eyes fixed on the pine – but beyond that daunting final hurdle her soul already embraced the light. *I am that, I am.*

"Free! Free!" the invisible chorus echoed while she headed towards her past, the place where it all began, like recognizing it for the very first time.

The huge tree groaned with emotion and opened its branches wide.

There it was: her nest, so close now and warm, and radiating a core of love. Piu Piu closed her eyes and released her deepest breath, extending her wings one last time. The old pine trembled as her feathered body tumbled through its branches . . . down . . . down . . . all the way to the ground. Into the silence.

With a loud triumphant growl, the caracal was instantly upon her and cracked her throat.

"Piu Piu!"

Pippa jolted up in her bed, tears spilling from her eyes.

"You're dreaming," MadMax whispered into the darkness, "go back to sleep."

"I'm not dreaming!"

"OK . . ."

"I'm sure it was . . ."

"Yes?"

"She could fly!"

"That's awesome!"

"She looked so happy!"

"So why do you cry?"

"I don't know."

After a moment she added: "Perhaps you were right."

"Is there a difference anyway?"

"Not really."

"Happy dreaming then!" He yawned and yawned until she yawned, too. He waited until her breathing eased; then turned his head in the direction of the big pine. Slowly, the silhouette of the tree with many branches peeled from the night.

"Do you see her?" Pippa whispered. "She's on the lowest branch."

"Yes."

"Just above . . . oh no!"

"Watch! The geese – they're everywhere!"

"They've all come!"

"Her whole clan!"

"They're so quiet; what are they're waiting for?"

"I dunno . . ."

"Shhh! Look at her!"

Piu Piu perched on a branch just above her killer, translucent and bathed in a bluish light. She watched him tearing her body apart, piece by piece, her feathers flying all over the place.

"Alright," she started off in a casual tone, "have my flesh. You'll never get my soul!"

He was not going to be fooled again, so he ignored her while he continued to deplume her, avidly drinking the blood spurting from her throat.

"Tastes divine?" she inquired, putting her head to the side and watching as he devoured her damaged wing as a starter.

"I never doubted your taste," he grunted, while her bones were cracking under his jaws. "Oh, sweet memories . . . They are the salt on today's meal!" He chewed them up completely then went straight for the other wing. Basking in the glory of his victory, he deliberately took his time. He licked his muzzle with relish once he had finished, and then he licked his paws.

Nothing ever tasted that good!

"Alright!" She sounded relieved. "That being out of the way, I would suggest you try my breast!"

"Funny you should mention that," he hissed. "Take it easy. I'm getting there!" Holding her carcass firmly between his claws, he ripped her breastbone apart and dived into the raw and tender flesh, closing his eyes in delight. "I always wanted your heart," he hissed, "I feel it beating on my tongue . . ."

"I know where my best parts are," she noted matter-of-factly; his carnal feast left her completely cold. "And you haven't even tasted the best part yet!"

"Ah?" The caracal looked up, perplexed, with blood dripping from his fangs. "What would that be?"

"Watch out, Charlot, you may seek what's seeking you!" she tweeted.

"Tell me . . . your best . . .?"

"Kiss my pokemon!" she breathed, touching his nerve.

"Ah! I've been waiting for that for a long time!" he grinned, turning her in his claws.

"Here's to your royal butt, Princess!" – with that he bit her butt off and munched it with closed eyes.

"Hmmm, so sad you've only got one of them; wish there were more."

"I'm flattered," she cooed. "What does the gourmet say?"

The caracal belched with utmost pleasure. "Out of this world, so deliciously tender. A slight flavor of lemon thyme, rosemary and . . ." He paused.

". . . and??" she whispered, breathlessly.

"and . . ." his eyes still closed, he was melting away.

". . . *escargots?*" she asked enticingly.

"Escar-what?" he asked blankly.

"Snails, stupid!"

"Ha!" he laughed, finishing his meal and spitting the mauled stomach away in disgust. This triggered an instant tremor in Piu Piu; she watched with bated breath. While the big cat contentedly spread the toes of his paws, licking up her last juices, she scanned the scattered pieces of her spurned organ. By now, her whole being was vibrating with anticipation.

Then she spotted it! Surrounded by a bluish halo, and shimmering from inside, it was moving ever so lightly on the blood-soaked earth: *The magic seed!*

It was breathing. It expanded. The seed coat burst and a root emerged, anchoring itself in the ground.

"I always wondered why you were so mad about that slimy pest," she heard him say from far away, pulling her from her contemplation. "I prefer them in your butt."

"I thought you would." With a note of subliminal ecstasy trembling in her voice, she whispered: "Want more?"

"More?"

He growled greedily, looking straight up at her: "I always want more!"

Plofffffffff! A big round of goose shit teeming with snails landed right on his face and more followed.

"More! More! More!" Piu Piu honked and kept the loads coming. "All for you! All for you!"

She was fired up by the cheers from all the other geese who were watching the scene from above her in the pine, stretching their necks and honking. The tree was vibrating.

The caracal did not know where to turn. He was bombarded with snails until they were all over him, even in his ears, on the tip of his nose and under his tail. He howled, boiling with rage and indignation; the creepy-crawlies were driving him mad.

Jeering and jokes echoed from everywhere in the garden.

Soaked, dripping with goose shit and blood, he scratched, jumped and rolled on the ground, snarling and snorting in disgust. As if that weren't enough, now he had Piu Piu's plumage plastered all over him and resembled a feathered faun! He yelped, wishing he could disappear in the ground.

"Hehehe," giggled the mongoose from a safe distance, "long live the goose!"

"A goose! A goose!" The words echoed through the pine. "Show us how you fly!"

The mythical garden exploded with laughter. The old tree bent over and Piu Piu had to hold on to her branch.

Mortified, the caracal sneaked back into the shadows and the curtain of obscurity closed.

"Piupidoo!" Piu Piu trumpeted, "thank you, Charlot! Thank you, each one of you!"

A thundering ovation spiraled up into the night. The geese were flapping their wings and honking with mirth. The old pine almost levitated.

One last time, the caracal appeared in the moonlight, majestic and strong. "*In the end,*" he growled, "*everything is a gag.*" Then he was gone.

"The game is up," Piu Piu called out. "Time to go home!"

A sudden flurry of wings whirled Piu Piu's feathers from the ground and swept her into the air, lifting her higher and higher, beyond the tip of the old pine, past the magic mountain, higher and higher, until she was just another luminous dot in the star-strewn night.

CHAPTER TWELVE

Into the Light

Oh, the freedom of being!

Exhilarated, relieved of all weight, she drifted towards the brilliant light, filled with a deep knowing and trust. The closer she got the wider it stretched, extending to infinity. Once its shimmering veils of whiteness enveloped her, a sense of timelessness expanded her soul. She hardly noticed when the familiar whirring of wings around her faded and the sounds of a celestial symphony that had always resonated within her, carried her on. Tears welled up in her eyes and when she wiped them away she realized that she did so with her fingertips. She became aware of her hands and arms. She felt her legs and feet washed by billowing clouds. She was becoming herself again: a unique spiritual being transcending earthly form.

As she floated through the supreme luminescence that words cannot describe, she picked up a familiar vibration. She knew he was there even before his upright stature and finely chiseled features appeared. Wearing translucent garments held by a silver belt, he was shining from inside. The magnetic pull was irresistible; it had to be him, Eiji!

"Welcome back, Anata."

His instant response crashed through her like a wave. "I must be dreaming," she thought as his eyes reached into her. "I waited so long."

Before she knew it, he had wrapped his energy around her. "You're waking up, my love."

"How I missed you," she sobbed, overwhelmed with emotion. "This unbearable longing. The loneliness. Pain."

"You are now here," he whispered tenderly, releasing her chignon to let her curls flow freely around her face. "It was just a moment. The wink of an eye."

"It's been an eternity to me."

She moved slightly away from him, taking with her a trail of his magnetic blue light. For some unknown reason, vague wisps of memories cascaded through her mind: yellow puffs of mimosa sinking onto a pond . . . drifting across the moonlit mirror of the night; a blue heron eclipsing the sky; a lonely goose lost in white . . .

All this happened so long ago . . .

With her eyes closed, and still trembling inside, she spread her arms upwards, her face bathed in light. Inhaling slowly, deeply, she felt its healing warmth stream over and through her, washing all heaviness away.

"I'm back!" At last, she felt realigned with the sublime forces permeating the eternal Now. "I am where I belong."

He was delighted to see that fiery sparkle returning to her eyes. Her whole being began to vibrate. He could hardly wait to begin a new life journey with her – and only with her – again.

There was an enthusiastic round of applause and cheers as, gradually, the other members of the close-knit group appeared. Depending on whether they, too, had completely returned into this realm, or whether they were just a fleeting presence through a dream, their energy patterns pulsated at different frequency levels, most of them manifesting in dim or brighter hues of white and blue. They had come to welcome her home, showering her with light.

One graceful figure was almost transparent yet filled with so much excitement that her energies swirled and flashed: it was Pippa. As she came towards Anata, brimming with joy and with an aura of blossoms and tendrils surrounding her, it was obvious that they were twins.

"You little devil!" She giggled as they hugged. "I will have to come up with something super spiffy to match your outrageous coup!"

"I won't go back anytime soon," Anata replied. "Thank you for being so kind and forgiving. I felt really bad. I still do."

"Relax," Pippa laughed, "I, we – me and my control freak – were giving you a pretty rough time."

"Oh, I could've easily spent my whole life on your foot!" Anata basked in the atmosphere of trust with no hidden thoughts nor any malice. "I needed that kick to break free."

"Hey! You deserve mega kudos for who you became . . . from a timid start to a fearless finale! Earth is a daunting place to be, you know!"

"Tell me about it!"

"Pancakes, pancakes all the way!" A tenor intoned and before Anata knew what was happening, she disappeared into his massive hug. "*O sole, 'o sole mio, sta nfronte a te . . .*" he continued to sing, putting his other arm around Pippa and pulling her close, while the musical notes kept spiraling in the air.

"Oh, my Pasharotti!" Pippa beamed with bliss. But soon she noticed that his energies were dwindling. "Please," she whispered, "just hang in there a little longer. We love to hear your voice!" But he was a big spender and she could literally see him slip away and disappear.

"I won't last forever either," she thought, eager to follow, but Anata held her back: "Don't you dare leave me just yet!"

She smiled, feeling their vibrant thought forms flow in complete sync: "I never will." They absorbed each other's energy presence for a moment, until Pippa suddenly laughed: "And then, who left whom behind anyway? I will cry my eyes out once I wake up and see you're gone!"

"You'll get over it," Anata winked. "You still have him!"

"Also," she added, apologetically, "our time is determined."

"I know," Pippa laughed. "You packed it to the limits! We will never forget your finale: offering yourself as a feast to make us laugh! It was your best departure ever!"

"There was more to it," Anata whispered. "Much more. You'll find that out one day."

Pippa looked at her lovingly. "Another secret?"

"I wonder," Anata said, "whether you will notice when I sneak into your life and whisper in your ear?"

"How could I not?" Pippa replied, her gaze drifting off to a greyish mass of energy molding from undulating space.

"Look who's here," she said in a low voice. "At least, he tries."

Anata recognized the turbulence he always caused within her, even before he appeared. She stood tall and composed, her arms folded across her chest. The picture of the silver airplane drawing a line across the sky came back into her mind. A web of treacherous clouds floating steadily towards a shore washed by a weeping sun. She shivered when his flight uniform and cap emerged from shimmering waves and their eyes met in a void.

"Forget pancakes, my girl," he tried his charm, panting. He was neither quite here nor there, but rather awkwardly, if not hilariously, suspended between the physical and spiritual realm.

She watched him, unmoved.

"Hmmm . . . forget it," he grumbled, patting his pockets for cigarettes. "Damn." It dawned on him that there were none.

"Anyone gotta smoke for me?" He looked around, staring suspiciously at the nondescript energy patterns with no physical extensions that were floating all around him.

Where am I anyway?

He turned back to Anata: "Is this heaven or what? And not even a smoke?" Gesticulating with his arms and hands, he was immediately lifted upward, which amused him. He kicked his feet – with the result that now he was aloft in the air.

"Here we go again," he chuckled, rising higher, higher. "Ha! I see the earth," he proclaimed loudly. "At last something real in the quantum soup. Now let's check Uncle Pete's parachute."

'Woomph!' He plopped down, got out of balance, stumbled and cursed. "Damn! I'm outta here! Heaven is a bad dream!"

"Wait!"

He recognized her voice immediately. Where was she? He gaped with sheer disbelief as some insignificant fragments of light transformed into a veiled African woman, her ebony features shrouded in white.

As she turned to look at him, her eyes flashed.

"Ha! So here's where you're hiding," he grinned, succumbing to her blue eyes, "on your magic mat again." His eyes wandered to Anata, giving her an appraising look. "That wasn't bad, my girl," he said, "not bad at all." As she remained silent he added, with a few whimsical chuckles: "For a duck *nogal!*"

She stood firm, breathing deeply, her hair flying untamed in the air. A lunatic greed lit his eyes as he looked her up and down a few times before exploding with laughter: "But you still have no meat on your bones!"

"Don't forget, Captain," she shot back, "all I got from you were snails!"

While everyone burst out laughing and welcomed Dad, Anata dived into Mom's arms. There was a gorgeous glow around her – the same blue as her eyes.

"I will never forget my last supper," she whispered, absorbing Mom's energy and thought waves. Oh, to see and feel each other, being just oneself! No fear of hidden agendas, no doubts or the need to be wrong or right or however one was supposed to be. No expectations, just a sublime aliveness exactly in the way one was.

From the corner of her eye, she observed an androgynous being somersaulting through light and flipping around the group, accompanied by a sound wave that darted through space in crackling circles and curves. It triggered a vague memory within her, soon to be absorbed by Dad's boisterous voice.

"Even in heaven I'd still go for a duck," he went on and on, shaking with laughter, pulling everyone along.

"And miss her as last time!" Mom and Pippa came to Anata's rescue.

"I'll get her," he thundered, amongst lots of merriment. "I'll darn get her in *some* life . . . but first gimme a smoke!"

"Your flight captain is speaking," Anata joked, now completely relaxed. "Always his life purpose at heart!"

"New role! New life!"

Everyone shouted and cheered as Dad faded away, protesting wildly: "To hell . . . I go again! Too bad, my lovelies, I gotta leave you now for a bit. I better first finish with this . . ."

"Deliciousssssss!" The sleek silhouette continued to somersault with endless energy, wrapping itself in trails of electric blues. Now and then it came to a brief halt, its limbs vibrating into stillness and a pair of empty eyes staring in reverse – like a *robo sapiens*.

"Oh, you!" Anata exclaimed, recognizing the lizard from her early days as a gosling. "I see where your energy went once you could no longer spy on me and pinch my food!"

She looked around for her other childhood friends: "Where are the killer monsters? Oh, and the tiny take-away freaks?"

"They need all their energies on earth," Eiji answered, "the rest is dormant here." And even before she could think or ask her next question, he'd already answered it: "And the roller is busy hanging himself."

"Again?"

"Again!"

She looked at him thoughtfully for a moment, overwhelmed by the depth of her emotion – inside herself and undulating around her. Now all was one. "You had a good time, checking it all out from a cloud while I -"

"Anata," he responded as her thoughts instantly entered him. "I love you. This will never change. But remember you chose that life, and its radical challenges, for your own growth. A life filled with emotion and limitation. You wanted the experience. The animal energy pattern and perspective. The vulnerability of an orphan searching for love, crushed by the most debilitating handicap imaginable for a bird. Besides, of course, no ego."

"Enough," she sighed, "I know I messed up pretty well."

"No, no. That's not true," he objected. "No one could have played this better than you in a world ruled by fear. Having the courage to turn around . . ."

His eyes tenderly embraced her face. How fragile she had become. This time, more than ever before, life had taken its toll.

"And I so much wanted to show you the spring blossoms in Kyoto . . ." Closing his eyes, he shifted right into that moment.

" . . . and the maple leaves . . ." she smiled.

Together, they floated through a dream of red and golden autumn leaves, teased by sparkles of light and a soft rustling of the wind.

"Anata . . ."

The sound of her name vibrated in the air, transforming into letters of light. A burst of ecstasy rushed through her and she opened her eyes. Through the fading autumn colors, the letters split into fractals. They were coming closer, resembling opalescent shells. Soon they were whirring all around her: snails!

Trailing wisps of light behind them, they pointed their tentacles at her, touching and tickling her, while their shimmering shells rotated with a gentle chime.

"Shame on me for what I did to you!" She tried to catch them but they slipped away. She burst into laughter.

"Who does this?"

She did not need to ask. She knew. It could only be one.

"All for you!" The others laughed. "Want more?" Everyone had fun with the harmless weirdos that looked at them from the eye spots at the tips of their tentacles, occasionally opening their abysmal mouths, filled with thousands of teeth.

"Looksssssss!" the sleek lizard-lady hissed, backflipping through misty veils, disappearing and emerging while painting a big white flower into the air.

Pippa was watching her and applauded when the shape of a small man with a bowler hat, a cane and wide trousers emerged from the center of the flower. As he wobbled closer, everyone stopped and turned. "*Escargots?*" he asked a few times, twitching his toothbrush moustache and lifting his hat to greet them.

He put his hand to his ear until the "Ohhhs" and "Ahhhs" came, nodding invitingly. Then he raised his cane and exclaimed: "*Escargots!* Welcome Piu Piu, the legend of Noordhoek!"

The vibrating creatures spiraled high into the luminous realm, bursting into millions of particles reflecting the light . . . then uniting to create a rainbow. Everybody stood, spellbound.

"The blue flower!" Pippa gasped. No one else seemed to notice that the white had turned into a dazzling blue – the exact color of her dreams.

"It's real," she whispered, absorbing the image as she herself faded away. "I knew it. I will always –"

Then she was gone.

Lifting his hat, the small man turned towards Anata, bowing slightly: "In her darkest night she remembered her soul's plan and followed her inner light: The one and only Piu Piu!"

Into the thundering ovation he added, with genuine admiration and a tongue-in-cheek smile: "You just did it again, Princess! A real pleasure to *play* with you!"

"Thank you for giving me that chance," Anata replied, "there would be no play without all players." She continued, with a mischievous smile, "I may have taken it a little far. Are we square?"

"You lost your fear of death – and I my appetite for geese," he grinned. "For that particular experience of life, that is," he added with a fierce growl and pirouetted, with a swing of his cane. Then he leant towards her and whispered, with a devilish twinkle, only for her to hear, "Normally, I don't leave anything on the table!"

Enjoying the expression of utter shock on her face, he lifted his hat and bowed: "Until we meet again!"

"Until we meet again," she repeated vacantly, blown away by his revelation. When she emerged from her shock she said, with a spirited smile, "Then we shall turn the tables!"

"Woo-hoo!" a tall man with feathers in his silvery hair commented, bowing first to the man with the hat, then turning towards Anata, placing his right hand on his heart. Everyone else followed him, floating around her and lifting her up.

"And she sure made us laugh!" A jolly fellow with glittering eyes and a high-pitched voice giggled. "She had us waiting until the very last minute, the witch!"

"Our differences are not destined to separate us," said the blind poet who stood like a timeless statue within all the movement, his face lit up, the epitome of joy. "They are the wings that lift us up, up. And – together – we soar!"

Sight and sound merged; ethereal silhouettes in orange and yellow hues melted into an overtone of deep chanting that had Anata floating on waves of bliss. The tinkling crystal bells and chimes reminded her of a secret garden, a mythical night with leopard toads celebrating the spirit of Life – long, long ago.

Or was it a dream?

Into the atmosphere of mirth the Elder appeared, emitting a purple light. She looked at him expectantly, still hovering above the ground. All sound faded away.

"Welcome back, Anata," the Elder said in his warm and distinguished way. "She truly excelled, our *Piu Piu of Noordhoek!* But she may descend . . ."

Ooops! Anata almost dropped, a little embarrassed. But as she courteously lifted her eyes to look into his, she was met with a loving smile. She felt his scrutinizing gaze upon her as he scanned the flow of her energy, the frequency of her vibration. She could not prevent herself from shivering; how tired she was.

Eventually, he nodded and spoke: "You expanded your potential considerably. You did this with remarkable courage and grace within a limited space of time. We advise you to take a rest – not only to refuel and to heal but also to become one with yourself again. You know the choices."

"Thank you," she answered, by now almost transparent. "Yes, I'd like to rest for a while . . . and sleep. Just sleep."

"Very well. Your spirit guide will now take you to your place of rest, reflection and restoration. You may stay as long as you wish. Once you're ready, we will review the immortal life of Piu Piu and consider future choices for further self-improvement and co-creation."

Following the sign of his hand, Anata saw a vague shape changing into a graceful human form, radiating a yellow light. Her favorite spiritual guide.

After a gesture of deep gratitude towards her group and a mental embrace with Eiji, she bowed her head reverently before the Elder. Then she turned and followed her guide through veils of whiteness glistening with filaments of gold.

Light to light . . .

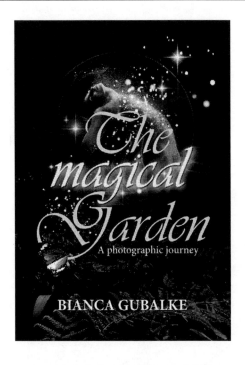

~ A GIFT TO MY READERS ~

Download '*The Magical Garden*' - 120 gorgeous
photos taking you into Piu Piu's secret world:

http://biancagubalke.com/free-book

STAY CONNECTED & WRITE A REVIEW

Visit my website: http://biancagubalke.com/
Updates & info: http://biancagubalke.com/blog
Reach out here: author@biancagubalke.com
Connect here: http://facebook.com/BiancaGubalke
Write a review: **http://amzn.to/2rb0Izc**

GLOSSARY

CHAPTER 1:

'Life is a desire, not a meaning.' Quote by Charlie Chaplin.

'Anata' in Hindi means 'eternal', 'immortal'.

' . . . *be in the world but not of it'*. – John 17:14-15.

CHAPTER 4:

Kirstenbosch National Botanical Garden in Cape Town, South Africa, was the first botanical garden in the world that was founded to preserve a country's unique flora (1913).

Rumi was a 13th-century Persian Sunni Muslim poet, jurist, Islamic scholar, theologian, and Sufi mystic.

Crane flower *(Strelitzia reginae)*

Pincushion *(Leucospermum)*

Silver tree *(Leucadendron argenteum)*

Sugar bush *(Protea)*

Double-collared sunbird *(Cinnyris chalybeus)*

Cape sugarbird *(Promerops cafer)*

Keurboom *(Virgilia oroboides)*

Water blossom pea *(Podalyria calyptrata)*

CHAPTER 7:

African iris *(Dietes grandiflora)*

Red disa *(Disa uniflora)*

Blue disa *(Disa graminifolia)*.

Himalayan Blue Poppy *(Meconopsis grandis)*

Ting Sha *(Tibetan prayer chimes)*

The Story of Queen Disa - Source: Wikipedia

Carl Peter Thunberg (1743-1828) was a Swedish naturalist. He was called *'the father of South African botany.'*

CHAPTER 8

Ralph Waldo Emerson (1803-1882) was an American essayist.

Antoine Laurent de Jussieu (1748-1836) was a French botanist.

CHAPTER 9:

Fynbos – small dense shrubs, heath-like bushes and a large variety of plant species that made this area of the Western Cape one of the world's significant hot-spots for biological diversity.

'The voice of the infinite in the small' ~ from 'The Lost World of the Kalahari' by Sir Laurens van der Post, 'The Heart of the Hunter', 1961, p.233 of 233

CHAPTER 10:

Fire lilies *(Cyrtanthus ventricosus)*

Table Mountain Beauty *(Aeropetes tulbaghia)*

'Mannenberg' – Cape Jazz by Abdullah Ibrahim

CHAPTER 11:

'In the end, everything is a gag.' ~ Quote by Charlie Chaplin.

CHAPTER 12:

"O sole, 'o sole mio, sta nfronte a te . . ." (The sun, my own sun, it's upon your face!) ~ *"O Sole Mio"* was composed by Eduardo Di Capua in Odessa, Italy, during April 1898, based on the poem by Giovanni Capurro. In 1961, Yuri Gagarin hummed *"O Sole Mio"* while becoming the first person in recorded history to orbit planet earth.

ABOUT THE AUTHOR

Bianca Gubalke is an award-winning screenplay writer and artist, a passionate gardener, photographer and metaphysics student.

Born between the Namib Desert, the Atlantic Ocean and the Milky Way, she grew up with a deep connection with nature and a desire to understand the dichotomy between the separation we see out there and the sense of 'Oneness' we feel within. Her first poem was published when she was twelve. An early fascination with spiritual healing inspired her to dive into ancient healing traditions, including shamanism, zen meditation, and clinical hypnosis, all of which is reflected in her creative work.

An advanced degree in Germany and France led to over two exciting decades as filmmaker for the European Film & TV industry, until she returned to South Africa to cultivate her own garden on the slopes of a magic mountain, to continue her studies and to focus on her writing.

She lives in Noordhoek, near Cape Town, with her husband, at least two cats, and the world's most curious Cape cobra coiling in her paper basket, pretending she's not there . . .

WHAT'S NEXT FOR PIU PIU?

AS IN REAL LIFE, THE MAGIC CONTINUES . . . So stay tuned because our heroes will be back soon, although in a different constellation that will have you wonder as to who's who? They've already embarked upon a new journey full of mystery, twists, and suspense. The tension between Anata and Charlot has been playing itself out over many lives. Will there be another tragedy or a happy ending?

It's still a secret . . . but you'll be surprised!

'The Soul of Man is Immortal' – Plato